OAK
APPLE

Roger Whale

Orca publishing

First published in 2011 by Orca Publishing
Ponsworthy

www.orcapublishing.co.uk
roger@orcapublishing.co.uk

Text copyright @ Roger Whale, 2010-04-13

The right of Roger Whale to be identified as the
Author of this work has been asserted by him.
ISBN
978-0-9562256-2-7

Printed by
Short Run Press Ltd.

The
OAK
APPLE

ONE

"Timmy, it's time we were going."

"OK Mum, I'm just coming."

Jacqui, standing at the foot of the stairs was looking up waiting for her son to appear. She had already opened the front door letting the spring sunlight in to form a pool of light on the floor of the front hall and the bottom step. Her low-heeled boots and jeans were also in the bright light and beside them stood a large hessian bag with the logo 'recycle, save the planet' in bright blue letters across one side.

Timmy appeared at the top of the stairs making his way down, slowly at first, but speeding up and skipping down the last few steps. He smiled bravely at his mother, hoping that she wouldn't see the tear in his eye, and picking up the bag said

"Let's go then."

Together they left the house and walked down the short path to the gateway onto the pavement. There they turned and Jacqui put her arm around his shoulders and gave him a hug. At twelve, nearly thirteen in fact, he was almost as tall as she was. A little skinny perhaps, he had been growing upwards rather rapidly of late, not outwards, and had a good deal of filling out to do. With his nearly jet black hair and dark brown eyes he was already beginning to get the looks of a handsome young man. She realised only too well how hard it must be for him to leave the house that had been his home for the last twelve years, his whole life in fact. Now they were off to a completely new life, leaving the noise and bustle of West London for the quiet and far less busy life of a Dartmoor village. She wondered how well he would cope and whether she was right in making this decision for them both.

Their car at the kerbside was laden with suitcases and boxes containing all their clothes and personal belongings, or as much as they could pack in, stacked up to the roof. They had spent the last few days sorting through and rejecting as much as they could, involving several journeys to the charity shops. Timmy had been amazed at how many plastic toys he still had, saved away in the bottom of a cupboard, toys that he had grown out of long ago. His books and sketch pads and all his other artist's materials were far more important to him now than any toys. But still, they evoked memories of past birthdays and Christmases, some of which made him laugh and others that made him feel sad.

Jacqui had found it surprisingly easy to get rid of so many of the items in her wardrobes. She had never been very good at discarding things that she hadn't worn for over two years, but this was for her the start of a new life and she found it therapeutic getting rid of old clothes. To have kept them would have only perpetuated that part of her life that she wanted to leave behind. Photographs and a few other mementos of the better times she was happy to bring with her, together with one or two of her favourite ornaments.

As they pulled away from the kerb Timmy said

"Can we stop by Jacko's place on the way Mum?"

"Yes of course, it's not out of our way; I just hope that I can find a place to park near-by."

"You should be OK, his dad will have gone to work and you'll be able to park in his space."

Sure enough there was a space and she waited in the car while Timmy went in to say cheerio to his best mate. This for him, she realised, was going to be the hardest part of their move away. He and Jacko had been friends all through primary school and into secondary school. She was well aware that Timmy was a rather quiet, sensitive boy, a possible target for bullying. Jacko, street-wise and black, had been as much a protector as a friend.

A few minutes later they both came out onto the street, looking a bit like Laurel and Hardy, one broad and short the other tall and slim. After various hand slaps and friendly punches Timmy turned and with a big smile on his face climbed into the car. Jacqui was a little surprised and pleased at this expression on his face. She had feared that he would blame her for breaking up his friendship and taking him away from his best friend. As she started the car and drove away Timmy said, rather matter- of-factly

"Jacko's going to America."

"What, for a holiday?"

"No, to live. His dad's got a job there. They move in about six week's time. It seems like everybody's moving."

Jacqui kept quiet; she felt like saying that he would have been parted from his friend, even if they had not moved to Devon, but she had seen from his smile that Timmy had already thought the very same thing. Was it selfish of her, or wrong to feel a little glad that he wouldn't be able to blame her?

The journey down the motorway had been uneventful. They had stopped at the services a time or two, and had eaten the sandwiches that Jacqui had made from the leftovers in the kitchen. But when they left the main roads and started the climb up onto the moor it was different altogether. There were no pavements or street lights, as they had been used to, instead at the sides of the road were high hedges, and the roads often seemed too narrow for more than one car. More than once Timmy felt sure that his mum was going to either hit the hedge or the car coming towards them. He felt himself trying to squeeze his body and the whole car into a smaller space.

Then they were out onto open moorland where there were no hedges, just grassy banks with the odd clump of dark green gorse bushes beside the road. To one side the land fell away gradually to fields and trees and beyond them in the haze Timmy imagined that he could see the roofs of houses. On the other side the land rose steeply to the top of a hill surmounted with a cluster of dark rocks. Dotted all around were small windblown thorn bushes, green

4

with the fresh leaves of spring. Grazing in small groups were ponies, some with young foals beside them, their long spindly legs looking almost too thin to carry them as they skipped and danced around their mothers. Some seemed to be perilously near the road and the traffic and Timmy was fearful lest one should run out in front of the car. A little further along the road they passed a flock of black-faced sheep, their long greyish wool almost touching the ground. Beside them lambs, looking freshly bathed their wool so white compared to their mothers, leaped and bounced over the rocks and grassy mounds.

They turned a bend in the road to see a view of more such rocky topped hills stretching as far as the eye could see.

"It's a bit wild Mum, what are all these mountains?"

"They are called Tors, they are really just hills where the soil on the top has eroded away leaving the granite rocks showing."

"And where do Gran and Grandad live?"

"Oh, it's not far from here, in fact we should be there in a few minutes. I forgot, you haven't been here to see them. When we last came down here for a holiday we stayed near the coast and Gran and Grandad came to see us in the caravan we rented."

Sure enough they soon dropped down off the higher part of the moor and into narrow lanes again for a while until they finally passed first a farm and then several cottages before arriving in the village centre.

TWO

Jacqui's parents, Walter and Jessica Blackmore, had been living in the village for nearly five years. They had bought the old smithy, a cottage with the blacksmith's shop beside it which they had converted into a tea room. The large double doors had been replaced with glass ones and the open windows had also been glazed. The forge with its raised hearth at one end of the building made an unusual display area, a sort of stone sideboard. In the centre of the room on a block of local granite stood the anvil, a reminder, if one were needed, of the former use to which the old building had been put.

In addition to the conversion of the blacksmith's shop, they had also added a wing on to the rear of the cottage. Just like the neighbouring cottages it had been built before the advent of bathrooms and flush toilets. When these modernisations had been added at least one bedroom had been lost. With the spacious gardens behind, it was not surprising that each cottage had had a wing built onto the back of the property.

Walter was a young sixty six and Jessica equally sprightly at two years younger. Nevertheless they felt that a pair of young hands around the house would be an asset. Running the tea room was not too arduous and they managed it very well, but sometimes the running of the house got somewhat neglected. So when Jacqui had telephoned a week before and dropped the bombshell that she and Timmy needed somewhere to live, her parents were able to say that they had plenty of room and would be delighted to have them to stay for a while.

Jacqui pulled the car into the drive beside the cottage and by the time she and Timmy had got out, Jessica was running towards them with arms outstretched.

"Leave the unpacking for now and come in and have some lunch" she said after hugging them both warmly. "You're looking well Dear, not too tired after the drive down I hope. And you Timmy, my word how you've grown since I last saw you. After we've eaten I'll show you to your rooms and Dad will give you a hand carrying things upstairs."

It was easy to see where Jacqui got her good looks from. Her mother was not only young at heart but also in appearance, with a trim figure and a very young looking face. Both women had the same wide spaced eyes and full friendly mouth. The only marked difference was that Jacqui's eyes were grey where her mother's were dark brown.

They went into the cottage and Walter welcomed them both and led them into the tea room where they sat and had lunch. Jessica had so many questions that she wanted to ask but she realised that the time wasn't right then and that she would have to wait, perhaps until after Timmy had gone to bed.

Nevertheless it was very hard to contain her curiosity. Jacqui had said so little on the phone, just that she and Timmy were leaving Alan and could they come down and live with them for a while. When asked why and what it was all about, Jacqui had said that she really couldn't say over the phone and would rather wait until she could explain everything face to face. This of course, had only made Jessica worry more and she had spent many an hour thinking and wondering what on earth could have gone so wrong. She realised that Alan had to spend long periods away from home and this probably put a strain on the marriage. Even so, Jacqui had never given her any indication in the past that anything was wrong. Obviously she had either been putting on a brave face, or something had occurred recently to upset the apple cart. She would just have to wait a little longer.

THREE

Timmy sat on the bed in his new room looking around. The room was bigger than the one he had had in London although the window was smaller and low down. Above it the ceiling sloped up a little way before levelling out. There was plenty of cupboard and drawer space where his mum had helped him to pack away his clothes. His other belongings were still in the boxes stacked under the window where he and his granddad had left them. Just at that moment he didn't feel like unpacking any more. He sat looking out of the window, lost in thought.

So much had happened in the last week; he found it almost difficult to believe. He and his mum had left home, left his dad and come to stay with his grandparents. He felt relieved that they had done so, and yet he couldn't help but feel a bit sad. Would he miss his dad? Could he miss someone who was for ever critical, always finding fault and never giving any praise? He had never missed him before, in fact he had almost dreaded his coming home some days, or was it more that he was missing what he had always missed; the sort of dad that he wished he had had. The sort of dad that his friend Jacko had, a dad who played with them without always wanting to win, who helped with homework, and when he got things wrong showed him how to put them right rather than picking on him and telling him he was no good.

Or was it his fault? Instead of thinking that his dad was a disappointment was it the other way round? His dad often complained that he wasn't sporty, didn't like football or cricket like other boys, that he was too soft. But he couldn't help it if he preferred music and art. Perhaps it was just that they were both different to the sort of person the other expected. And different surely didn't have to mean disappointment, did it? Tears were running down his face and he turned and threw himself onto the bed burying his face in the pillow racked with sobs.

After a while he sat up, wiped his eyes and went to the bathroom and washed his face. Then, hoping that nobody would notice that he had been crying, he went downstairs and said that if it was OK he was going out for a look around.

"Don't get lost" said Walter with a smile, "There's no mobile phone signal here."

Timmy laughed and gave a brief wave as he opened the door and went out. He turned left into the centre of the village. The older residents called it The Green, some others referred to it as The Square. Neither was an apt description there being no grass or greenery apart from a large horse chestnut tree. This stood in a paved section with outward facing benches in the centre of what was a large triangular area of tarmac. On his left was the village hall, formerly the local school, with a notice board full of colourful posters giving details of forthcoming events. Next to it were two new looking houses and beside them gates across a private drive that led to Edworthy Hall. The road led on out of the village with several other dwellings on either side, but Timmy crossed it to stay in the green, passing three granite cottages, the village shop and the New Inn that formed the second side of the triangle.

The shop seemed busy, it seemed to sell most things: newspapers, fruit and veg and other items of food and drink as well as being the village post office. It reminded him of Mr Patel's shop on the corner of the street back home. He stopped and smiled at himself, it wasn't home, of course, London wasn't home any more.

He crossed the second road out of the village and made his way along the third side of the triangle. First there was the gateway into the Old Rectory through which he could see up a sandy drive beyond the rhododendron bushes to an expanse of lawn. Finally the parish church, with its lichen encrusted tower topped with four pinnacles, proudly overlooking the whole of the village.

Timmy was back where he started outside the Old Smithy so he turned right and set off along the third road out of the village passing a B&B and another cottage as he left the village. He paused to watch a flock of jackdaws squawking and fluttering around the church tower. Two girls on ponies came riding up behind him. They looked to be about his age. The older one was on a grey pony and the other was riding a chestnut with a light mane and tail. They were happily chatting away and as they passed they smiled at Timmy and said hello. He, somewhat surprised, hesitated before replying. He wasn't used to strangers greeting him in this friendly fashion. Was this how people acted here in the country?

They rode past him, giggling and talking non-stop as they went. A short way on they turned off the road, passing through a gate on the left. The girl on the grey had turned her pony and was about to shut the gate when an empty plastic water bottle blew along the road, bouncing and making a hollow rattling noise. Her pony spooked, turned away violently almost unseating her and jumped away from the gate. Timmy seeing all this ran forward saying

"Alright, alright, I'll shut the gate for you. You OK?"

"Yes, thanks, thanks very much,"

They rode on, chattering and giggling all the more it seemed. Timmy couldn't help wondering if he was the object of their mirth, and he felt himself blushing. He followed them along a gravelled track with a stone wall on either side and fields beyond. After a while the track turned slightly to the right and went downhill while to the left the fields came to an end and were replaced by moorland. Looking down the track Timmy saw that after a few hundred yards it went through a gate and then through two fields in which was a collection of buildings nestling in a small valley. Beyond the fields the land rose steeply and was scarred with deep heather covered gullies on either side of the valley. Thinking that he was on somebody's private drive, he turned off the track onto the moor and followed the two girls. They were cantering up a wide grassy path that led to the top of the tor. On both sides the short grass was just beginning to show the dark green, thick leaves of bluebells that would soon carpet the whole of the lower slopes with their bright colour. As he walked higher Timmy saw these give way to heather and gorse with granite rocks of all sizes scattered amongst them. It was a sort of scenery that he had never encountered before; he felt a strange sense of fear and unease and yet of freedom in the wildness and vastness of all that was around him. Looking ahead he felt, like all mountaineers, that he just had to go right to the top and stand on the highest rock. He scrambled up, finding footholds in the crevices in the layer-like rock formation, and then like the king of the castle he was on the very top.

From that vantage point he could see tors and valleys stretching away into the distance, horizon after horizon each seeming more hazy and purple the further away they were. He saw the two girls below him, passing a large wooded area, and back were he had come from, the tower of the church. Well at any rate he wouldn't get lost as long as he could see that. His granddad needn't have worried.

He sat on a rock soaking in all the sights and sounds around him. There seemed to be ponies with their foals on the lower slopes and sheep and lambs everywhere. He laughed at the way the ewes called to their lambs as they grazed, making their '*baah*' call, sound more like '*wow wow wow*'.

"You shouldn't talk with your mouth full" he said, laughing some more. Then on a nearby gorse bush he saw a small bird. It was saying '*tsick tsick*' as if telling him to go away. He wished that he had his sketch pad; he would have to remember to bring it next time he was out. He would try to carry the image of the bird in his mind. Black head, brown back and orange breast and a white collar. He had no idea what sort of a bird it was but he felt sure that his granddad would know. He was used to blackbirds and robins but this was totally new to him. Then another bird landed on a rock not five yards away. This one was light grey with a black line through its eye and a pale cream coloured breast. It stood very upright, looking for all the world like a gentleman in a frock coat and cream waistcoat off to a wedding. Timmy drew a mental picture of this one and then set off down to where he had last seen the two girls before they disappeared. It was, he discovered a small gate that led into a lane. Stone faced hedges on either side topped with bushes and small trees that grew in many places to meet at the top forming a green tunnel. He went down it and found that it joined the road beyond the village.

His granddad met him as he went indoors and asked him if he had had a good time exploring. Timmy excitedly told him of his exploits and asked about the buildings in the valley.

"That's Braggator Mine or was. There was tin mining there up until about nineteen fifteen I understand. All gone now, of course, the house used to be the mine captain's."

"Does anybody live there now? I didn't like to go too far along the path in case it was somebody's private drive."

"Oh, it's only private after the gate into the fields. Yes, there's a chap lives there, a blacksmith. Quiet sort of a chap, keeps himself very much to himself. Got silver grey hair."

Then Timmy described the birds he had seen.

"D'you know what sort of birds they are Grandad?"

"You certainly described them very well Timmy. I think I know what they are, but just to make sure I think you had better look them up in the bird book. You will find one on the second shelf of the book-case in the dining room. Then you will better remember them."

Timmy ran off to find the bird book, excited and delighted that his granddad had given him such praise. He was also pleased to see that his mental pictures of a stonechat and a wheatear were so similar to those in the book. He went up to his room and sat on his bed again, thinking that perhaps living here in this wild countryside wasn't so bad after all.

FOUR

Walter had decided to go to the pub that evening and have a natter and a few beers with his friend Charlie. Although he prided himself that he had a good relationship with his daughter, he knew that his wife would probably be the one that Jacqui would be most at ease with, especially when it came to explaining the break-up of her marriage. So after they had had their evening meal, Timmy had gone to bed and Jacqui had been up to say good-night and see that he was OK and comfortable in his new bedroom. Then when she came down again Walter had smiled knowingly at his wife and left them to it.

Sitting in the comfort of their cosy lounge, and with a cup of coffee each, Jessica said

"Don't feel you've got to tell me any thing that you feel unhappy to tell me. I want to help, and I feel that to do so, I need to know. Your Dad and I both need to know just what has happened in your marriage and why you have had to come down here. Don't think that we don't want you; we're delighted to have you and Timmy living with us. It doesn't matter if it's for a week or a year or for ever. But if we don't know the whys and wherefores we'll be tiptoeing around you all the time, afraid in case we say the wrong thing; d'you understand?"

"Of course I understand Mum, and I know that you and Dad will understand my position and what has happened to bring us down here. It's a long story so if you're sitting comfortably I'll begin."

Jessica realised at once that her attempt at humour was a way of Jacqui overcoming her nervousness, so she just nodded, smiled and shuffled in her seat, as though to get into a more comfortable position to fall in with the joke.

"Well this is something that has been building for a long time. Alan's behaviour towards me has never been violent, at least not physically. Mental cruelty I suppose some would call it. The problem is and has always been his jealousy, insane jealousy. At first, when we were first going out together and then married, it seemed almost a sort of flattery. To think that he loved me so much that he couldn't bear to share me in any way, even if it was only my smiling at somebody that upset him. But it got progressively worse, and the fact that he was away for a week or two at a time didn't help. I suppose he was worried that I would be unfaithful to him in some way while he was away for such long periods. At least that was what I used to think. I couldn't understand it; after all it was no different for those hundreds of army wives who are separated from their men for months at a time.

Every time he came home, if we went out any where, just shopping or to a pub for a meal, it was always the same. If I so much as smiled at some man who had stepped out of my way in the street or the barman in a pub, he would get all ratty and fire questions at me. 'Who is that man? Is he a special friend of yours? Oh, don't tell me you were just being polite…' and so on. It got to the point when I dreaded him coming home. It was rare for him to make a scene when we were out, but he would really go for me when we got home. It was awful Mum. It was so wearing, and also it was bad for Timmy to have to hear such things, such ridiculous accusations. And hear them he did. But that wasn't the worst as far as Timmy was concerned. If he had been left out of it, things might have been different, though probably not.

Alan thought of himself as a very male type of man, very macho in his outlook. He may not have taken part in a lot of sport, but he loved a kick around with a ball and watching football on telly. So when Timmy showed no inclination to take part in any sport at all, he couldn't understand it. He picked on the lad a lot, criticised him at every turn. The only game they played together was the odd game of pool in our local pub. Even that ended up as no good, because Timmy got to be better at it than Alan and regularly beat him, so Alan wouldn't play any more. Childish, jealous little man."

"Oh, I'm so sorry dear. I had no idea, but even if I had I don't suppose that I could have done anything to help."

"No, there was nothing anyone could have done, it was up to me, and it took me too long to pluck up the courage. The last straw, well there were two really, came last weekend when he came home. We went to the pub, as we often did, for a meal and a drink or two. Timmy went off into the pool-room for a game and Alan started off at me for smiling at the barman when he brought our drinks. Then, after we had eaten, the place was getting busy. A couple came and asked if we would mind if they shared our table. There was plenty of room so I said of course not, and as you can imagine that was no good. Not long after that we left, Alan was in a foul mood, grumbling that I had spoiled his evening again, as usual.

Once home Timmy went up to his room and Alan really laid into me about the way I behaved towards other men, total strangers even like those who wanted to share our table. 'Would you have preferred it if I had told them to go and sit somewhere else?' I had asked. Oh, he had shouted and ranted and finally Timmy had come down, crying and had told him to shut up and leave me alone. He said that all Alan did when he came home was to find fault with us; picking on me for smiling, and picking on him for not being a 'silly footballer' as he called it. He said it would be a lot better if he didn't come home at all; life was much nicer and more peaceful when he was away.

Alan went mad, I was afraid he was going to hit Timmy, something he had never done. I jumped in between them and berated Alan for the way he treated his son. And then he said he wasn't sure that Timmy was his son. With his black hair and dark brown eyes he didn't resemble Alan who has blond hair and blue eyes. Well that did it. Timmy burst into tears and said

"You horrible man, I hate you, I hate you." Then he ran off up to his room and was still crying several minutes later when I went up to him. I told Alan that that was unforgivable, how he could say such a thing to his son, and he is his son, I haven't slept with any man other than Alan. He may not want to believe it but I know it's true. But one thing was certain; I wasn't going to sleep with him that night or any other. He had to sleep on the settee. It was a terrible thing to say, terrible. It would have been bad enough if he had said it to me about Timmy, but to say it to Timmy; well…."

"Oh you poor darling, it must have been awful; but you did the right thing leaving him and coming here."

"That wasn't all, that was only the half of it. The next day he was off to work. He used to come home for two nights at least but lately it has been for only one, something to do with feeder runs or something. I never bothered to understand about coach driving. Well after he left I was cleaning up the sitting room and I found this, slipped down in the side of the cushion of the settee."

She pulled a small blue mobile phone from out of her hand bag.

"I thought at first that it was his works phone; the coaches are that sort of blue, and I knew it wasn't his mobile. I was about to ring his office and say that he had left it behind, but something made me look at it more closely. There was only one number in the 'phonebook' and that was for S, who ever S might be. Then I started to play with it a bit

20

more and found that there were a few messages in it, all from S and all of a very explicit nature. 'Looking forward to our next night together' and the likes of that. Well that did it for me. When Timmy got back from school that evening we had a long talk. I had to make sure that he really would be happier living away from his dad, and when I was absolutely sure that that was what he wanted I started the difficult process of moving out.

Two days later I rang the number in the phone, S's number. A woman answered and I said, 'is Alan there?' She said that he was at work and wouldn't be back for a fortnight. So that was that, proof positive if proof were needed. I left him a note saying that I had left, that it was pointless following me, and that he would be hearing from my solicitor as I was suing him for divorce. I didn't mention the mobile; I'm keeping that as a surprise up my sleeve for the moment. And I haven't said anything to Timmy about it either; in fact I don't want him to know about Alan's infidelity at all, not yet and not from any of us. The last thing I want is to involve him any more in a battle between his Mum and his Dad, that wouldn't be right."

"You're absolutely right, after all, in years to come he may want to renew his ties with his dad, and it might be difficult for him if you had made a big point of trying to set him against Alan. It's a mistake that so many couples who split up make. They are so full of anger, quite understandably, that they use anything, even the children, as weapons in their battles. It's the children who are the most

21

vulnerable. They are the victims who have no understanding of all that's going on and no way of knowing how to deal with it all. No, you are quite right to keep him out of it as much as possible and Dad and I will back you."

"Thanks Mum, thanks for everything. For listening to me without telling me that I ought to do this or that, and most of all, for giving us a home here."

They had been sitting opposite one another, Jacqui in an armchair and Jessica on the settee. Jacqui got up and crossed over, to sit beside her and they both threw their arms around each other, hugging each other and crying softly. After a few minutes they pulled apart and, having wiped their eyes, Jessica said

"Thank you so much for telling me all this; I realise how difficult it must have been. I only wish that you had told me about Alan's jealous behaviour before."

"What would have been the point Mum? There was nothing that you could have done except worry. You wouldn't have been able to change him; he has never seen his behaviour as being wrong. He sees himself and his opinions as being right always, and if anybody disagrees with him, well, they are wrong. That's the sort of man that he is. My mistake was that I didn't realise early enough, like before we got married."

She laughed at herself and squeezed her mother's hand as she said

"But it's not all bad; after all I've got one really wonderful thing that has come out of our marriage, my lovely sensitive understanding Timmy. I only hope and pray that he won't be too damaged by all this. Going to a new school and making new friends will be difficult enough. I hope that he can find that living here, which is so different to the sort of life that he's used to, is enjoyable and fulfilling. I shall have to keep a close eye on him."

At that point they heard the front door open and Walter very soon joined them.

"Many in the pub tonight Dear?"

"Yeah, a fair crowd. I had a nice chat with Charlie. He's a wise old man, seen a lot in his life, both good and bad, yet he seems to hold no grudge against the hardships, and what we might think of as injustices that he's had to face."

"Did you say anything to him about Jacqui and Timmy being here?"

"No, I didn't know exactly how you wanted to deal with the subject. Mind you, I know what Charlie would have said."

"What's that?" said Jessica.

"He would have said tell the truth, don't try to make it sound like something that it's not. But at the same time, keep it to the bare facts, no details."

"And is that what you would advise Dad?"

"Yes Jacqui, I think I would. I don't know all the facts, Mum will fill me in on what you've told her, and knowing you, my girl, you'll have told her everything. Something that I felt you might have found difficult to do if I had been here."

23

"Thanks Dad, I'm sure you're right. It would be silly to make out that we were just down here for a few days holiday, or something, and then how would we explain things when we didn't go home."

"If we go to the shop tomorrow morning" said Jessica "I generally go to get the paper and one or two things, we are bound to meet Sal and Edna. They are nearly always there to pick up what ever gossip is going around. I can introduce you and you can tell them, or I will if you prefer, and then you won't need to say anything more to anybody."

Walter laughed, "Yes" he said "Those two work better than any jungle drums at spreading news. Mind you, Charlie, that's Sal's husband, won't let her slander any body, and since Edna found her grand daughter again she has been a lot more careful as to what she says. Yeah, that's a good plan Jesse, if those two are in the shop it could save you having to tell quite so many people."

FIVE

Mick Cribbett had lived at Braggator for five years. The place had been pretty run down when he bought it, but the challenge of doing it up had been just what he needed. He felt that he needed to bury himself in hard work; preferably a completely different sort of work from that which had been his normal up to that time. He hoped that by doing so he might overcome his pain and heartbreak. So he set to and had spent six weeks working, sometimes as much as eighteen hours a day, gutting and then modernising the place. It was by no means a large house, the dwellings of a nineteenth century mine captain were hardly sumptuous, but when he had finished it had become a very pleasant and modern two bed-roomed dwelling. Although from the outside it still appeared to be the same old Dartmoor building.

The previous owners had had it as a holiday home. They had thought that the isolated position was perfect as a place to escape to from the hustle and bustle of city working life. They hadn't counted on the Dartmoor damp; damp that would invade any house that was left empty for only a matter of a few days. Eventually they had admitted that the struggle to dry out everything; beds, bedding and comfy chairs every time that they came down, just wasn't worth it. Especially as it would take at least two or three days to get the place properly dry, and they were often only down for a weekend or at best a short week. But for Mick it was exactly what he wanted with the small amount of land to grow and raise things and some useful buildings for his workshop and forge.

Mick was a stocky man, of about five foot ten, with broad shoulders and narrow waist and hips. He had a well tanned, clean shaven face with eyes that were a shade of steel grey, as cold as the steel horse shoes that he made and all was topped with wavy silver grey hair, a lock of which always seemed to fall over his right eye. It was possibly a younger face than the hair colour would suggest. He had broad capable hands with strong looking fingers that showed that he was a man who worked with his hands. On the fourth finger of his left hand was a plain gold ring.

He drove his van out of the barn and checked the contents. As a travelling farrier he had to make sure that he had enough nails and shoes for the job to which he was going, and several spares, just in case. His portable gas forge and anvil were always in the van. Then he was off, up the lane. As he went he looked up across the moor as he always did. A group of ponies caught his eye, they were galloping; their ears back, weaving in and out of the rocks and gorse bushes. A dark chestnut stallion was chasing them, neck outstretched and lips pulled back whistling and whinnying as he went. Mick would have to mention this to Pippa, her two girls often rode up on this part of the moor.

He had been a farrier ever since he left school, learning the trade from the village blacksmith. At first it had just been a childish interest during school holidays. He had loved watching the horses being brought into the small yard by the forge, their coats gleaming, tails swishing and heads nodding. The way the smith had talked soothingly, touching them gently, rubbing them behind their ears, waiting to see the calm return to those beautiful soft large eyes before he stated his work. Off would come the old shoes, often with enough life in them to go back on. Then the hooves would be inspected and pared. And then the part that Mick had always found the most exciting as a boy, when the red-hot shoe was held onto the hoof and clouds of acrid smoke would rise up, making the smith's head disappear in the swirls of yellowish smog. Then back into the trough of water would go the shoe, hissing and spluttering, to be nailed on a few minutes later when it had finally cooled down.

But later it became a passion. His mentor had been more than pleased to have a strong young man to help him, and had been equally happy to train him. Mick's father was the gamekeeper on a large estate in South Devon and had taught his son well, so his knowledge and understanding of the ways of the country had grown as he had. From an early age he had followed his dad through the woods, checking on both the wild life and the pheasants that he raised. The variations in work, the jobs to be done and the way the days were filled due to the seasons, were to him as second nature as eating and sleeping. As was the fact that farming and wildlife could fit together in the countryside without difficulty, though maybe with a little effort, was to Mick perfectly normal.

His first call that day was to be at the riding stables on the other side of the village. They had a string of nearly thirty horses and he had found it best to visit every week. It was a lot easier to tend to the shoeing of four or five, and the needs of the odd one that had thrown a shoe, rather than try to see to them all together every six weeks. Pippa was there to meet him, as usual, and straight away he told her about the stallion on Braggator. He was concerned for her daughters, whom he had often seen riding in the area. An aggressive stallion could attack and upset their horses, possibly unseating the riders. If this were to happen, even if they weren't injured they would be badly frightened. Apart from that, he talked only when the job required him to, as was his habit, never getting drawn into local gossip, and never ever mentioning anything to do with his own personal life.

So it was hardly surprising that he had become something of an enigma, a mystery man about whom little was known but, as is so often the way in a small community, much was assumed. It suited him well, though he would surely have laughed at some of the theories put forward about him and what he had done with his life before coming to the village. Did he have something to hide? Was there some crime that he had committed? Was he running away from something or somebody? That he was a good farrier was without doubt, and that he had a wonderful way with horses. But he took no part in any of the social life of the village and was not often to be seen in the pub either. It was as though he had built an invisible wall around himself and his personal life, and although he was charming and polite to all that he met, nobody had managed to find out what was on the other side of that wall.

SIX

It was a beautiful spring morning; a song thrush was singing its heart out from the top of one of the trees in the garden of the Old Rectory, repeating each phrase three times before moving on to the next equally exuberant one. The chestnut tree in the centre of the green was ablaze with white floral candles. From somewhere in the shady depths of its branches came the distinctive *teacher teacher teacher* call of a great tit. The sun had been up for long enough for the ground to feel warm beneath their feet, warm enough for a lone bumble bee to drone its way passed them.

Jessica and Jacqui walked slowly across the green to the village shop, savouring the moment.

"D'you think that you will be able to settle down here after the hustle and bustle of city life?"

"If I can wake up to mornings like this every day, I don't think that it will be too difficult" said Jacqui with a laugh.

"I can't promise that it will be like this every day, but if you are happy here it may well feel like this. I remember the day that your dad and I moved in. It was raining and blowing, a typical Dartmoor rainy day, as I later came to recognise it, with gusts of rain blowing horizontally across this green. We struggled with the move, desperately trying to keep all our things dry as they came out of the lorry and into the house. But we loved it, we were so happy to be moving into this village and our new life that we didn't notice the rain. One of the removal men, a little cockney chap with a face like a ferret said 'If this is Dartmoor, give me 'ell any day' as he blew the rain-drop off the end of his nose. Your dad and I roared with laughter, we couldn't help it. I expect that little man thought we were absolutely mad."

"Well if I can be as happy here as you and Dad obviously are, I shan't have anything to complain about."

They entered the shop and after picking up her paper Jessica introduced her daughter to John Hunt, the shop keeper. As they turned to go a smart looking lady came hurrying in. She was wearing a green sweatshirt, with the logo of the stables on the front, jodhpurs, half chaps and riding boots. Her long blond hair was held back in a pony tail and her grey-green eyes seemed to be alight as she said a brief but happy hello to Jessica.

"Oh, Pippa, have you got a minute?"

"You'll have to be quick; I've got the farrier coming this morning. Why, what is it?"

"This is my daughter Jacqui, she's moved in with us. She has a twelve year old son who will have to go to school, the one your girls go to. I was hoping that you might be able to give her some pointers and such like."

"Sure, delighted to, and pleased to meet you. Give me a ring and we'll arrange a meet. Sorry I can't stop...Bye."

31

With that she was out into the sun and gone. Jacqui and her mum left the shop in a slightly more leisurely fashion and once outside she said

"So tell me, who is Pippa?"

"Pippa is a farmer's daughter who is top hand at the riding centre. Her husband has an agricultural supplies business and is the nephew of Charlie Blundell, the chap Dad was having a drink with last night. Her sister Beatie is the district nurse who lives two doors from us and is married to an American."

"My word, is every body related down here? It seems like it from what you've just been telling me."

"It does seem a bit like that, but I can assure you that none of them have webbed feet" said Jessica with a grin on her face.

"Mother really…. you can't say things like that."

"No, it's not that bad, but it is as well to be aware that there are a lot of people here who are related. We'll give Pippa a ring later, perhaps ask her round for a drink and a chat. She's a lovely girl."

SEVEN

George and Edith Hamlyn had lived at West Furzes since the day that they had got married after the war. It had been a hard life with little time for leisure; but then, that was normal for those who farmed a small Dartmoor farm. As the decades passed and farming became more mechanised George stayed firmly in the past. Not for him the sprays and modern fertilizers used by so many. He did have a small tractor and a few implements, though for major tasks such as baling hay he relied on contractors. Eventually, without any conscious effort on his part, his ways caught up with the modern fashion, or it with him; he was farming as he always had done, organically, it being the only way he knew.

Retirement was not something he or Edith had ever thought of. With no children, farming was not just a way of life, it was their life. As age caught up with them and they found some jobs more difficult, they reduced their stock and cut down on the amount of work that they had to do every day. On one occasion he said somewhat philosophically to a friend,

" Us goes to bed saying; tomorrow us'll do this, that and 'tother. But then when tomorrow comes, us does this an' that an' 'tother most likely has to wait for another day".

Eventually George died suddenly. Neither he nor Edith had ever been ill for any length of time, but at well over eighty and after a hard-working life it was no surprise. Edith accepted it, though that didn't mean that she liked it. Having worked with animals all their lives they knew that death was a part of life, part of the natural cycle. For a short while she had carried on the farm, it helped to combat the loneliness, but it became more and more difficult. Getting part time help had been the biggest problem, so finally she gave in and sold up.

The farm sale drew a good crowd. Landrovers and tractors were parked in the lane and the field nearby. All the implements, machinery and tools were laid out neatly in rows in the field behind the house and a makeshift ring had been set up in the yard for the selling of the livestock. Bidding was brisk for the cattle and sheep, as the old blood lines were in great demand and also her neighbours were pleased to help Edith.

A lot of the implements and tools should have gone to a museum, so many of them were of an age that had long passed. Apart from a few personal items everything, indoors and out, was sold. It was a hard but inevitable end of an era for Edith. Grieving for the loss of her husband would be with her for the rest of her life, as would be the loss of the only lifestyle that she had ever known . She took a last look around the house after all the people were gone, memories of past years in every room. Most poignant were those in the kitchen, now bare of its scrubbed top table and wooden Windsor chairs. This room had been the hub of their life when indoors. Meals were prepared and eaten on the table, as had been the doing of the ever increasing paperwork, so prevalent in recent years. The stove had not only cooked their meals, heated their water and dried their wet clothes; it had often warmed and restored to life many a new-born lamb. The bedroom had been where they had done most of their talking, discussing what should be done and how, as they lay in bed. They had never found it difficult to talk and both had the knack of listening to the other's point of view. It was hardly surprising that their marriage had lasted so well for so long.

Grace, the vicar's wife, had stayed after the sale to be with her in those last few minutes and had accompanied her as she took her last look around. Then she drove her to what was to be her new home; a bungalow in Dawlish where she would be living with her sister who was also widowed.

Most of the land was sold to the neighbouring farmer at East Furzes on the advice of the local agent. The farmstead with two small fields was sold separately. Curiously the new owners were not seen for many months and the place stood empty. There was no dog barking when anybody passed and no smoke from the chimney. It was worse than empty, it seemed to be deserted. It seemed such a shame when there were local youngsters who were desperately looking for somewhere to live. Eventually a middle-aged couple were sometimes seen staying there for a weekend but they didn't use the village shop or frequent the pub. To the local inhabitants it was all very mysterious.

Charlie Blundell was in the habit of going for walks, it kept him fit, got him out from under Sal's feet, and gave him a chance to keep up to date with what was going on in the area. One day he was passing and saw the new people in the yard. To Charlie it seemed a golden opportunity to find out a little more about them. Unfortunately they didn't seem to want to tell him very much about themselves. So where they came from or what they did still remained a mystery.

EIGHT

Holidays are never long enough when one is of school age. Since moving to the village the days had flown by and the start of the summer term was upon him almost before Timmy was aware of it. He had settled in to the new life well, happy with his own company, never lonely when out in the open countryside with all that it had to show him. His granddad had lent him a small pair of binoculars for bird watching, and Timmy had spent many a happy day out on the moor with his sketch pad. It was all so new to him; the scenery, the wild life and country activities of which, up until then, he had had no experience.

His sketching was limited to pencil work only, but he still managed to create some remarkable pictures, coming home each evening with his eyes shining with excitement as he described to Jacqui all the things that he had seen. He was full of questions for Walter who unfortunately, being relatively new to the area, was not always able to give him an answer.

Although she would have loved to accompany him to the school bus, Jacqui knew only too well that that would be a mistake. The last thing that Timmy wanted was to be seen by the other children being escorted *by his mummy* on this first day at his new school. So she stood in the tea-room in the relative darkness, watching him as he walked across the green to the seats under the chestnut tree where all the other children where waiting for the bus. When it arrived she was pleased to see that he was not the last to get on board, mixing in with the others, laughing and joking as they all scrambled up the steps. And although she felt a slight pang of disappointment she was glad that he didn't look back in her direction as though for support.

When the bus had gone she went across to the shop for the paper and was pleased to meet Pippa there.

"Timmy get off alright?" she asked.

"Yes, he seemed OK. I watched him go, I was probably more nervous than he was. He was chatting to your two girls as they waited for the bus."

"Margaret and Helen think the world of him. He did a picture of Margaret's pony, Sandpiper, did you see it?"

"No."

"It was amazing, just the head and neck really. Somehow he had captured the character of her pony. The way he had done the eye, there's something about a pony's eye, that wonderful deep, soft, almost liquid eye that seems to lead you into the soul of the animal. He can certainly draw alright."

"Well he always did a bit of drawing before we came down here, but now that he has discovered the moor and all it has to offer he seems to be doing a lot more."

"He ought to get lessons, I'm not sure what the art classes are at school, if any, but his talent shouldn't be ignored."

"Thank you" said Jacqui, pleased and proud at the praise her son was getting from Pippa. "Have you got time for a cuppa, or do you have to dash back to the stables?" Since arriving in the village Jacqui had found it easy to make new friends, and Pippa had been the first. It was she who, having children of similar age to Timmy, was able to advise Jacqui regarding the school, its uniform and so on.

"I think I can spare few minutes; I'd love a cuppa, thank you."

So, with their children on their way to school, the two mums strolled across the green in the spring sunshine. In the chestnut tree a blackbird was singing, seemingly trying to outdo the robin for their attention as it hopped in front of them. All around birds were tweeting and warbling and flying busily, taking food to their young. In the churchyard and the gardens new life seemed to be exploding. The daffodils in the front garden were nearly over but the tulips and grape hyacinths in the tubs on either side of the door to Walter's cottage were a blaze of colour.

"D'you think that you will settle here, I mean permanently?"

"It's hard to say, it's early days yet, but I feel more settled than I have felt for a long time. Whether that is to do with me, or this place, or the kind people like yourself who have welcomed Timmy and me, I really don't know. Right at this moment, with all this around me, I can't think of a better place or one where I would rather be. These beautiful spring mornings seem so much richer than any I experienced in town."

"It has been good this year, but don't get too complacent, it can change here very quickly. We often say that you can get four seasons in one day on Dartmoor."

Pippa's remark was to come true sooner than expected, though it wasn't the weather that changed the day for the worse. Jacqui was waiting table in the tea-room and had just come out of the kitchen with an order for a couple who had come in a few minutes earlier. As she approached their table she saw to her horror that Alan was sitting at a table in the corner. She couldn't ignore him and went over to see just what he wanted, hoping that he wouldn't make a scene.

"I need to talk to you Jacqui... now" he said in a hoarse whisper.

"That's not possible, can't you see that I'm working?"

"Take a few minutes off, or would you rather I made a scene and we had a right old row here in front of all these people?"

"Oh alright then, go outside and I'll meet you in a few minutes. I can't just walk out without organising things here."

She went up to her room, her heart pounding as the adrenaline pumped through her body.

Although this was the moment she had been dreading, at least Timmy was in school and wouldn't have to be involved. She looked out of the window at the beautiful scene of the village green in the spring sunshine and thought to herself, 'nobody's going to take this away from me, especially not Alan.'

Seeing her reflection in the mirror she said 'you can do it, you have the strength and you know you're right, you should have done this years ago and now you can.' With that she went downstairs and out into the sunshine.

He was sitting in the shade under the tree and she felt the nerves building up inside her, a knot in the pit of her stomach. She knew that she would have to get in with the first words or her courage might desert her. So she walked towards him with her head held high, trying desperately to portray an air of self assurance that she wasn't really feeling.

"So, what is it you want, why are you here?" she said with forced fake confidence, her mouth so dry she wasn't sure that the words would come out.

"I should have thought that it was obvious, I want you to stop this silly nonsense and come home" he said gruffly, his head thrust forward, his chin jutting out belligerently.

"Home! What d'you mean, home? This is my home now."

"Don't be silly Jacqui, this may be alright for a few days holiday but it isn't your home. Home is with me, back in town." He had moved closer and was looking down on her with a superior, confident look on his face.

"You have an amazing gall, d'you know that. After all you've said and done to me and to Timmy, d'you honestly expect me to want to be anywhere near you? I would have thought that my note made it perfectly plain, I have left you for good. I'm going to divorce you. I should have left you years ago, you're nothing but a bully." Her anger was giving her more strength by the minute, anger at his attitude, his arrogant self assurance.

"Don't be silly Jacqui, what possible grounds do you have for divorce? I know you say that I'm jealous of anybody you smile at or talk to, but that's just because I love you, don't you see?"

She wanted to hit him, she felt so angry that he was still trying to put all the blame on her. Taking a deep breath and with all the effort she could muster to stay calm she said almost quietly, spacing out the words

"I'm divorcing you on the grounds of adultery."

"What! Are you at last admitting that I was right? Have you been having an affair all along, as I suspected?" He laughed a sort of forced false laugh, a laugh that annoyed Jacqui even more.

"No, you horrible, self-centred, conceited liar. I haven't been having an affair..... You have."

"Me, whatever makes you think that?" he said, eyes wide and his eyebrows raised in mock innocence.

42

Jacqui took the mobile phone out of her pocket and held it up to Alan's face.

"This is what makes me think that. It not only makes me think it, it proves to me what I should have realised years ago."

Alan's face changed in that instant, the colour drained from it and his head fell forward slightly. Then he made a sudden move to try and grab the phone but Jacqui was too quick for him. Turning away she put it in her pocket again saying

"All your jealous accusations were just a blind to cover your affairs, and yes I say affairs because I expect that there were many more than one. So go back to your girl friend and get ready for the letter from my solicitor. Go on, I don't ever want to see you or speak to you again."

Her confidence was rising. She felt at last that she didn't have to fear him or any thing that he had to say.

"What about my son, what about Timmy?" he asked almost plaintively.

"He certainly doesn't want to see you after all you've done and the bullying way you've treated him. If in years to come he should change his mind, then I won't stop him contacting you. Now I think that you'd better go."

With that she turned and walked across the green and back to the cottage that was now her home. It was hard not to look back to see what Alan was doing, but she was determined not to give him the satisfaction of thinking that she was wavering at all. However, she managed a glance at the shop window and in its reflection saw him get into his car. She heard the engine burst into life and turned to watch him back out and then drive away with a squeal of tyres, as if in a bad temper.

Back in her room once more she sat on her bed, the adrenaline rush had passed and different emotions took over. Holding her head in her hands she started to cry. But her tears were of anger, anger at him for being such a lying, cheating, selfish man; tears of frustration that she hadn't been strong enough to say more of the things that she now wished that she had said. Tears of anger at the pain and suffering that he had caused to Timmy by his bullying over so many years. And finally tears that he had managed to spoil what had started out to be a beautiful spring morning. After a while she dried her eyes and restored her make up.

"You may have managed to spoil today Alan, but you are certainly not going to spoil the rest of my life."

So saying, she went back downstairs. She tried to look normal as though nothing had happened, and resumed her job in the tea-room.

"Are you alright?" asked her mother, who had seen her go out to meet with Alan.

"Yes thanks, I am now, though it was touch and go for a while. I was afraid that I wouldn't have the strength to say what I needed to say. I suppose I was angry enough and that helped."

"Good for you, I doubt if you need it, but Dad and I are always here to support you and give you strength."

"Thanks Mum, and thanks for giving us a home here."

NINE

Although Jacqui wanted to know how Timmy was getting on in his new school, whether he was enjoying it, had made new friends and liked the teachers etcetera, she was well aware that to ask him would be wrong. Timmy could well see it as, not just prying, but a sign of her being over-protective. So she had to wait for him to tell her in dribs and drabs what was going on and how he was feeling.

It was over a week since he had started and he seemed cheerful when he came home. A quick wave and 'Hi Mum' as he came in and if he got the chance he would grab a bun or small piece of cake as he passed through the kitchen. He was very good at doing his homework, there always seemed to be plenty of that. Jacqui was pleased that both she and her parents were always on hand to help if necessary, if they could. Off he would go up to his room, change and then do his homework before they ate.

This evening he had seemed more inclined to talk as they all sat down for their evening meal.

"Good day in school today?"

"Yeah, it was OK. I'm not too struck on the chap who teaches us history, but Mrs Sharland our art teacher is brilliant. She has shown us a lot of new techniques, ways of seeing things that I had never thought of."

Timmy's face was alive with excitement as he went on to describe what had happened in his latest art lesson.

"She asked us to do a painting of what we could see out of the classroom window, just with basic paints. Well, I was sitting a little bit away from the window, so I thought I'd use the window itself as a sort of frame for the picture."

"Good idea, like a frame within a frame eh?" said Walter

"Yeah, something like that Granddad. Anyway, when she came to look at it she said that she liked it, the idea that is, but I had got the window wrong. I couldn't see what she meant until she explained. You see, I had painted the window frame white, and the tree and bit of a building that I could see outside, the green and sort of grey that they were."

"So what was wrong with that?" said Jacqui.

"Exactly, just what I thought. Like the window here, it was a white window, so I painted it white. But she said, 'look at the window with half shut eyes, now what colour is it?' So I did. You do it Mum, the window frame looks grey now doesn't it, see what I mean? She said I was making a classic mistake, I was painting what I knew, not what I saw, and that's what I must learn to do."

"This Mrs Sharland sounds like a very good teacher to me" said Walter, "She has certainly got through to you."

47

There was a pause in the conversation as the family continued their meal. Jacqui was delighted at how Timmy had opened up. She knew she had been right to wait for him to tell her all that was going on without her asking. She was also pleased that his interest in art was being encouraged. Then, with a slightly perplexed look on his face Timmy said

"We've got a bit of a strange chap driving the school bus. He seems very kind and.... well.... nice. The other kids laugh about him, if not exactly at him, and refer to him as Soft Sid. His name's Sidney Something or other. Some of the older girls say that they reckon his mum buys all his clothes for him; mostly at charity shops. I admit he does look a bit of a nerd, with his hair stuck down with gel or something and his old sports jacket with the leather patches on the elbows. He looks a bit like he stepped out of a black and white film." Timmy laughed briefly at his description. "I suspect he was bullied at school, he seemed to be particularly concerned when I started. He would ask me if I was enjoying school and so on. I just got the feeling that although he couldn't protect me, he wanted me to know that he understood if I was having trouble."

"Sidney Turner, lives with his mum in the last cottage on the right as you go out of the village on the Princetown road" said Walter. "Very quiet sort of a chap; a whizz kid with computers. In fact he has a small business helping folks with their computers, teaching them and sorting out their problems."

"So why does he drive the school bus?" asked Jacqui.

"I understand that he had several jobs after he left school, got into driving almost by accident, and when he started up his business he kept on the school bus job just as a sort of financial cushion, so to speak. It all happened before we came here, so I can't say for sure."

"He could be a very useful bloke to know when my computer goes wrong."

"Yes Timmy, in fact I have recently asked him to join our drama group. Not as an actor, but to help us with sound effects and so on. I don't know if he will come, he tends to shun the limelight, but I would dearly love to have his expertise on board for our next production."

TEN

May had been a miserable month. For farmers it was probably an excellent month based on the old adage 'A wet and windy May, a barn full of hay'. But Timmy was not a farmer and he had missed the opportunity to get out on the moor, walking and watching and exploring the area around his new home. But now at last the sun was shining and he was out with his bag on his back and generally full of the joys of spring. The weather was warm, almost hot, and he set off in his jeans and light blue T-shirt, his new trainers completing his outfit.

In the bag on his back he had a couple of sandwiches, a can of coke, his sketching materials, a bird book and his granddad's binoculars. His quest today was to find and hopefully get a good enough view of a ring ouzel. These moorland blackbirds were known to nest in the cliff-like rocks forming the edges of the gullies made by the tin miners on the lower slopes of Braggator.

Unsure of exactly where to look he was prepared to watch and wait for a long time. That was the first thing that he had learned. To see nature at work he had to sit patiently and wait, wait while the birds and animals got used to and ignored his presence. He had turned off the main path that led to the top of the tor and was following a narrow track made by sheep through the heather. In places these tough bushes were up to and even above his knees. Keeping to the high ground he passed the top of the first two gullies and then looked for a vantage spot above the third and deepest one. A large rock with a patch of short sheep-cropped grass in front of it looked perfect, so he sat down to watch and wait.

Below him he could plainly see laid out like a map the fields and the old mine captain's house of Braggator mine. Looking over the side of the hill and into the next valley he could see the roofs of West Furzes and beyond the buildings and the fields of East Furzes. A pair of buzzards circling over head had taken no notice of his arrival, nor had the skylarks singing high above, and it wasn't long before other animals and birds appeared around him. The sun on his back was beginning to warm not only him but the rock against which he was leaning. He had taken the things out of his bag and decided to eat half of his first sandwich and have a drink of his coke. It might not be lunch time but so what, explorers ate when they felt like it didn't they? Several birds flew by but none of them were the black bird with the white collar that he was hoping to see. Looking down the vast cutting before him he thought that some cliff-like rocks about a hundred yards away would be a more promising place to watch. So, gathering his possessions he scrambled along the side of the gully keeping to the opposite side. He had to be careful not to loose his footing and slide or tumble into the bottom some thirty feet below. The ground above was no better to travel on there being mounds of stones and spoil partly overgrown that would trip up the unwary.

Again he waited and the time ticked by accompanied by the song of the birds and the droning of a bumble bee. Suddenly he saw, or thought he saw what he had come for. A black bird, slightly bigger than a garden blackbird had just landed on a ledge on the rock face in front of him. No sooner had it landed than it disappeared into the heather that seemed to hang like a curtain over the rock. Timmy found himself holding his breath. If the bird came out it would be facing him and he would be able to see its breast with the white bib. He seemed to have to wait for ages, and he daren't take his eyes off the spot for a minute, almost afraid to blink. Finally his patience was rewarded and the bird re-appeared, pausing as if to give him a good view, before flying off. Timmy breathed a sigh of relief, he hadn't realised how tensed he had been. He quickly from memory did a sketch of the bird as it had stood for that brief period before flying off. Then with a huge smile on his face he tucked in to the rest of his picnic.

The warm sun, his lunch and the relief after the tension of the waiting all contrived to make him sleepy and it wasn't surprising that he soon nodded off.

Down below him in the nearest field Mick Cribbett was repairing a gap in the stone wall. Sheep would often try to get in from the moor for the better grazing. Goat-like they would try to scale the wall and if one or two stones became dislodged they would soon knock down more and have a running gap to pass through. As he worked he looked around, ever watchful, noticing any changes that had taken place since he was last there.

He had seen Timmy in his light blue T-shirt scrambling around as he arrived at the top of the gully, and curious as to why he was there and what he was doing, he had kept an eye on him. He was about halfway through the job when he saw the sky begin to darken from the west, behind Braggator. Although it was time for lunch he decided to stay and finish the job, hopefully before the rain came. By the looks of the black clouds it could well be a really heavy downpour. He had just replaced the last stone when almost without warning the wind got up and the first few heavy drops fell.

Up on the hillside Timmy was awakened by the wind and the rain. Splat on his sketch book fell a drop the size of a fifty pence piece. Hurriedly he packed his things into his small bag and then looked to see which would be the best way to go. There might be a bit of shelter in the bottom of the gorge, but right where he was the drop was too steep. He would have to go up first and then along a little way before attempting to go down. With his bag on his back he started off but he soon found that the rain had made the ground much more slippery than it had been when he set off earlier that morning. Hanging onto the tough heather he slowly inched along saying to himself 'take your time Timmy, don't try to rush'.   Then suddenly he slipped and lost his footing. The piece of heather that he was holding onto came away in his hand and with a weak cry of 'Oh shit' he went sliding and tumbling down, bouncing on half over-grown rocks and through bushes that scratched and tore at him as he passed. He landed winded and bruised in the bottom of the deep gorge. After lying in a tangled heap for a moment or two while he got his breath back he tried to get up. Most of his body felt fine and he was relieved until he tried to put his weight on his right foot. A sharp stabbing pain shot through his ankle and he let out a yell. He sat down again and gingerly felt around his right ankle. He had no idea if he had broken anything, but it was already feeling hot and swelling somewhat.

All the while the rain was pouring down in sheets, not the regular horizontal rain usually associated with Dartmoor, but a thunderous cloudburst. He knew he had to do something. He was miles away from home and besides, what was worse, nobody knew where he was. He couldn't walk, that was obvious, but he could hop and crawl. If he could get to some shelter where he could rest until the storm passed, maybe then....

Down in the valley Mick had seen the drama unfold. He had watched as the rain flushed Timmy from his resting place, his scramble and subsequent fall into the bottom of the gully. He laid his tools beside the now repaired wall and walked to the top of the field and out through the little hunting gate that led onto the moor. It was two hundred yards to the foot of the gully and a further five hundred from there to where Timmy was. With the water now running down the sheep track that he was following he couldn't move as quickly as he would normally have done. So it was a good ten minutes before he reached his goal and saw Timmy sitting shivering and looking thoroughly miserable.

"Hello there, are you badly hurt?"

Timmy was sheltering under an overhanging rock to which he had crawled in an attempt to get out of the rain. He hadn't seen or heard Mick coming and was startled by the question.

"Oh, hello…er…it's my ankle, I'm not sure what I've done to it, but it hurts like hell when I try to walk on it."

"Better get you down off here before you get any worse. Haven't you got a coat? You look like a drowned rat."

"No, I didn't bring one; the sun was shining when I left home." He sniffed, near to tears.

"Well put this on" said Mick taking off his waxed jacket "and as you can't walk I suppose I'd better give you a piggy-back."

"But you'll get wet if I have your coat."

"With you on my back at any rate that part of me will stay dry" he said with a gruff laugh. "Come on boy, climb aboard."

Timmy lifted himself up onto the broad back in front of him and felt the strong arms lock under his backside.

"If I slip on this wet ground we'll both sit down with a bump, that's a chance we've got to take, OK?"

"Yeah… fine, thank you, I'm sure you won't slip."

And slip he didn't, getting down to the hunting gate slowly but without any mishap. There Mick put him down and had a brief rest before setting of once more with him on his back across the field to his home. Once inside the front door, in the warmth and dry of the house, he put Timmy down again and said

"Can you hop over to that chair by the stove?"

"Yeah, sure,

Mick disappeared for a couple of minutes, returning with a large navy blue towelling bath robe.

"You'd better get out of those wet clothes and put this on."

He disappeared again and came back a few minutes later having changed into dry things. Timmy looked at him, almost for the first time. He saw a strong looking man with a tanned face topped with silver grey hair. He was looking down at Timmy smiling slightly as he said

"I'll make us a hot cup of tea first, then we'll see what we can do for you." As he put the kettle on he turned and looking over his shoulder said

"So, what's your name?"

"Timmy."

"And where d'you live? I think I've seen you about, haven't I?"

"At the Old Smithy. My mum and I moved down here a few weeks ago."

"You must be Walter Blackmore's grandson, right?"

"Yeah, that's right Sir."

"You don't have to call me Sir, my name's Mick, I'm a blacksmith and I live here."

Having made the tea he arranged Timmy's wet clothes on the top of the stove and then produced a large round tin from the sideboard. He opened it and offered it saying

"Have a bun, may help to warm you up a bit. Now let's have a look at that ankle of yours."

He eased off Timmy's sock and trainer to reveal a puffy hot ankle. Timmy grimaced but kept quiet despite the pain. Then holding the heel in one hand and the toes in the other he gently moved the foot in a circular motion.

"I can't say as I know a lot about human breaks and strains, but I don't think this is more than a bad sprain. You twisted it when you fell, I reckon."

He moved away and came back with a bottle of clear liquid and a large crepe bandage. He gently wiped some of the cooling liquid onto Timmy's swollen ankle with a piece of cotton wool and then bound around both the ankle and the instep with the bandage. Timmy meanwhile was looking around the room. It was a fairly large kitchen with a big cream coloured stove against the wall opposite the door. On one side of it was a cupboard, topped with a stone coloured work top, beside which was the large leather chair in which he was sitting. On the other side was a door, possibly leading to a utility room, he couldn't see a sink in this room. There was a

57

window in one side wall under which was a table and two chairs. Some papers and a magazine or two were tidily stacked on the table by a telephone. Against the other wall was a large dresser with beside it a small cupboard on the one side and a fridge on the other. On the wall above the cupboard were three framed photographs. The largest one, in the centre, was of the head and shoulders of a very pretty woman with long wavy light-brown hair. To its right was a picture of the same woman standing by a pony on which was sitting a child of about six, looking as proud as punch with a happy smirk on his face. The third showed a man on a beautiful dapple-grey horse, wearing a red coat, white riding breeches and highly polished black boots. He had a hunting horn in his hand and he was looking slightly towards the camera and at the pack of hounds that were all around him.

It was a warm comfortable room, the sort of room that Timmy felt he would like to have as a kitchen. It was clean and tidy if a bit bare; a man's room, without the clutter of handbags and piles of washing that Timmy associated with the kitchens he knew. The floor was wood and the walls were painted off white. Apart from the three pictures there were no other ornaments or decorations. Though he had only been there for a few minutes he was already beginning to feel warm and a lot more comfortable.

"I think it's time that I took you home young Timmy" said Mick as he left the room again. "I'll get you a change of clothes first, your shirt is nearly dry, but your jeans are still soaking wet." He came back with a jumper and trousers saying with a laugh

"These are probably far too big for you but they'll do to get you home. You put them on while I get the van."

As they drove out of the small yard Timmy asked

"D'you keep any animals here?"

"Yep"

"What have you got?"

"Two horses, a few sheep and some fowls."

"What d'you mean, fowls?"

"Hens."

"Oh" said Timmy, he had never heard them referred to as fowls, as was common in Devon.

"Don't you have a dog? I would have thought that you'd be bound to have a dog, seeing as you've got sheep."

"Yes, I've got a collie, she's in a shed, just had pups."

"Oh, can I see them someday, someday soon?"

Mick laughed at the sudden eagerness of the boy and the way that his whole face lit up when he mentioned the pups.

"I daresay you can, when your ankle is well enough for you to walk over here."

They had reached the gate where the lane joined the road. As the van came to a halt Timmy made to get out to open the gate.

"You stay where you'm to" said Mick "Your ankle isn't well enough yet, I know."

When they got to the Old Smithy he helped Timmy out of the van and up the path to the house door. He looked a bit of a scarecrow in Mick's clothes, too big and bundled around him. As he went in he called out to his mum. Just like all kids he expected her to come to him when he called, rather than go and find her. But it was Jessica who came out of the kitchen to greet them. Mick had stayed just inside the door and nodded to her as she said to Timmy

"What on earth have you been up to, and whose are those clothes? I thought…"

"I got caught in the rain and then I had a fall and hurt my ankle. Mr …er…Mick here rescued me…these are his clothes."

At that point Jacqui joined them and Timmy went through his description of his day and accident again, ending up saying

"Mick thinks it's just a sprain, he put some stuff on it and bandaged it up."

Mick was backing out of the door and said

"Just a bit of witch-hazel. I'll be off now… things to do… bye."

"Oh no, please don't go, you'll have a cup of tea surely?" said Jacqui. "It's the least we can offer you after all you've done to help."

"No thanks, kind of you but I must be getting on. I think I should get that ankle seen to though, perhaps the nurse?"

And with that he was gone.

ELEVEN

It was three days later; Timmy's ankle had meant that he was on crutches for the next week or so. An X-ray at the local hospital on Beatie's advice had shown that Mick's diagnosis had been correct and that it had been only a bad sprain. Timmy had gone to school and Jacqui and Jessica were finishing their breakfast when there was a knock at the door.

"You see to that love, will you?" said Jessica.

Jacqui went to the door and opened it to find George, the postman standing there with a packet in his hand.

"Hello, sorry to bother you, this packet needs to be signed for."

As Jacqui signed on the strange little mechanical box he said

"I don't think we've met, have we? My name's George."

"Oh... yeah" said Jacqui, unaccustomed to this sort of familiarity from a postman. In London she couldn't remember ever meeting with the man who delivered the mail, let alone have any sort of conversation with him.

"I'm Jacqui, Mr Blackmore's daughter."

"Oh right, I'll see you around." With that and a friendly wave he was gone and Jacqui rejoined her mum, who had overheard the exchange.

"Are all your postmen as chatty as that chap?"

"We do have a nice trio of postmen, but George is definitely the most friendly. He's a widower, lost his wife ten years ago or more. I don't think he has any children, never heard of any. He is also very good at looking after elderly people on his round. He will check to see that they are alright, and if he's in any doubt he'll make a point of knocking even if he has no post for them, just to make sure."

"That's very good of him. So he's providing a sort of community service" said Jacqui.

"Yes; and if you're away on holiday you can be sure he'll keep an eye on the place. The other good thing that he does, in fact all our postmen do, if you are out and he has a parcel or something large, he'll leave it next door with your neighbour, rather than take it back to the sorting office. Yes, all in all he's a very nice chap."

"Certainly very different to London" said Jacqui.

A few days later she met him again as she was coming back from the shop. He was by his van outside the village hall.

"Morning Jacqui, are you coming to the Midsummer Ball? It's usually a good evening" he said, pointing to the poster in the glass-fronted notice board.

"Oh yes, we're going as a family" she said "Dad's got the tickets. No doubt I'll see you there."

TWELVE

The Midsummer Ball was one of the main events of the summer calendar in the village. Each year a dance was held, not to commemorate any particular event but just to give the villagers a chance to get together and have fun. It had all started when the village school, like so many in the country, had closed. Sir Harold Edworthy, the lord of the manor and local landlord, had bought the old building. It was a fact that he had managed to keep secret. He vehemently believed that it should stay a part of the village for the use of the villagers. He feared that if it had been put on the open market it would be bought by a developer from outside the region and turned into something hideous. For quite a long time it had stayed empty and unused, a sad reminder of past times. However when the old wooden village hall that stood next to it had been destroyed by fire, he surprised every body by giving it to the village to be used as their new village hall. Everybody had rallied round, giving materials such as paint and so on and helping with the decorating. After the work of renovating and transforming it to its new use was completed, a dance was held in celebration. People so enjoyed this happy occasion that it was decided to make it an annual event, though not necessarily on the same date each year.

A band from a neighbouring town called The Pixielanders were the group of choice. They were essentially a square dance band playing music that was a mixture of Country 'n Western and Irish folk but with a strong hint of rock in the beat. With a caller to help dancers learn the steps and the essentially toe-tapping beat of the music, they were very popular and few could resist getting up and joining in.

It was a very pleasant June evening. A few clouds were slowly drifting across the sky, a reminder of the shower that had fallen earlier that day. Jacqui walked the short distance with Timmy, now at last free of crutches, beside her. He hadn't been altogether sure if this dance was the sort of event that a cool twelve-year old should go to. His grandparents however had seen his disappointment of a few days earlier and had hinted that Mick just might be there. Their ruse had worked and in jeans and a clean shirt he had joined them with a little more enthusiasm.

Some days previously he had gone to return the clothes that Mick had lent him. It had been quite a tiring journey, with his bag on his back and on one leg and elbow crutches. He had arrived at Mick's only to find nobody at home. He looked in one or two outbuildings, calling out Mick's name, being careful not to disturb anything. He had been hoping to see the new pups that Mick had spoken of, but he was out of luck and his dispiritedness was plain to see when he returned home.

The place was buzzing when they walked in, small groups of people standing around chatting and laughing, or sitting on the chairs that were around the walls. In a small room, leading off the entrance hall, a bar had been set up and a dozen or so youngsters were buying drinks. Jacqui looked around the hall, seeing a few faces that she recognised, though there were many more that she didn't. Amongst a group near the stage she saw Pippa who turned and waved, beckoning them to join her. Her two girls were there and Timmy moved with them a little way away from the grown ups. He had been scanning the faces all around, hoping to see Mick. Pippa introduced Jacqui to her husband Jim and to another couple, Frank and Linda, who had joined them. Jim had an agricultural supplies business and Frank helped his mother run their small farm, though his main business was as a motor mechanic servicing and maintaining the local vehicles.

Then Phil German, Pippa's dad, climbed up onto the stage and started the proceedings. A few chords from the band and the caller announced the first dance and the evening got underway. The band, consisting of an accordion, a fiddle, a banjo and two guitars was backed by a drummer whose antics reminded Jacqui of the animal who played the drums on The Muppets. She danced with several different partners, as is often the case with square dancing and found herself really enjoying herself. It seemed the first time that she felt really relaxed since her recent, somewhat heated conversation with Alan. Timmy was also enjoying himself, she was glad to see. He might not have imagined this sort of evening to be 'cool' but it was certainly fun and he seemed to have forgotten that he had hoped to see Mick. Her only worry was his ankle, so recently had he left off his crutches.

There was a break for refreshments at half time and as usual the good ladies of the village had produced a wonderful spread of quiches, sandwiches, sausage rolls and cakes of all descriptions. These were available in a large side room, buffet style. Tea and squash to replace lost body fluids were in demand by those who didn't want alcohol, and one or two small tables had appeared in the dance hall for people to sit around. George came up to Jacqui asking her how she was enjoying herself and offering to buy her a drink. She declined and he stayed for a while chatting before moving on to the bar. Later, when the dancing started up again, he asked her to partner him, and she found him to be good company. He was not particularly handsome but he was by no means ugly, and he had a pleasant smile and was polite and courteous, thanking her when he took her back to her seat after their dance. Jacqui judged him to be in his late fifties going by his thinning hair, greying at the temples, and the lines on his face.

She sat out for a while, happy just to listen to the music and watch Timmy and the other dancers enjoying themselves. She found herself looking around the room at the other men there, not looking for a partner exactly, but just looking. Most if not all their faces seemed to be happy and smiling like George's; probably brought on by the happy atmosphere of the evening. It all helped to make her feel good and relaxed; pleased that she had moved down to live in this village. However the last thing that she wanted at that moment was to be tied into a relationship with another man, any man. They would have baggage, just as she had baggage with Timmy, and just like her would be set in their ways. Ways that could be difficult and hard to live with.

Then she found herself thinking of Alan, trying to remember when or if they had ever enjoyed an evening together like this. She smiled to herself at the thought of him racked with his stupid jealousy. He would have been completely unable to cope with her dancing with another man, a normal and frequent practise at this sort of dance. He wouldn't have lasted five minutes; he would have stormed off home, expecting her to follow him without question. Then once home, the accusations would have started; accusations that she found hard to understand because they were so ridiculously untrue. Once long ago, she had laughed at him, telling him how silly he was to even suggest that she had designs on any other man. He had slapped her across the face telling her not to laugh at him. Almost immediately he had apologised, but it had made her careful of what she said when he was in one of his jealous moods. She should have moved out there and then, but Timmy was not very old and where would she have gone? So fear kept her from leaving, and besides if she had left him it would have been an admission of failure, in a way. And then there was also the strange inexplicable fact that she loved him still, and her hope was that she could change him, persuade him that his jealousy was unnecessary and unfounded. But the accusations became more frequent and more difficult for her to cope with, and occasionally the violent outbursts re-occurred. Even so, it had been several more years before she had finally left him, and then it had only been possible because of the way he had treated Timmy which had made him want to leave too.

She was awakened from her reverie by Timmy who came over asking her to dance with him.

"Are you sure your ankle is alright, you're not doing too much on it are you?"

"No it's fine Mum, besides I've not been dancing as much as you."

So mother and son got up and joined the dancing, skipping and swinging to the music. Jacqui was glad that they did, as it turned out to be the last dance of the evening. Then somewhat out of breath they said farewell to their many new friends and tired but happy left for home.

Once outside they discovered, what was for them both, another new experience. Walking home in the dark, no pavements, no street lights, just the thousands of stars gleaming above them. Stars which in London they had never been able to see.

THIRTEEN

The next morning was one of those beautiful summer mornings when lying in bed just isn't an option. Strong almost hot sunlight was blazing down on the dew-soaked grass, sparkling and dazzlingly bright. On the other side of the green the roofs of the houses were steaming, adding to the early morning mist that filled the valleys. It all foretold of a hot day to come.

Jacqui was up early, and was helping Walter with the daily baking of cakes and scones. Although she had been working with him for several weeks she was still not quite sure of the ways of his business, so she asked

"Are you expecting many today Dad?"

"This afternoon, hopefully, Sunday mornings are never very busy."

"So you won't mind if I go out with Timmy this morning?"

"No, not at all, where were you thinking of going, somewhere nice?"

"I want to go and thank Mick properly for the way he helped Timmy, I feel I ought to take him a little thank you present, a bottle of whisky perhaps, what do you think?"

"Yes, that would be good, always assuming that he drinks."

"Oh, I think he does, Pippa was saying something about him occasionally going to the pub."

"Are you really only going to thank him, or is there another reason for your visit?"

"What d'you mean?"

"Well, I suspect that like any mum you want to see what and who it is that Timmy is so taken with and satisfy your natural concerns. Am I right?"

"Yes, I suppose you are. I haven't said anything to Timmy yet, I wonder if he will object to my going with him."

"I doubt it; if anything I reckon he'll be pleased to show off his new friend and rescuer."

So it was that after breakfast they set off up the road and through the gate onto the track that led to Mick's place. Walter had been right in his judgement of Timmy's reaction and he happily carried the bottle of whisky in the small rucksack that he habitually carried on his back. All the way along the lane he pointed out to Jacqui the birds and plants most of which he had sketched. Jacqui was impressed with his knowledge, knowledge acquired so recently. She was grateful that he had taken to their new life away from Town. He had always been somewhat of a solitary kid, but his previous interests had taken place mostly indoors. True, he had played with Jacko and occasionally they had gone to the nearby park with Jacko's dad. But now he seemed to want to be out on the moor all day, every day.

As they started going down hill towards the two fields and the house that was the home where Mick lived, Jacqui was struck by the idyllic beauty

71

of the place. It was like an oasis of tranquillity miles from anywhere. The soft green of the fields with their dry stone walls were surrounded by the darker colours of the bracken, the heather and the gorse. Sitting squarely between the fields the small stone buildings with their slate roofs nestled snugly together, looking for all the world as though they had grown there. It was a small, almost level patch of ground near the head of the steep sided valley with a small stream tinkling through it all. Beyond the holding were great scars; the furious efforts of former inhabitants, trying to wrench from the earth some of its wealth. The small canals known as leats, that used to carry water to turn the huge wheels that powered the operation, could just be seen as faint horizontal lines across the hillside, and in places mounds of rocky spoil showed grey amongst the heather.

"So where were you when you slipped and fell, hurting your ankle?"

"I was in that big gully, the third one from the left. I don't know if you can make it out Mum, but there's a big sort of rocky cliff about half-way down on the right."

"Yes, I think I can see it."

"Well that's where I saw the ring ouzel, and near there is where I was when I slipped and fell."

"So Mick had to carry you all the way from there? Wow, d'you think a bottle of scotch is enough?"

"I don't know Mum, I don't know what he likes, he doesn't say a lot. He seems to be very kind

72

and caring, like the way he helped me but he's quiet. It's like he just doesn't want to talk for some reason. "

As they got nearer Jacqui saw in the first field two horses, a grey, now almost white with just a hint of dapple, and a dark bay, their coats shining in the sunlight. They walked towards her, nodding their heads and swishing their tails. In the field beyond were several sheep of various colours, some looking more like goats than sheep, with lambs now almost as big as their mothers. The lane led straight into the farmyard where they were met by a collie dog, barking and wagging its tail. The yard was clean and tidy but without any window boxes full of flowers or ornaments of any kind, showings clearly to Jacqui the absence of a woman's touch. The house was typical of the period when it was built, with three windows upstairs, and downstairs a front door with a window on each side. A lean-to extension on one end looked to be a later addition. Outbuildings formed two other sides of the yard and from the open door of one of these buildings came the ringing sound of hammer on anvil; a rhythmic *clang, tap tap tap.* This soon stopped, the barking of the dog telling Mick that he had visitors, and he came out into the sunlight a hammer in his right hand.

Timmy, patting the dog, almost ran forward, saying

"Hi Mick, can I see the pups?"

"Wait a minute Timmy, give the man chance to breathe, we've only just got here." Jacqui smiled at Mick and said

"I hope you don't mind us butting in on you like this and disturbing your work. I just wanted to say thank you for rescuing Timmy the other week. I felt that I hadn't said enough then, and I feel bad that I haven't been to see you before. I hope that you'll accept this small gift from us both."

Timmy took the bag off his back and produced the bottle of whisky.

"You didn't need to do that Mrs...."

"Jacqui, please....please call me Jacqui."

"Thank you, it was no trouble, just got a bit wet, that's all."

"I'm sure it was a lot more than that. All we hear about from Timmy is how you rescued him and carried him for miles; like some modern-day St Christopher."

"Oh, I don't know about that but thank you. Anyway, you want to see the pups do you? Well come on, they're in here."

Putting down his hammer he led them to a small shed adjoining the house, his dog trotting ahead. As they approached they could hear several squeaks and high-pitched yaps. Mick opened the door and five small black and white bundles tumbled out, bouncing playfully around their mother.

Timmy crouched down among them stroking and petting them as they sniffed and licked his hands and arms. Looking up at Jacqui he said what she was expecting him to say

74

"Aren't they lovely Mum?"

She had to admit that they were, and before he could ask his next predictable question she said

"No, we can't have one."

"Sorry Timmy, they're all spoken for" said Mick "I'm keeping that one on the left with the most black on its head. She'll be company for her mum, so you'll be able to see her when you come, that's if your mum is happy for you to go home smelling of dogs. The others will be gone in a couple of weeks; they are nearly eight weeks old now." He was looking down with a warm smile on his lips and in his eyes at Timmy crouching amongst the pups.

"Are you sure you don't mind him coming here, he won't be a nuisance, interfering and interrupting your work."

"No, he's no trouble, if he were I'd send him home."

He was looking at Jacqui now and she noticed that the smile was no longer in his eyes. It wasn't that he had become cold exactly; it was more as though a wall had dropped down between them. As though he could allow his emotions to show when he was talking to a child but not when he was talking to her.

"I won't be any trouble" said Timmy with a ready laugh "I'll be glad to do anything to help."

"Well as long as you're no trouble and can be of help here it's OK with me. Now I must be getting back to help Granddad and you must be home for lunch, it's your favourite, Sunday roast, so don't be late."

She turned to Mick and holding out her hand said

"It's been good to see you again, good to see the place that Timmy has been so excited about, perhaps you'll visit us one day soon."

He nodded graciously, almost an old fashioned bow, taking her small hand in his large calloused one for a brief moment, and then she turned and set off up the track towards the village. She felt happy and almost relieved to have met Mick and seen the place he lived in. It was obvious to her that he had made a huge impression on Timmy and she had felt the need, as her dad had said earlier, to see him again and get a fuller impression of him.

He was hardworking, of that there was no doubt, and by the looks of his well kept animals, cared deeply for them. He seemed to be fond of children, as was evident by the way he smiled when looking at Timmy. But at all other times she noticed that the smile left his eyes to be replaced by what seemed to be sadness. She wondered if it was loneliness or pain from something that had happened in his past. What if anything was his secret and would it really matter if she knew?

He was without doubt a handsome man, and although his grey hair made him look to be in his fifties, his unlined face would put him at least ten years younger than that. And why was he on his own? Was he like she soon would be, divorced? Had he ever been married or was he a loner, or maybe gay? She laughed at herself for thinking these things, what or who he was didn't matter to her at all, as long as he was good for Timmy. After Alan, and all the bullying and pain that he had put him through, Timmy needed a good man as a role model

She walked on, enjoying the warmth of the sun and the sounds and smells all around her. A gorse bush in full bloom was a blaze of gold giving off, to her surprise, a strong smell of coconut. She was beginning to understand what Timmy saw in this wild landscape and what had attracted her parents to leave their busy life in The City and come here to live. She could feel a sort of comfort in the emptiness; feel that although there were no crowds of people around she didn't feel at all lonely.

FOURTEEN

John Badcock was a countryman through and through. He disliked towns and cities and rarely set foot in either, except perhaps to attend a market on a rare occasion. He was of a past era; one of the old moorland characters no longer seen. He lived on his own, in a caravan with a row of wooden and corrugated iron sheds behind it in a field that he had acquired many years before. Those of a generous nature said that he had inherited it from a distant relative. Others less kind said that he had been left it by a grateful former employer; a lady with whom he had shared a great deal of time, both indoors and out. How he had come by it was really of no consequence, he kept the place remarkably tidy. His tractor and trailer and his small horse box parked neatly beside piles of wood, ready to be sawn into logs. There was usually a pony or two in the field, keeping his riding horse company, and a few chickens scratching around.

Jay Bee, as he was commonly known, was about sixty, nobody was really sure. In fact it was doubtful if he knew himself exactly when he was born. His hair streaked with grey hung below his ears and looked as though he cut it himself. His beard, also grey, was full face and like his hair, roughly trimmed. He normally wore a pair of corduroy trousers, an old sports jacket, which had seen better days, and wellington boots. He drove an old four by four truck and whereever he went he was accompanied by his two faithful dogs, a lurcher and a Jack Russell.

How he made his living was not entirely obvious. He sold logs and did odd jobs for anybody and everybody, being in demand because he could turn his hand to almost anything. One of his talents was as a pest controller. He was particularly good at getting rid of moles; the scourge of lawns and farmers fields that were to be cut for hay or silage. He knew his way around most of the fields in the area and was also welcomed for keeping the rabbit population in check. Several farmers had surreptitiously availed themselves of his night-time lamping, when a rogue fox or badger was troubling them.

Phil German farmed the Manor Farm just out of the village. Over the years, many neighbouring farms had been sold, and often the new owners had only wanted a country residence with perhaps one field; so Phil had been able to add several acres to his holding. He was a good and successful farmer, who knew and understood the land and his livestock.

In one of his fields above the village he had a large flock of ewes and lambs and several of the lambs were just about ready for market. As he walked around the field, on the morning after the dance, he noticed that one or two of the ewes seemed to be bleating rather more than usual. All the sheep were up on their legs, running without their heads bobbing up and down; which would have been a sure sign of lameness. So he went to the gate into the next field and with his dog gently bringing them on, ran the flock through the gate slowly, counting them as they went.

He was six short, so he ran them through again, this time just counting the lambs. Again he was six short. He walked around both fields looking everywhere and then in the neighbouring fields. No sign of the six lambs anywhere, no sign of wool where they might have gone through a hedge. They had just vanished; six lambs fit for market and for many a family meal. He went back to his truck, parked in the lane outside the field gate, and had a good look around. There were wheel-marks, apart from those that his truck had made, but he had driven over them and it was difficult to make out much detail. But one thing that he did notice straight away, although the ground was fairly hard he could see several faint hoof prints of sheep, both in the lane and the gateway.

His guess was that somebody had driven a bunch of sheep out into the lane, where they had already parked a suitable truck; and there they had picked out and loaded up six of his fat lambs. He would have to report this to the police, though he had little hope of their being able to catch the culprits. He would also mention it to his neighbours. They would all have to keep watch, although it was very difficult to know how to combat this sort of crime. He just hoped that this was a one off, not the start of a wave of such thefts.

As he drove back to the farm he met Jay Bee and stopped to have a chat as usual. After the normal familiarities, the weather and so on, he said

"I've lost half a dozen lambs, Jay Bee; looks like someone has pinched them."

"That's bad, when was this?"

"Last night, so far as I can tell... they was all there yesterday. It looks like somebody drove a few out into the lane and loaded them up there... hard to tell for sure."

"What sort of a vehicle, could you tell from the tracks?"

"No, no idea. I was just hoping that you might have seen or heard something, you being out a bit at night and that."

"No, can't help you there I'm afraid, I aint seen nort, sorry."

"Well, keep your eye out will you? Let me know if you do see or hear anything."

"Sure will, it's a bad business...been a long time since we had any rustling around here."

With that Phil said cheerio and drove on home, knowing that he could count on Jay Bee to tell other farmers of what had happened. But what could any of them do? They could hardly lock up all the animals in sheds every night. The only thing that might help would be to keep them in fields that were difficult to get to with a vehicle.

When he got home he went indoors and rang Frank Narraway. He was a dear friend, the son of his oldest friend, with a small farm some way out of the village. He and Phil helped each other out occasionally and so he was naturally the first person to be contacted, even before the police.

FIFTEEN

Six o'clock on a July morning is always a good time to get up if the weather's fine. Mick dressed and went out across the paddock with a head collar in his hand. His two mares were standing by the single hawthorn at the edge of the field and as soon as they heard him call they started walking towards him, their heads nodding, almost in time with each other. The grey, Osprey, was the younger of the two hunters and his main riding horse. He had had and her since she was four years old and now at fifteen she was in her prime, both in strength and knowledge. Sure-footed and way-wise she was a perfect horse for Dartmoor, able to pick her path between rocks and gorse bushes without faltering. Ptarmigan the bay was six years older, and although just as reliable a mount, he had in recent years ridden her less and used her for breeding.

Mick walked a few yards into the field and met the mares, talking to them all the time. Then after a few minutes patting and petting he slipped the head collar on Osprey and walked back to the yard and the stable, leaving Ptarmigan snickering softly to herself. He tied Osprey up in the stable and started grooming her, whistling as he brushed her getting a pleasurable feeling from the closeness and warmth, admiring the shine on her coat. Every now and then she would turn her head around and nudge him gently, reinforcing the obvious bond between man and beast. Then he saddled up and was soon off to the hunting gate and out onto the moor. Way over to the West dark clouds were gathering and if he were to get a ride in before it rained now was the time. He liked to take Osprey out at least three times a week for a short hack to keep her fit. If time allowed he would go for a longer ride a couple of times a month. He had sometimes felt that it would be good to go on a long distance ride, stopping overnight at designated farms and livery yards on the way. But a ride like that really should be shared with someone. All the best things in life are better when shared. Even a short morning hack, like the one he was on, would be more enjoyable with a companion. Maybe one day he would again be able to share his life with a special person. For now he had to content himself with his horses and dogs.

He turned Osprey across the stream and up the hill beside one of the tin miner's gullies. Then over the top and down into the next valley and the small road between the fields that led to West Furzes. The road ran right through the farm yard. The long-house, the cart linhay and another small stone building being on the one side, while across the road was a much larger barn with lean-to sheds adjoining it. All seemed deserted, no smoke from the chimney, no dogs barking or hens cackling, so unlike the other farms in the neighbourhood. Grass was growing in the yard and a large bunch of nettles in one corner gave home and food to a number of caterpillars and other insects. It all looked very desolate and forlorn, and yet the large barn across the road from the house had recently had a new pair of large doors fitted, substantial looking doors with a heavy looking padlock in the hasp holding them shut. Perhaps the new owners had brought down some of their possessions and were storing them there. 'But why not in the house?' he thought. Living on his own, as Mick had done for so long, he tended to see puzzles and try to work out their meaning. As a born country man he was naturally observant, noting any changes that he saw as he went around the area. 'Maybe' he thought 'they've let the barn, as they don't need it themselves for a while'.

He rode on along tarmac and through East Furzes before turning off the road and onto a bridle path that would take him back to the open moor. A long grassy path that led up to the top of Braggator gave him and Osprey the chance to have a good gallop before they turned for home and breakfast. The clouds had reached them now and it would not be long before there was a shower or two. Ahead of him he could see the figure of young Timmy walking down the lane, coming to see Meg, and Floss the one pup that Mick had kept. He liked the boy, he was quiet and sensible; willing to listen and learn. He also seemed to have a natural touch with animals, almost an affinity. He wondered what he'd be like with horses and if he would like to ride. There was plenty of time, time to find out what other interests he had. He was aware of his love of drawing and his new found fascination for Dartmoor. It wouldn't do to push too many ideas on him, besides the boy might well stop visiting, might find some other interest elsewhere. He smiled, almost laughed out loud at himself, as he realised that he was getting fond of Timmy, looking forward to his comings and feeling slightly sad at the thought that he might go somewhere else for his entertainment. But was that really so surprising? After all he was about the same age as Sam would have been.

And then there was Jacqui. What did she think of him, was she happy for her son to be all his time with some old man who lived on his own? He was well aware of what people might think and if he was honest he couldn't blame them. And what about Timmy's dad? Neither he nor Jacqui had ever mentioned him. Did he have a dad, was he ever around? Perhaps he and Jacqui were separated or maybe divorced. That got him thinking about Jacqui. They had only met a few times and it was difficult to make a judgement on such a brief acquaintance. She was a very attractive lady, of that there was no doubt. If he were to go by looks alone she would score top marks. From what he had seen she was capable and caring, but she seemed a bit cool, as though hiding something, hiding herself maybe.

Was he looking for a relationship with her, or with anyone for that matter? Was he ready for that yet and if he were would anyone want him? After all, he had a past, he had been hiding behind the wall that he had built up around himself and his emotions ever since he had come back to live in Devon. Jacqui might or might not be hiding something; he certainly was.

As he reached the lane he caught up with Timmy who looked up at him with his usual wide grin.

"Had a good ride Mick?"

"Yes thanks. You come to see Floss?"

"Yeah, if that's alright. Are you going out shoeing today?"

"Not today, I've got to make some shoes though, would you like to help?"

"Oh yes please."

As Mick dismounted he asked

"Would you like to try riding one day?"

"I don't know, Osprey looks very big to me, I think I'd be better on something a bit smaller, like the sort of ponies that Margaret and Helen ride."

"Perhaps first of all, you could get used to being with my two mares, grooming and so on. They may big too big for you to ride but they are quiet and fairly sensible and you could learn a lot. I'll just take off her tack and then why don't you lead Osprey out into the field for starters, I'll come with you."

So they set off, Timmy holding the rope of Osprey's head collar. Mick looked on with a smile, it was more than likely that Osprey was leading Timmy, but the boy was happy. When they got back to the yard Timmy ran to his bag that he had left by the stable door and reaching inside it said

"Look what I found this morning. As I was walking here this morning I heard a strange noise coming from a tree beside me, I looked in to see if I could see what it was that was making the noise and I saw this."

He produced an oak leaf with a small red and yellow ball, about the size of a marble stuck to it.

"What is it Mick?"

"That's an oak apple."

"An oak apple? I didn't know oak trees had apples, I thought they had acorns. Can you eat it?"

"No, I wouldn't, I doubt if it would taste very good. It's a sort of shelter for a little grub to live in while it grows into a small wasp. The wasp, called a gall wasp, lays its egg on the leaf and the tree sort of defends itself and the grub by building this gall around it. Later on, like a caterpillar grows into a butterfly, the wasp hatches out and flies away."

"Fascinating. I'll take it home to show Mum, I wonder if she knows what it is."

He put the leaf back in his bag and then went to see the pup while Mick went in for his breakfast. Old and young, tutor and pupil, comfortable and unquestioning in their relationship together.

SIXTEEN

Sidney Turner was thirty three and lived with his mother Hilda. His father Norman had tragically been killed in a car accident two weeks before he and his mother were going to be married. The tragedy had been the talk of the village for several weeks. Who could fail to feel sorry for the bride-to-be at the peak of the excitement of her forthcoming wedding? All her hopes and plans for the future cruelly dashed in an instant. The cause of the accident was unknown, the car had been found on a stretch of open moor several yards from the road on its side and wedged against a large rock. The impact with the rock had been such that the roof of the car had been pushed down suddenly and with force onto Norman's head. Death had been instantaneous. Nobody could understand how the accident could have happened. Norman was a careful driver not known for driving fast, he hadn't been drinking and the road was dry. It was as though something· or some one had forced him off the road. Maybe an animal on the road caused him to swerve. It was all very puzzling.

Hilda had to deal with all that, the uncertainty of his death, the loss of her husband-to-be and the cancellation of the wedding. Not only that, but there was the awkwardness of returning wedding presents. Awkward and embarrassing not just for her, but for those who had given them. Most people were happy for her to keep the gifts, feeling that it would be adding to her distress if they were to take them back. Although there were a few less charitable souls who were happy to have their gifts returned.

Her friends and family did the best they could to comfort her but overnight she went from being a happy-go-lucky young woman into some one withdrawn and introverted. She gave up her job as barmaid in the local pub and spent her days sitting at home doing nothing. Her father found this more than a little difficult. He was of the old school, having no understanding of mental illness, inclined to say 'get a grip of yourself and snap out of it'. Her mother was more inclined to wait and give her more time to recover.

But two months later, Hilda found out that she was pregnant. Having confirmed her condition with her doctor she went and had a long talk with her old friend Mary at Ashworthy. Afraid to tell her parents she had to unburden herself on someone. Mary quite rightly told her to tell her parents right away, they would find out soon enough and would only be more upset that she hadn't told them before. The only other alternative was to have an abortion, and that was a course that neither Hilda nor Mary agreed with.

As she had feared, her parents were none too happy at the news that they were to become grandparents. It was bad enough having their daughter living at home, moping around the house all day and relying on them for her existence. As her dad said, it was one thing when she was working and bringing in some money to pay her way, it was totally different having her and a new baby depending on them. They were after all, nearing retirement. They hadn't expected to go back to a house full of nappies, baby clothes and toys all over the place. But they knew that there was no alternative, she was their daughter and they would stand by her, 'that's what you did'. They would have to put up with what they saw as the shame and embarrassment.

But as soon as the baby was born their attitude changed dramatically. Not only was he a little charmer, but their friends and neighbours seemed so proud of them and so full of admiration for the way that they had helped Hilda. After a year she was able to go back to work and young Sidney was looked after by his doting gran and gramp. But even this happy state of affairs was doomed, for Hilda's dad died suddenly of a heart attack just before Sidney reached his fourth birthday. So the boy was brought up in a house dominated by women and with no male role model. By this time his gran had taken over the role of his main carer, acting as both mother and father to him and Hilda.

At primary school he did well and joined in all the school activities, but it all changed when he got to secondary school. There he was ridiculed and bullied, mostly because he was quiet and studious. However, he was always good at maths and science and his salvation came when he discovered computers. Then he really came into his own. He loved them and everything about them. Because of his expertise he was able to help his classmates and soon his tormentors ceased their bullying. But his self esteem was low, he was not good at projecting himself, maybe because his grandmother had always done it for him, so when he left school he didn't go on to university. Instead he did a course at a local college in IT. In any case his mother would never have consented to him being away from home. He wanted to set up his own business using his skills, but at the same time he needed to earn some money. After several dead end jobs, like shelf stacking in a supermarket and van driving, he took the job of driving the local school bus. Despite them sometimes poking fun at him, he knew that they referred to him as Soft Sid, he felt an affinity with the children, but the job was only part time. By this time, and partly due to his gran's recommendation, he started helping friends and neighbours with their computers. Any time she heard someone saying that they were having difficulty she would say that they should get in touch with her Sidney. He was a veritable whizz kid with computers. This eventually led to him having a thriving though modest business, but still keeping on the bus driving job for the security of a weekly wage.

Although his business was doing well his social life was not. He had a few male friends but he never seemed to have any luck with girls. It always seemed to start well, often in company with one of his male friends or in a group, but on his own and one-to-one, things just seemed to go wrong. His gran was largely to blame for this, though Sidney would never have said so. On more than one occasion she had warned him of the dangers of getting too closely involved with some young girls.

"You take care young man, if you get yourself tangled up with one of they fast hussies you'll bring shame and disgrace on this house."

The life style of his contemporaries was so different to his, again largely due to the way his gran had brought him up. On one occasion he was going to go to a club with a nice girl, as he saw her, and another couple. They all came to his house to collect him and came indoors to meet his folks. When they were asked at what time Sidney would be coming home his girl friend said

"Oh, about half past one or two o'clock I expect."

His gran was horrified at this and told them that Sidney was not a young man for that sort of thing, he was used to being in bed before half past ten, like all decent people. They laughed at this, after all, half past ten was when things only just got started. If he couldn't stay out with them he would have to stay home. They were going anyway and would go without him. So they turned and left but he ran after them saying to his girl friend

"I'll see you tomorrow."

"Don't bother, I don't want a mummy's boy."

It was sad because he was a different man when he was out on business away from the shadow of his overbearing grandmother. More than once when he was younger he had complained to his mother, begging her to remonstrate on his behalf, but all she would say was

"Don't upset your gran, she's been very good to us, bringing you up and minding the house so that I could go to work. If it hadn't been for her and your grandad I don't know where we would have been."

So he had grown up, trapped in a life that was not really of his making nor really what he wanted either. But because it was what he had always been used to he felt safe; it gave him a feeling of security and he was naturally a bit afraid to break away.

When Walter asked him to come to the drama group to produce some of the backing music and the sound effects he was quietly delighted. But none the less it was with a degree of uncertainty that he entered the hall that evening to join in the discussion about the forthcoming show. It was to be a three act play, a thriller with a fair amount of comedy and it would require lots of sound effects such as thunder and lightening and ghostly groans.

Sidney was in his element and soon had an eager audience around him as he demonstrated his skills. One of the female members of the cast, a blond girl of twenty-something called Marilyn, soon asked him if he could help with her computer. She was at her wits end. While it was going it was fine, but it was misbehaving and she had no idea what to do to put it right.

"Computer engineers from town are so expensive and they have to come such a long way... I was wondering...." She smiled at him.

"Of course, I'd be happy to come and have a look at it."

So the next evening, after he had had his tea, he went over to her place. He was surprised to find that she lived in a large house with three other girls. Marilyn showed him into a small but cosy living room with the offending computer on a desk in the corner.

"Shall I get you a cup of tea?"

"Thank you; that would be very nice."

He didn't like to say no for fear of offending her, despite the fact that he'd just had one before he left home. He got to work and soon had the problem solved. Like most of the jobs he was asked to do, he found that usually it was the fear of doing something wrong and losing valuable material that had caused the owner to call him out. When he was finished Marilyn suggested that he sit back in an easy chair, he wasn't in a hurry to go was he? So he did, sitting somewhat stiffly, bolt upright with his knees together. Sensing his shyness and wishing to help she said

"I'm no good with electrical or mechanical things, I never have been, they are all Greek to me. It's so good that you could help me like this. We had computers at school and I could never get on with them, not like some of the other kids, I was always afraid of them I suppose. The other kids used to laugh at me and that only made matters worse."

"I think I know what you mean, I was bullied a bit at school. I always found it difficult to express myself and stand up for myself. I used to try and hide away from everybody. Fortunately computers were what saved me. I found that I had a natural gift for working with them. That meant that I could help the other kids and they then left me alone. But I'm surprised that people would laugh at you, you seem so composed and self assured."

"It's what I taught myself to do, I suppose. I have a lot of friends who are into complimentary therapies of one sort or another. It seemed good to me, so I studied and I'm now a fully qualified Reiki master."

"Reiki, I don't think I've heard of that, what is Reiki, what does it do exactly, would it help me? I get a bit shy and tongue-tied at times."

"Reiki is a system of healing developed in Japan. In it the practitioner gently places her hands non-invasively in a sequence of positions which cover the whole body. The whole person is treated rather than the specific symptoms. It would probably help you to relax."

"Is it expensive?" asked Sidney, worried because it sounded as if it probably was.

"No more than your charges for fixing my computer. In fact if you like I could give you a treatment session as payment for what you've done for me this evening."

"When would that be, tonight?"

"No, I can't manage tonight, let me look in my diary and we'll make an appointment."

So a date was fixed for two days later and Sidney said goodbye and went off home feeling remarkably good and more sure of himself than he had felt for a long time. Marilyn may not have practiced her Reiki on him that evening but something had given him a feeling of confidence. When dealing with his other customers he was always sure of himself while doing his job, fixing their troublesome computers. But when or if it came to social chit-chat afterwards, he got embarrassed or tongue-tied and tried to get away as soon as possible. Would she be able to make him feel like he now felt all the time, or was that too much to ask?

SEVENTEEN

The end of July and the beginning of the school summer holidays. Mick remembered well those long hot days when he was at school, helping with the harvest on the estate, or out with his dad ferreting. His dad had always kept a couple of ferrets in a hutch in the shed by the back door. They used to go out with a bag full of nets and a box with the ferrets in. Although his dad had a shotgun he never took it on those occasions. He always said that a gun and ferrets didn't mix. They would arrive at the hedge or bank that his dad knew was full of rabbits and drape the nets over all the holes they could find. They looked like straw coloured spider's webs in amongst the campions and the stitchwort. Then the ferret would be put down one of the holes and they would wait, he on one side of the hedge and his dad on the other. Sometimes the ferret would pop out after a very short time, his little head looking from side to side as if to say 'why did you put me in here?' Sometimes the rabbits would be bolting out almost immediately, they would get tangled in the net and if it was on his side he would have to grab the rabbit and break its neck. His dad had taught him at an early age how to do that.

"If you've got to kill something, do it quickly and cleanly, don't cause the critter any more pain than you have to."

Some evenings they would go home with as many as twenty rabbits. These would go to one of the local pubs that served rabbit on their menu.

Then there were the days out riding, mostly in the evenings, with the landlord's son. He was a couple of years younger than Mick and needed someone to go with him. They would ride for hours along the bridle paths that ran amongst the fields of the estate and beyond. Sometimes they would go down to the beach, after most of the day trippers had gone home, and ride along the sand, galloping and laughing with the salt spray stinging their faces. He remembered one occasion when they had taken off the saddles and ridden out into the waves, their ponies plunging and snorting the boys getting their trousers soaking wet but all of them enjoying every minute of it. Yes, he remembered his summer holidays had been great fun, could Timmy's be equally as good?

Mick was going over to East Furzes shoeing, with these thoughts running through his head, when he had an idea. They had a nice quiet welsh cob that their daughter used to ride. He was just standing in the field as company for their other two horses, not doing anything since the daughter had left home. After he had finished shoeing he asked if, instead of charging them, he could borrow the cob for the summer holidays. It wasn't the first time that he had done a bit of bartering in exchange for his services.

They were very pleased with the idea, so later that evening he rode over on Osprey and led the cob, Dillon, back to Braggator. As he passed West Furzes he saw, standing by the big barn, a light blue horse box. Naturally interested in any one with horses, he looked to see if he could see the driver. A man was by the box, but instead of looking his way and waving or in some way acknowledging him, he turned his back on Mick. This seemed most peculiar, surely the natural thing to do would be to look and see who it was that was passing on a horse? Oh well, if he didn't want to be neighbourly there was little Mick could do. They had always seemed a bit strange, these new people. Another thing that puzzled him was that Osprey took no notice of the horse box, and on reflection Mick realized that there had been no smell of horse at all.

Once home, he watched the three horses out in the field getting to know one another, glad to see that they settled down together. There had been a little twitching and prancing, then they had raced off down the field, kicking their heels in the air before standing in the far corner blowing a little.

As he watched them he wondered, was he doing the right thing? He had taken the precaution of checking with Jacqui when he had met her in the village a few days before. He wanted to make sure that she had no objection to his teaching Timmy after he had said that he would like to learn to ride. Subsequently he had encouraged Timmy to spend a good bit of time with Ptarmigan, grooming her and learning a little about looking after a horse. He

100

certainly seemed to have a natural way with animals; he had none of the nervousness that Mick had thought that a city boy might have. No, he felt sure that Timmy would be happy. It wasn't that that was worrying him. Was he, Mick, getting too close, too emotionally involved with the boy? He wasn't a relative, he wasn't Sam, he was just a lad who seemed to like the things that Mick had; the pup, the other animals and also the whole area where Mick lived.

What did his mum think of him spending so much of his time down here? Without quizzing Timmy, he had discovered that they had left his dad in a bit of a hurry and moved down to stay with his grand parents; but for how long? How well did they all get on together? It couldn't be easy, three generations in one house. That used to be the norm years ago but not now. And he had noticed very clearly how Jacqui had said that they couldn't have a pup, even before Timmy had asked for one. Was that because it wasn't her house? Would they be moving on, and if so did

building up this friendship mean that the pain of parting would be made all the greater? That was the last thing that he wanted.

And what did Jacqui think of him? She seemed not unfriendly, if a little cool towards him, but that might just have been the natural caution of a mother. Then again it might be because of the break up of her marriage; and a feeling of wariness towards any friendship with a man. He hadn't seen her that often but he had to admit, and not for the first time, that she was a very attractive lady. So much so that he felt he would like to get to know her better, and that was a feeling that he hadn't had for many years.

EIGHTEEN

Sidney had been lying on Marilyn's couch for just over an hour with his eyes shut as Marilyn had asked. As far as he was aware she was standing behind him, totally silent. Strange sensations filled his body, a rumbling in his tummy and the odd twitching or muscle spasm. Images filled his head like dreams, yet he was fully awake, and he had the impression of colours, reds and blues and yellow. Above all he felt completely at peace, very calm and relaxed. Finally Marilyn's voice broke the silence

"I should think that that's enough for now. Sit up and wait a moment, then you may want to go to the loo, it's quite normal, you'll find it through that door in the corner. Then when you're ready you can join me in the living room for a chat, OK?"

She left the room and after a moment Sidney did as she suggested. He felt a little disorientated at first but after a few minutes he went into the small living room which he remembered from his previous visit. Marilyn was sitting in one of the armchairs and said

"How are you feeling now?"

"Fine, very calm and relaxed, and at the same time a feeling of safeness, if that's the right word. It was rather weird at times... the colours I

felt I could see even though my eyes were shut...
and the twitching in my legs. "

"That's all very normal, though it does affect
different people in different ways, so it's really hard
to say just what is normal. It's good that you felt
those sensations, I wasn't sure how much you would
feel, especially on your first visit."

"I'd like to do it again if I may, I think it
helped, it made me feel good."

"You certainly look well, do you take any
exercise, walking or cycling?"

"No, but I think we eat well. Gran is a very
traditional cook, plenty of fresh veg and that.
Always home cooking, no junk food and plenty of
fruit. She's a great believer in an apple a day. Not
that it has done her a great deal of good; she's been
crippled up with arthritis for the last ten years."

They carried on chatting, Marilyn asking
most of the questions but in such a way that Sidney
was barely aware that she was asking questions at
all. They exchanged their views on music, books and
films, discovering a good deal of common ground.
Finally Sidney felt bold enough to ask

"So where did you live before you came
here?"

"I used to live in London. After I left school I
trained and worked in a social services hostel for
children; children who came from broken homes.
Some of them were really bad, not the kids, the
homes they came from. I was there for three years
and then I moved to the other end of the age group
and worked in a day centre for elderly people. Most

of them had mental health problems, dementia in one form or another, so they came in for one or two days a week to give their partners or carers a bit of respite."

"So how and when did you get into Reiki?"

"Oh, I met up with a couple of old friends from school. They were living in Totnes and were into alternative therapies of one sort and another. I got interested, did the training and…well…here I am."

"Fascinating. I really have enjoyed this evening, chatting away; I hope I haven't bored you too much."

"Not at all, it's been fun."

"I was wondering… would you care to …" he paused, head down, looking at his hands in his lap, embarrassment holding him back.

"Yes?"

"What I mean is, I would like to take you out to dinner, would you…?" The effort of asking and the fear of his request being rejected had his heart beating fast.

"I'd love that, thank you for asking. Where were you thinking of going?"

"I thought the pub in our village, The New Inn." He was looking straight at her now, a smile of relief on his face.

"Sounds good to me, we went in there after the drama group meeting the other day, it looked very nice. When would this be?"

"Next Monday; if that's alright with you." He had picked Monday because he knew it was the least busy night of the week and hopefully there would be less people there who would know him. Marilyn got up to look in her diary and said

"Yes; Monday's fine, I'm looking forward to it already."

"I'll pick you up at half past seven. Now I really must be going, I've taken up enough of your time. Thank you once again."

She walked with him to the door where he somewhat hesitantly took her hand as he said goodbye. A final wave from his car and he was gone.

All the way home he wondered what his gran and his mother would say. He felt that this girl was special; someone he wanted to get to know properly. He didn't want her driven away like the others. It all depended on his gran and what she thought of Marilyn. He knew that she was only thinking of his own good, but she was so old-fashioned. Was she trying to protect him, he wondered, or was it that she didn't want him to leave? More than once he had asked his mother to take his side and remonstrate on his behalf. But all she would say was

"Don't upset her, if it wasn't for her where would we be?"

"But if I don't say anything, it upsets me" was what he wanted to say, but he knew that wouldn't help, so he just said nothing and went along as he always did. When he got home supper was ready on the table and the two women had obviously been waiting for some time.

"We were just beginning to wonder if you had had an accident or something" his gran said with her usual biting sarcasm.

"Sorry, I was busy and wanted to finish what I had started tonight, rather than having to go back again another day."

"Didn't you have your mobile phone with you?"

"I didn't realise how the time had gone by until I was in the car on my way home" he said as he walked in to the kitchen to wash his hands.

Supper was eaten in frosty silence and the atmosphere only warmed up when, after the meal, he helped his gran into her room and then read aloud to her one of the stories from her magazine.

In bed that night he lay worrying about how he was going to tell his gran and his mother about Marilyn. He knew that he would have to tell them about his dinner date before it happened. It would never do for them to find out from somebody else. His only hope was that they would like Marilyn; but that would entail bringing her to meet them and he was half afraid to do that.

"Why does life have to be so difficult, why can't it be easy like computers?"

For the next few days all Sidney could think about was his impending date with Marilyn. He seemed to be walking around in a dream, nothing else seemed to matter and it was a wonder that his clients didn't say anything to him. But his strange behaviour could always be put down to the fact that he was a computer geek, or so some of them considered him to be, and he was almost expected to be in a strange world of his own from time to time.

He worried as to what he should wear for the evening. He had always dressed in the rather old fashioned clothes that his gran had encouraged him to wear. He didn't have many close friends with whom he could confide or from whom he could get advice. One of his customers called Terry was a friend who had been at school with him. So on the Saturday before the impending date, while working on his computer he plucked up courage and asked him

"If I was going out on a date, what d'you think I ought to wear?"

"Are you telling me that you're going out on a date?"

"Yes"

"Well good for you, it's about time you got yourself fixed up with a nice young lady. Who is she, do I know her?"

"She's called Marilyn and she comes to the drama group. That's where I first met her. Then she asked me to help her with her computer and …well… that's how it all started I suppose."

"I didn't know you were in to drama, when did this all start?"

"They wanted help with the sound effects and things, I was asked to help 'cos they knew I could do that sort of thing with a computer."

"I though that computers had to come into it somewhere."

"Yes, well, never mind all that, I need to know what to wear and so on. I like this girl and I don't want to make a mess of it."

"If you really want to know, and don't take offence, you have always dressed far too old fashioned. You almost look like you've stepped out of a nineteen forties film. You need to get yourself some more modern clothes. This warm weather you won't need a jacket, but if you do have to wear one lets get something more up to date. That one you always wear looks like it was your granddad's anyway. Perhaps a pair of jeans, have you got any?..."

"No."

"...and a T-shirt. I think the best thing we can do is to go to town after we've finished here and get you some things to wear, OK?"

"Yes, I suppose so."

"And one other thing, before you go out on this date, we need to sort your hair out. You always stick it down so flat; perhaps we ought to go to the barbers while we're there. Maybe he can get you into the twenty first century."

"But it looks a mess if I don't stick it down."

"Believe me; he will make it look a lot better, besides the fashion today is for hair to be less formal. So when is it that you're going on this date?"

"Monday, but please Terry, don't go spreading it around, keep it to yourself."

"OK, but if it's that soon we had better go now. We need to get you fixed up with your new image. Don't worry, I wont tell anyone."

So Sidney quickly finished the work he was doing for his friend and they went off to town together. It didn't take them long to find the right outfit, looking through the many items available on the rails.

"You might need a light-weight jumper or a casual jacket in case it gets a bit cold later" said Terry, picking a suitable one off the shelf.

"There, I should think that will do you. What d'you think?"

Sidney felt almost like a naughty schoolboy, getting something for himself without asking permission from his gran or his mother. When he got home later he tried it on again in his room and was very happy, standing in front of the mirror, posing and looking at himself from all angles.

The forty eight hours until that Monday evening were the longest forty eight hours in Sidney's life. He helped his gran and his mother around the house on the Sunday morning. They didn't go to church any more, it was too difficult for his gran, and she didn't really like to be seen in her wheelchair. After they had finished their traditional roast Sunday lunch he helped her to her bed and then read one of her short stories to her. She soon fell asleep and Sidney told his mum that he was going out for a walk; the weather was far too nice to stay indoors.

He walked up onto Braggator and sat for a long while watching a pair of buzzards, circling and wheeling high up in the sky, their mewing cry sounding so very mournful. There were quite a number of other people out enjoying the afternoon sunshine. Two girls on their ponies passed behind him. He could hear their chattering and laughter for some while after they had gone. A young couple, hand in hand, walked by nodding to him and smiling as they made their way up onto the top of the rocks. He wondered if he and Marilyn would go for walks on the moor. She had said that she liked Dartmoor, liked the wildness and the openness of the scenery. He just hoped that he would be able to share it with her; that nothing would happen to destroy the relationship that had barely started.

The next morning he was up early, finding it hard to stay in bed, and ate a small breakfast. His stomach was churning with nerves, not at the thought of his dinner date that evening, but at how he was going to tell the two women in the house. He collected his things together for work that day and then as he was about to leave the house said

"I shan't be in for supper tonight."

"Why's that then?" said his gran

"I'm going out for dinner." With that he opened the door and was gone. The last thing he heard as he shut the door behind him was his gran saying

"Did you know anything about this Hilda?"

But that evening, much to Sidney's surprise, he was not subjected to an inquisition before he went out. It was as though his gran and his mother were waiting for him to speak first. As though they thought that if they said nothing he would have to break the silence and tell them all that they wanted to know.

He came down the stairs and into the living room wearing his new outfit and carrying his jacket. He smiled at his mum and nodding to his gran said

"I'll be off now, don't wait up for me."

To his surprise she smiled at him and said

"Have a nice time."

He drove the few miles to Marilyn's place and, realising that he was far too early, pulled in at the side of the road. He sat listening to the radio for a while. It was a request program with several young men declaring their love for their girl friends. He knew that he was a long way away from that sort of relationship with Marilyn but a man could wish and hope, couldn't he?

When he got to her door the nerves hit him again and the butterflies were doing a dance in his stomach. With his heart beating nineteen to the dozen he knocked on the door. It seemed to be an age before she answered. Then there she was, a picture of loveliness in a short dress that showed off her long tanned legs. Her golden hair brushed her shoulders as she tossed her head and the scent of her perfume seemed to waft over him like a narcotic wave of sensual beauty.

"Wow, you look fantastic, just like a fashion model...beautiful."

"Thank you" she said, feeling slightly embarrassed "Come in, I'm nearly ready. You look pretty good yourself, I like the new image." She turned and led the way into the living room, disappeared for a few minutes and then bounced back into the room with a jacket over her arm and clutching her hand bag. Sidney led the way out to the car and held the door open for her, getting another glimpse of her beautiful long legs as she swung them in.

'He may be a little shy and old fashioned, but it feels nice to be treated with old fashioned good manners. It makes one feel more special and respected' she mused to herself as they drove to the pub.

He led her to a table near a window, there being plenty of daylight left, and after getting her the drink that she had asked for they chose their meal from the menu. It was a lovely evening, better than Sidney could ever have expected. The food was new to him, he sampled dishes that he had never had before and found them to be very tasty. Gran's meat and two veg was perfectly alright, but this was exciting and particularly tasty. Maybe the company had something to do with it.

They talked even more than they had on the previous occasion after his Reike session. Sidney was totally oblivious of all other people around him, entranced by his beautiful companion sitting opposite him. He couldn't help looking at her eyes,

113

intrigued by the way she used them as she talked, just like some people used their hands. And the curl of her lip as she smiled, a little bit to one side as though she was almost apologising for her mirth.

All too soon it came to an end; the bar emptied and they were the only ones left. The evening had flown by quickly, hours seemingly condensed into minutes, both of them engrossed in the conversations that they had been enjoying.

"I think we ought to be going" said Marilyn, giggling slightly.

Sidney jumped to his feet and stood beside her as she got up, smiling broadly at him.

"I didn't realise how the time had gone by" he said. Then taking her hand for the first time he led her out to his car. They stood for a minute gazing up at the stars, a myriad of tiny silver lights twinkling in the deep purple summer night sky. He wanted to put his arm around her, but didn't for fear that it would be a move too soon. Instead he just stood holding her hand, drinking in the moment. A shooting star flew across the sky, its streak of a trail almost lost before it began.

"Wow, did you see that? You must make a wish."

"I've never seen a shooting star before. I wonder if it's an omen of some sort."

They stood for a while, drinking in the atmosphere and then as they moved slowly to the car he said

"I hate to spoil this wonderful moment, but I must take you home."

"Before I turn into Cinderella" she said, laughing.

"Just don't lose your slipper as you get into the car."

He stopped outside her house and walked with her to the door saying

"This has been a wonderful evening, I don't think that I've ever enjoyed myself so much. I feel as though I'm going to burst with joy."

He put his hands on her shoulders and looking into her eyes said

"Thank you, thank you so much."

"Not at all, I should be thanking you. I have enjoyed it myself, enormously." With that she moved closer and taking his face in her hands, kissed him softly and tenderly on the lips. Then she stepped back and turned to open the door

"Will I see you again?" he said anxiously.

"Yes please."

"Soon?"

"Yes" she said and with that she was gone, a dark silhouette passing through the pale yellow rectangle of light that was her open door.

NINETEEN

Sal Blundell and her best friend Edna Marriot were busy in the village hall arranging the furniture for the meeting that evening of the village ladies group. The group were in the habit of meeting once a month, mostly for a good old natter, but also to listen to a guest speaker. Topics such as 'Hut circles' and 'Somali embroidery' had been brought to their attention and listened to with varying degrees of interest, depending on the personality of the speaker.

Sal and Edna were neighbours, living next door to one another in two of the cottages on the green next to the shop. Always keen to help, they could be relied upon to prepare the hall or provide modest refreshments at village events. They could also be relied upon to collect and distribute local news and events, together with, as they saw it, suitable comments.

"I hear Sidney Turner has got himself a young lady friend."

"No, you don't say, where did you hear that Sal?"

"My Charlie. He said that Walter told him."

"Who ever would have thought it? Sidney Turner with a young lady, has he ever had a young lady before and who is this party and where do 'er come from?"

"She's one of those girls that live over to Sandycombe in that big house, you know the alternative ones. Charlie said that he has been out with one or two girls before, but always with another couple, if you know what I mean. "

"You mean the ones that practice the funny medicine?"

"Yes, that's the ones. Apparently this one has joined the Drama Group."

"So how did Sidney get tangled up with her then?"

"Probably fixing her computer, I should think."

"What's Hilda goin' to think about that I wonder? I know she's always singing Sidney's praises when it comes to things to do with computers and the likes, but taking up with one of his customers and a young lady at that, well.... Here, give us a hand with this table will you? I think we need it over there."

"Right.... this where you want it?....Well, I don't think it's got very far yet, so far as I know they've only met a few times, but it certainly is a start."

"I should think it's high time, if you ask me. What is he now, thirty two is it?"

"No, he was born the same year as Beatie, our nurse. That makes him thirty three."

"Well, you would know Sal. I suppose that was a year or two before I moved in here. By the way, what's tonight's topic, d'you know?

"Yes it's Crop Circles."

"Oh, that should be fun …. Look up, I think I just saw Close Up coming this way."

She was referring to Grace Russell, the vicar's wife, a small bird-like woman with the unfortunate habit of standing right under the chin of the person to whom she was speaking. This had earned her the nick-name of Close Up. She came from a long line of clergymen's wives and was a good organiser of church and parish events. Too good for the likes of some people. She came in to the hall with a cheerful

"Good day ladies, I've just brought a few flowers from the garden. I'll just put them in a vase; I won't get in your way."

She went into the kitchen and came out with the flowers arranged in a big vase. Then moving a small table to a position in front of the stage she put the vase on it saying

"There, that should do. Yes, I'll see you ladies tonight I hope. I can't stop now, I'm off to see Hilda, it's a pity we can't persuade her to come."

"How's her mum?"

"I heard she'd taken a turn for the worse Sal" said Edna.

"That's why I'm going over there now. I fear the old dear won't be with us much longer, she's very poorly, so I understand."

"Well give her our best wishes and tell Hilda we're thinking of her" said Sal.

As she walked away from the stage Grace repositioned two of the chairs that Sal and Edna had set out. Then she was gone and the two women continued with their job of setting out the furniture.

"She always has to move something, doesn't she? It's like we can't do it properly" said Sal moving the chairs back to where they had been.

"She can't help it, she means well, it's just her way, she's a busy beggar. Poor Hilda though, I didn't realise her mum was that bad. What ever will the poor soul do if her mum dies and Sidney gets married and moves out? She's cared for those two all of her life almost."

"Well, just because Sidney's got himself a girl friend at last, it don't mean that he's going to get married soon, if at all."

"No, perhaps not…. Course if he does, he and his wife could always move in with Hilda."

"No Edna, there's no way a modern young woman would want to move in with her mother-in-law, especially one as old fashioned as Hilda. No I can't see that happening in a month of Sundays."

"I don't think its Hilda that's old fashioned, 'tis her mother more like. After all 'twas she as brought up Sidney wasn't it? You've only got to look at the way he dresses and does his hair, all stuck down with brylcream or whatever. "

"Yes, my Charlie says he doesn't have a shampoo, he has an oil change instead."

They chuckled at this as they moved into the kitchen and started taking out the cups and saucers from the cupboard. Sal being the shorter of the two bent down and lifted them out while Edna laid them in neat rows on the worktop.

"Then there's Walter's daughter, Jacqui" said Edna "I hear the postman…. whatshisname…George, has been showing an interest in her."

"Oh I can't see that happening, he's a nice fellow and a good sort; looks after the people on his round, right enough, but he's not her sort at all. Too old for one thing."

"We'll just have to wait and see….Well I reckon we've done all we can here….I'm off home….'you coming?"

TWENTY

Grace left the village hall, carefully closing the door behind her. She hesitated as she passed her car but decided that she would rather walk the short distance to Hilda's house. The houses and cottages that she walked by were all proudly displaying window boxes, tubs and hanging baskets full of flowers. Few of them had any garden against the road; in fact most of them had only a rudimentary pavement between the building and the traffic. Outside one cottage were two tubs of lavender, the scent pouring out from them as they stood bathed in sunshine.

It had been over two weeks since she had visited Hilda and her aged and ailing mother, and she felt a pang of guilt at this. It was easy to visit the more vociferous of those in need, it kept them quiet and she had to admit, it made her life easier. But it also meant that the more silent ones could get put to the back of the queue. As a family the Turners were less well-known than most, seemingly keeping very much to themselves. Sidney had always been a quiet, shy young man only recently becoming a more visible member of the community through his driving of the school bus and his computer business. Hilda had in the past worked in the local pub but that was several years ago. For the last few years she had been caring for her mother, which had kept her very much at home. In fact her only outings had been to the village shop and that not very often. Her mother had suffered from debilitating arthritis for many years, which had rendered her virtually house-bound, and sadly out of sight tended to mean out of mind.

She arrived at Hilda's front door and knocked. From inside she could hear old Mrs Turner's voice calling to her daughter that they had a visitor and then footsteps and the click of the latch as Hilda opened the door.

"Hello Hilda, I hope I haven't called at a bad moment, I was wondering how your mother is."

"Oh, Mrs Russell, do come in, mother will be so glad to see you. She doesn't get many visitors." She lowered her voice and almost in a whisper said

"To tell the truth, she's none too well."

She led the way into what used to be the sitting room of the house. It was a nice bright, cheerful room with a large bunch of flowers in a vase on the small bedside table. But despite the bright appearance the room had the tell tale smell of an elderly invalid. The bed was opposite the window which faced south, over-looking the road. This not only let in the sun but also gave her a view of people passing by. It explained how Mrs Turner had seen Grace arriving before she knocked at the door. Behind the bed was a new extension that had recently been built consisting of a small toilet and shower room which had made it possible for Mrs Turner to stay in her own home for as long as she had. There was a chair at the foot of the bed which Grace took and moved nearer to the head of the bed before sitting down.

"How are you today?" she asked, not sure what sort of an answer she would get. On one occasion when she had asked the same question of an elderly man who was fresh out of hospital, the answer she had received had been 'none the better for your asking'.

"Not too good. Doctor said I had one of they there mini strokes. Fact he reckons I've had more than one, it's left me weak as a kitten, I can hardly sit up, leave ago get out of bed."

"Oh, a TIA, I am sorry, it's a good job you've got Hilda here to look after you. I could sit with you for a while if Hilda needed to go to the shop or anything, would that be a help?" she said, turning to Hilda who had come in to the room with a tray of tea and cakes.

"Thank you for the offer Mrs Russell, but Sidney can generally pick up what ever we need when he finishes his bus run. Also he has taught me how to use the computer to order most of what we need from the supermarket, so I don't really have any need to go anywhere. You'll have a cup of tea and a piece of cake won't you?"

"Thank you, yes that would be very acceptable" she said taking the proffered cup. "The supermarket ....oh dear....yes ...well I realise that it is a great help to some people to have goods delivered, in fact I've seen the supermarket vans in the village from time to time. I can't help feeling that it's a shame to take the business away from the local shop keepers."

"Trouble is, they don't have all the things we need. If I can only get a quarter of the things I want, I've got to go on to the big shops in town, so I just as well have gone there in the first place. Besides, it's cheaper as a rule, see?"

"Oh I do see, I see only too well and I sympathise with you. I also see Post Offices, village schools and pubs every where closing down. It may be an unavoidable sign of the times, but it saddens me to see it."

Grace could see that she needed to change the direction of the conversation so she asked if there was anything that she could get Mrs Turner, a book from the library or something like that.

"No, but I tell you what you could get for me; my copy of the People's Friend magazine. I do like the stories in them, they'm so real, if you know what I mean. It hadn't come in when Hilda went for it 'tother day."

"I'll go and get it for you as soon as I leave" said Grace, taking a piece of cake and passing her cup to Hilda for a refill. "I won't bother coming in when I get back, I'll just push it through the letter box." They carried on talking for a while as they drank their tea and ate Hilda's cake. It was difficult to have a long conversation with them, because they had little knowledge of village affairs, and Grace was certainly not one to gossip. Also they had so few shared interests.

Finally she said goodbye to the two women and let herself out into the sunshine again. As she walked back to the village she pondered the fate of Hilda and her mother. Both were prisoners in their own homes, the one through ill health and the other through caring for her. No doubt when Sidney was at home Hilda could get out to go to the local shop, but it was hardly likely that in such a short visit she would make any great social contact with the rest of the community. The fact that he had taught her how to order her needs from the internet really only made matters worse. Her mother seemed to be a kindly soul, sitting up in bed with her crocheted shawl around her shoulders, but Grace knew from what her husband had told her, that she was a very demanding person. It was she who had brought up young Sidney and was probably responsible for the old fashioned way that he always dressed. It was a very sad state of affairs and she wished that there was something positive that she could do to help.

TWENTY ONE

Jacqui and her mother were sitting enjoying a cup of coffee before the morning customers started coming in. There was often a lull after the early birds, the Full English Breakfast brigade and the few walkers who wanted a home-made pasty to take with them. It was an opportunity to have a little chat without Walter, who always seemed to be busy in the kitchen at this time, or Timmy who was as usual out sketching wild life and Dartmoor scenery, or over at Braggator with Mick.

"You haven't said any thing lately and I haven't liked to ask, but how is your divorce going?"

"It should be all over and done with fairly soon now Mum. According to Clare Holdsworth, my solicitor, because Alan hasn't contested it and has agreed to the way I asked to divide our modest finances and estate, it has all gone remarkably smoothly. So it looks as though I will be footloose and fancy free again soon."

"Does that mean that you will be moving on from here? I appreciate that this job here, working for us as a waitress, is really only a stop gap. Your career up until now had been working in a bank and then for an estate agent. Did you want to go back to something like that?"

"I don't really know. I do appreciate what you and Dad have done, taking us in off the street, so to speak, and giving us a home and me a job. I don't know what we would have done if you hadn't."

"Well, it worked both ways, we got to see more of you and young Timmy for one thing, and you being here meant that work wasn't such a burden for us. It has also shown us that if you do go, we will have to get someone to take your place, work wise. We used to think we could do it all ourselves, now we realise that we can't. It's quite a busy little business, and we aren't getting any younger."

"Oh, I don't know about moving on. It would be nice to have our own place obviously, and I know you understand that that's no reflection on you. But Timmy will soon be a hormonal teenager with all the problems that that brings. I wouldn't want to subject you and Dad to that. Just imagine him coming in at half past two in the morning, or playing his loud music when you were trying to get some sleep. Then he will want to bring his friends home and that would double the noise. It doesn't bear thinking of, does it Mum?"

"Oh, I'm sure he wouldn't be that bad, you never were."

"Maybe not, but then I'm not a boy, and anyway I made sure that you and Dad never knew of all the things I got up to. If I did move into a place of my own, you're right, I would have to go back into some sort of a job like I used to have. But if it meant moving away from this area, I don't know...."

"It could mean moving Timmy to another school, that would be an upset and he seems to like it where he is now."

"Yes, and its not just school that he has taken to, I never thought I would see him so happy in this very quiet rural environment. He only knew of a life in a city before, now all I hear about is Dartmoor and all the wildlife that he sees around here and his art work. His paintings are very good you know."

"And Mick" said Jessica, raising one eyebrow and looking straight at her daughter to see what reaction she would get from mentioning his name.

"Yes, its true, Mick has become quite a big thing in Timmy's life. I'm not really worried, but I do wonder sometimes if it is a totally good thing, his spending so much time there."

"Oh it's just a sort of hero worship. Nothing wrong in that, in fact it's quite normal, looking up to and admiring an older person. I remember you were the same with your English teacher at one time. Though I must say in your case it was a bit wearing at times."

"Wearing, how do you mean, wearing?"

"Oh you know, all that 'Miss Latham doesn't do it like that' and 'Miss Latham says this' all the time. I sometimes used to wish Miss Latham would feed and clothe you, if she was so good at everything.

"I'm sorry, I never realised I was such a pain."

"You weren't a pain Jacqui, just a normal girl growing up; now Timmy is going through the same phase."

"I was wondering if he was beginning to look upon Mick as a substitute for his dad, and if so, would that be something that I should be worried about."

"I don't think that would be anything to worry about, in fact I would have thought that Mick is as good a role model as any mum could wish for her young son to follow and aspire to."

"Yeah, he seems a nice enough chap, it's just that I don't know much about him. In fact I've not met anybody here who does know anything about him. He seems to be a man with a secret, something in his past that keeps him shut away from the rest of the world."

"Would you like to know him better?"

"You're fishing now Mum, aren't you?"

"Well, he's a very attractive man, and you are single, in fact to all intents and purposes you have been single for quite some time; emotionally if not in reality."

"So if you are asking do I fancy him, the answer is 'I could if I knew a bit more about him and his mysterious past'."

Both women laughed at this and Jessica said

"The only way you'll get to know more about him is for you to get to know him better. To do that you've got to see more of him, go and see him teaching Timmy to ride. Timmy would love that, he wants you to see his friend, he wants you to see how he's getting on with his riding lessons. And I expect that Mick wants you to see just what and who he is, without him having to tell you."

"Thanks Mum, that's a great idea, and thanks for everything. Now it's time to get back to work before Dad starts shouting."

She got up, walked round the table and gave her mum a kiss, happy to have such an understanding relationship with her.

So it was that that evening after tea, when Timmy said that he was hoping to go for a riding lesson, she asked if he would like it if she went along too. Most days Mick was working, shoeing or occasionally helping at the riding school leading small groups out for a ride. So Timmy's lessons had to be in the evenings.

"That would be great Mum, are we going in the car or do we walk down?"

"I think we'll go in the car, I've been on my feet all day waiting table, I think I've walked far enough for one day."

They drove down to Braggator and Mick sent Timmy off with a halter to catch Dillon. He and Jacqui stood leaning on the gate watching him confidently walk up to the three horses. He talked to all three in turn and then, after patting Dillon a few times on his neck, put on the halter and walked back with him, the other two horses following behind.

"They all seem to know him."

"Yeah, they know him alright, they know that he doesn't fear them and has no wish to harm them and so they trust him. It's good to see, he has a natural way with animals, something that not many boys have at his age. Did you have any pets before you moved down here?"

"No, we didn't, though I think his best friend Jacko had a dog." She smiled inwardly, noticing the mild interrogation about their former life, wondering how soon it would be before she was able to ask him a similar sort of question.

Timmy rejoined them and Mick held the pony while he put on the saddle and bridle and once mounted they went out into the small field away from the other horses. Jacqui stayed by the gate, watching with pride as her son rode around in a large circle. He appeared to be doing what Mick told him to do and after a short while Mick said

"D'you want to try a little canter?"

"Oh yes" said Timmy, his eyes shining brightly with excitement.

"Right then, walk him around once more and then when you come past me turn and push him into a canter, like I showed you, and canter to the far end of the field. Then bring him back here at a walk. Make sure you keep control of him at all times, I don't want to see you galloping like some racehorse jockey. He may want to go, you've got to show him that you are in charge, and that he can only go when you say so. Or in this case, when I say so, OK?"

Timmy grinned delightedly at his mum and set off walking in a big circle and then as he passed them again he urged Dillon into a canter. At first he looked to be a little unsteady, swaying a bit from side to side, but soon he was into the rhythm, moving his body in unison with the movement of the horse.

"I don't know anything about it, but he looks to be doing alright to me" said Jacqui.

"Yes, he's doing well, he needs to build up the muscles that are needed for riding, muscles that he hasn't had to use before. That may take a week or two, then by that time he will have learned a bit more and will be able to go out on the moor."

"What, alone?"

"Oh yes, if he wants to, but I'll go out with him the first few times to see that he's alright. He'll need to be shown where to go and what is safe and so on. As he has discovered from his fall when he hurt his ankle; Dartmoor has to be treated with respect. It doesn't do to go out on your own without telling someone exactly where you are going. Of course it's much more enjoyable with company, sharing is always good. He may want to go out with Margaret and Helen, Pippa's two girls, d'you know them?"

"Yes, well I can't say I know them, I've seen them on the school bus, and I've met Pippa several times."

"Nice kids, good riders too, but then they were born to it."

Timmy had joined them again and asked what he had to do next.

"Take him down to the end again at a canter, and this time I want you to come back at a trot."

"This is really very good of you to take so much time and trouble on Timmy like this" said Jacqui.

"Its no trouble, in fact I think I get almost as much enjoyment out of it as Timmy does. He's going to need some proper riding gear if he's going to keep this up, breeches and boots etcetera."

"Where do I go to get that and will it be very expensive?"

"Pippa's husband Jim has an agricultural merchants store, they have a section of second hand riding gear. You'll probably get all you need there. If I were you I would ask Pippa to go with you, she'll know what will be best to get Timmy, and you never know, she may be able to get you a better deal as a friend."

"Well, he's got a birthday coming up soon, his granddad may be pleased to help as part of his present."

They stood watching Timmy riding up and down the field for another half an hour, doing the various exercises that Mick told him to do. Then it was felt that he had done enough for one day and Dillon was unsaddled and turned back into the field with his new companions.

"So you've got a birthday soon, a teenager and a rider all in one year."

"Did I do alright? Can I come again tomorrow evening?"

"Yes, but remember, if any time I'm not here, don't go in with the horses, talk to them over the gate."

"Why, they know me?"

"I know they do, but they can be unpredictable, flies may bite them and make them a bit skittish. I don't suppose that they would mean to hurt you but I don't want you to take any chances, right?"

Later, on the way home in the car, Jacqui told Timmy what Mick had said about getting the right sort of clothes to wear.

"I don't want to spend a lot of money if this is just a fad that you are going to grow out of in a month or so. You have to be sure that this is what you want as a long term pastime, OK?"

"I see what you mean Mum, in all honesty I don't know, but the way I feel at the moment I want to continue riding for a long time. Dillon is such a lovely pony, so soft and kind. Did you see the way he came up to me in the field? He knows me already. Well, so do Osprey and Ptarmigan."

Jacqui smiled at his enthusiasm, glad that he had found something to be so happy about. After the pain and misery that he had suffered from his father, the teasing and belittling, it was wonderful to see the change in him. It was heart-warming to see the huge increase in his self confidence that had happened since they had come down to Dartmoor to live. If it was due in large part to Mick, his animals and his influence generally, then who was she to complain?

No, as usual her mother was right; Mick was hardly a reason to worry where Timmy was concerned.

TWENTY TWO

Frank had always liked the early mornings; to walk across the fields with his dog, the fresh dew on the grass and the only sounds to be heard those of the natural world all around, was to him heaven on earth. It was also the time of day that he reserved for the farm before getting on with his business mending and maintaining cars and tractors. Skylarks were singing in a sky, blue with just a few aeroplane vapour trails criss-crossing it. Few other sounds could be heard, just an odd bumble bee droning along, woken up by the warm sun.

The farm didn't carry a great deal of stock; twenty five ewes and their lambs and just a few head of cattle. His father and grandfather before him had built up a herd of prize Red Rubies, the famous Devon cattle. They were a small, dark reddish brown, slow growing breed of cattle, famed for their meat. He passed through the field where the cows with their new calves were; all up and grazing contentedly. It always amused him the way that they all faced the same way as they grazed, moving forwards slowly in an almost regimental line. Everything seemed fine so he went on to check on the rest of the stock.

In a small field, at the end of the lane that led to the farm, was his small flock of sheep. The advantage of having a small flock was that they were a lot less trouble for him to tend to, especially with his other business as a car mechanic. Several of his ewes had had two lambs and they were all looking well. The lambs would soon be going to market, and Frank was very proud of them. He got to the gate and looked over, surprised to see that they were at the far end of the field, stood up and looking his way, not grazing like they should have been. He jumped over the gate and they moved, startled by his sudden movement and it was then that he was able to see that there were not as many lambs as there should have been. He went forward and sent his dog to round them up; then he counted them as they passed between him and the hedge. There were five missing so he walked all around the field, looking carefully at the hedges to see if he could see where they had got out. Nothing; there was no obvious sign but a good part of the hedge was a solid stone-faced Devon bank and it might not have shown much of a mark. By the same token, it would have been hard for an animal to get out over such a wall. He had always prided himself on keeping his hedges in a good enough condition to keep any animal in.

He walked back, checking all the fields to see if the lambs had got in with any of the other stock, but he knew it was a waste of time, he had seen them all earlier. Then he spent an hour looking around the outskirts of the farm on the open moor. It was no good; if the lambs had escaped they would eventually try to join up with some other sheep, being herd animals. He would just have to spread the word and hope that somebody would find them.

Later that morning he met Pippa, and told her. He hoped that if she was out riding with a group on the moor she could keep an eye open for the lost lambs. Likewise if her two girls, Margaret and Helen were out riding on Braggator, they could do the same. Then he drove over to Phil's place, he had not been able to contact him earlier. Phil was in the yard with his workman Jeff, sorting through some sheep.

"Hello Frank, what brings you here?"

"Had some sheep get out last night, I doubt if they would have come this far but I thought I'd better let you know, in case you saw or heard anything."

"What, ewes and lambs?"

"No, just lambs; five of those fat ones I was thinking of sending off in a day or two."

"Could you see where or how they got out?"

"No, not a sign anywhere. I've been all over the place looking for them, can't see any trace, wool on the hedge or anything. It's a mystery to me, sure enough."

"Just a minute Frank…. can you manage here for a while Jeff?" and with that he left the sheep and led Frank off into the house. Once in the kitchen he told Frank to sit down and he made them both a cup of tea. Like so many farm kitchens the kettle was on the side of the Aga and was near to boiling so it didn't take long.

"Now, tell me, which field were these lambs of yours in?"

"The one at the end of the lane, by the damson tree. Why d'you ask?"

"I didn't like to say anything in front of Jeff, don't want to start a rumour, if you know what I mean. That field has a gate leading onto the lane doesn't it?"

"Yes."

"Well you remember I had six lambs stolen a few weeks ago...."

"You think someone has stolen my lambs as well?"

"Could well be, they were quiet, like all your animals. You've always treated them like babies, you and your dad before you. Anybody with a good dog could round them up and pick five of them out into a truck or trailer."

"Yeah, but just a few lambs, it hardly seems worth the risk. I mean, what could they do with them, unless they've got their own slaughter house?"

"Well maybe they have. Meat isn't cheap these days, an unscrupulous butcher might be glad to get his hands on some free livestock, especially good stock like our lambs. Or maybe the thief is killing them himself and selling meat to a restaurant; who knows?"

"Wow, I dare say you could be right, but it does take a bit of believing. Who the hell would be doing it? It's got to be someone who knows this area."

"Yes, and someone who knows and understands stock. It won't do any harm to keep looking, they still may turn up I grant you, but in the mean time I think you ought to tell the police, like I did about my lambs. You never know, they might be able to help. Besides, with all the red tape there is today, you've got to explain why you haven't got the animals any more."

TWENTY THREE

Timmy had been sitting on the hedge overlooking the field with the horses in. They had been standing peacefully in the shade of the single thorn tree by the boundary wall against the moor. He had his pad on his knee and had been carefully painting with water colours. Every now and then he had to go to get more water to wash his brushes. This was his third attempt, the earlier ones had not been to his liking and he had thrown them away, screwed up into a ball in the bottom of his rucksack.

He wanted to paint the horses under the tree with the open moorland behind and had been desperately trying to somehow capture the atmosphere of the heat and the flies. There the three horses stood, heads nodding, swishing their tails and occasionally stamping the ground with their hooves. Each time one of them stamped the ground there was a click as the shoe hit a stone and a small puff of dust from the well worn dry ground. Behind them the bracken and gorse covered slopes of the tor seemed to lose detail in the heat haze that passed a smoky-like cloud over it all.

In the distance he heard the clunk as a car door shut and he knew that Mick was at the gate at the top of the lane and would soon be home. He climbed down off his perch, put his belongings in his bag and carefully carrying his wet painting ran towards the house to meet his friend. Mick stopped the van and climbed out reaching over to ruffle Timmy's hair with his big hand.

"What have you been painting today, eh?"

"Mind, it's still wet. It's not very good."

"I think it's excellent; I can see just what it is, and I can almost feel the heat. You've got the way the horses stand to a tee."

Though there wasn't a great deal of detail, he could recognise the three horses and get the mood of the hot summer's day. There was no doubt about it, the boy had a talent. Timmy beamed with pleasure at the praise he was getting. It meant a lot to him to be recognised by this man whom he had come to look upon as more than just a friend and teacher.

"So when's this birthday of yours?"

"Next week, on the seventeenth."

"Really, now there's a coincidence."

"Why?"

"Well, mine's on the eighteenth, the next day."

"You're joking, is it really? You're not just winding me up are you?"

"No, straight up, mine's on the eighteenth, day after yours. Now are you going to have a ride or not?"

"Yes please" said Timmy, his eyes bright with excitement.

"Well go and catch Dillon then, and you can have half an hour before I get my tea."

As Timmy went home later his head was full of an idea that he wanted to put to his mum. He almost forgot to show her his painting as he asked her

"Mum, you know you said I could go to the pub for a meal as a treat for my birthday."

"Yes, if that's what you would like, why?"

"Can I ask a friend, can we ask Mick? You see it's his birthday the next day."

"Oh, I don't suppose he'd want to come, would he?"

"Well you don't know till you ask him do you? I'd like him to come, he's taught me a lot, riding and that."

"It's true, he's been very good to you and it would be a nice way of saying thank you. Alright Timmy, I'll ask him tomorrow. I think it would be best if I do, if you ask him he'll only come back to me to check if it's genuine."

"Thanks Mum, I think you could get to like him in time" he said with a little smile at the corner of his mouth. 'Little monkey' thought Jacqui he's worse than my mum, trying to match make. But she had to admit that the idea of spending a bit more time with Mick might be good. Away from his home environment he might just loosen up a bit and let his guard down. She was interested to see what lay behind those cold steel grey eyes of his. What made it possible for him to be so warm and friendly to his business customers and to Timmy, but so cold to those that he came into contact with outside of his work, such as her? And if she was honest with herself, she had to admit that it wasn't just the element of mystery that attracted, he was a very handsome man. She might well catch him in the shop tomorrow when she went for the paper.

The next morning Jacqui kept an eye out for Mick's van, delaying her visit to the shop until she saw him drive past and park on the green. Then she went out and managed to bump into him as he came out of the shop.

"I'm so glad I caught you" she said "as a birthday treat Timmy is going to have a meal in the pub. As his first day as a teenager I thought it would be nice for him, and in any case he said it was what he wanted. Last night he asked me if he could have a friend along too and of course I said 'yes'. When I asked which friend he said that he wanted you to join us, especially after all your kindness to him and as it is your birthday the next day."

"Well, that's very nice of Timmy and of you too."

"Will you join us then?"

"Yes, thank you I will. I haven't been 'out' so to speak for years, it will be very nice. What time and where shall I meet you both?"

"Oh, in the pub I should think, and shall we say seven o'clock, I don't know if that will be too early for you, I know you're a busy man."

"Seven o'clock will be fine, I'm looking forward to it already. I'll see you then if I don't see you before."

With that he was off in his van and Jacqui strolled back to the café with a smile on her face and a warm feeling inside. There was definitely something very attractive about the man and something that intrigued her. Maybe if she got the chance to see a bit more of him he might let his guard down and she would see the real Mick. Sharing an evening meal with him could be just the occasion when he would feel relaxed enough.

TWENTY FOUR

Sidney had met Marilyn a couple of times since their meal together in the pub. They had been for walks, talking all the time about the various things that they liked, and he had been more than a little surprised at how many interests they shared. So far in his life he had never found a girl who was really interested in him. He knew that many looked upon him as a bit of a geek, wrapped up in his computers almost in a 'virtual world'. And, if he was honest with himself, his life was greatly dominated by his grandmother, a fact that would seem strange to many. He could hardly believe his luck that this delightful and pretty girl should have any time for him at all. Yet she clearly wanted to be with him and now she wanted to meet his mother and grandmother. He had parked his car at the crossroads outside the village and they had been for a walk up on Brown Tor. He liked it up there; liked the solitude and the feeling of space. The rest of the world seemed miles away. The view all around was breathtaking, the rolling hills and rock topped tors. The dark patches of the forestry plantations, the lighter patchwork of the fields and the wooded valleys with their fast flowing streams. He often wondered how many of the local people ever bothered to go up there as he did, or did they take it all for granted just because it was on their doorstep? Perhaps he should be glad if not many other people came up onto this special patch of moorland; special to him that was, because it wouldn't have been the same if he and Marilyn had had to share it.

He had found a clump of whortleberry bushes and had picked two handfuls of the small purple berries for them to eat. Marilyn had never tasted them before and was delighted to try them. She had expected them to taste like blueberries, but she found that they had a deeper, more subtle flavour. Afterwards they laughed at the way the berries turned their tongues a deep purple.

Now they were walking back down to the car, hand in hand, the purple of the heather and the yellow of the gorse a riot of scent and colour all around them. The lines from a poem that he had learned at school came to him

'The Assyrian came down like a wolf on the fold

His cohorts were gleaming in purple and gold.'

Once at the cottage he helped Marilyn out and escorted her in to the living room. His mother came bustling up to meet her, smiling and bobbing saying

"Do come in… come in we're pleased to meet you."

His grandmother was sitting in the armchair in the corner with her multi-coloured crocheted shawl wrapped around her shoulders. She looked at her over the top of her glasses with half shut eyes and after a moment said

"So you're Marilyn, eh? Sidney tells me that you're in to this alternative medicine."

"That's right, Mrs Turner, though I would hardly call it medicine, more a form of treatment. I do like your shawl, did you crochet it yourself? It's beautiful."

"Yes."

"My gran used to do a lot of crocheting, cushion covers and the likes. She made me a special cushion when I was small, crocheted wool on one side and silk on the back. I used to carry it everywhere with me with the silky side against my cheek; it was my sort of comforter I suppose."

"Is she still crocheting now?"

"No, she died when I was ten. I'm not as lucky as Sidney; I lost all my grandparents before I was fifteen."

"Yes, well you see, I brought up Sidney. His mother had to go out to work so it was down to me you see, him having no dad and all. Fed and clothed him I did and gave him a roof over his head. Not that I minded, of course not, 'twas what you did."

"And a very good job you did too, he's a credit to you."

Hilda meanwhile had shown Marilyn to a seat and said

"I'll get us a cup of tea; I expect you'd like one wouldn't you?"

148

"I'll give you a hand Mum" said Sidney, embarrassed by his gran's outburst yet proud of the way Marilyn had handled the situation.

"No that's all right, I can manage, you stay and talk to Gran, she hasn't seen much of you lately."

"No" said Marilyn with a smile "he's been too busy seeing me. Have you always lived here Mrs Turner? It's a lovely cottage and so handy, close to the village centre. I expect you've seen a lot of changes here in your time."

"Oh yes, when I first remember, there was no running water and no electricity. It was hard work in they days, I can tell you, none of your modern machines. Mondays was the hardest, wash day. We had to carry in buckets and buckets of water for the copper and get it lit up with black sticks. Then there was the rinsing in baths of clean cold water, I tell you that was no fun on a cold winter's day. But I think we were just as happy then as folks are today, more so in fact. Folks may have got a lot more these days but that only means they've got more to worry about"

"It's difficult for people like me to imagine what it was like in those days, before television and washing machines. What did you do for entertainment, how did you pass the time in the evenings?"

"Oh we had plenty to do; patching and darning, knitting and sewing. If we weren't working we'd play cards or read or do jigsaw puzzles."

"Did you go out at all?"

"Yes, we'd visit friends and neighbours, and there were whist drives and a few dances from time to time. But we never went to pub to eat out like you folks do these days. In fact women rarely went to pub at all. That was for the men folk."

Coming from the city and being two generations younger Marilyn found it hard to visualise life in the country in the nineteen forties. She was fascinated by the tales that Sidney's grandmother told and encouraged her to go on. In turn, the old lady was delighted to have such an appreciative audience and to be the centre of attention. Tea was poured and cake cut and the afternoon passed with far fewer problems than Sidney had expected. No doubt he would be subjected to a lengthy interrogation when he got back after taking Marilyn home. But she had managed to make quite a hit with his gran and that was more than he had expected or even hoped for.

TWENTY FIVE

Mick was sitting on the seat under the chestnut tree when Jacqui and Timmy walked over to the pub. The midges had just started biting and he was glad to get away from their savage little teeth and join them in the safety of the inn. Jacqui chose a table at the far end of the room under a window, from where they could see the whole of the bar. She and Timmy sat on the window seat facing the bar with a seat for Mick opposite them across the table. He had gone straight to the bar to get a round of drinks ordered and then joined them with three menus. As it was Timmy's first time in a proper pub and his birthday, he was allowed to choose anything he wanted. When they had been to the pub in London with his dad, it had always been to sit in the children's area or the games room. The food that they had had was generally junk food with chips and peas. So this was all very new and several of the items on the menu were strange to him so Jacqui had to help him to choose. Finally the decisions were made and he was sent up to the bar, as large as life, to place the order.

On his way back he stopped to look at the hunting prints on the wall, showing horses and riders galloping over the countryside in full cry, leaping over fences the riders' coat tails and horses' tails streaming out behind them. He wondered, with his little knowledge of horse riding, what that must be like. It looked as though it would be exhilarating and exciting, the thrill of the chase, galloping off into the unknown, so to speak. When he got back to the table he asked Mick

"Did you ever go hunting Mick?"

"Yes, I used to."

"Don't you now?"

"I haven't since I moved down here."

"Oh, why is that?" asked Jacqui.

"A number of reasons" said Mick guardedly.

"Are you against hunting then?" said Timmy. Mick hesitated, seemingly thinking for a while before answering

"It's a difficult question that…. I'm against some aspects of it and some of the people that take part, but I realise that the number of foxes needs to be controlled. I don't agree with the government ban on foxhunting, but I don't like to see animals being chased and killed just for sport. So you see I'm not quite sure which side of the fence I sit on."

Jacqui was fascinated to hear him saying so much. Usually the most she had heard Mick saying was a blunt 'yes' or 'no' in answer to a question. But she realized that it was probably because Timmy had asked the question that he had been so abnormally talkative.

"What about badgers, do you think that they ought to be culled?"

"Again I'm not sure Timmy. Where they are concerned it's a bit of a 'chicken and egg' situation.

Do badgers give TB to cattle or do the cows give it to the badgers? I think the most important thing is for the scientists to get a vaccine against TB that they can give to the cattle and other animals. But again the number of badgers has got way out of control lately and some sort of a cull will have to come soon."

"Are there many badgers around here?" asked Jacqui.

"It's funny you should ask that, I was just going to say that there's a set not far from my place where there's a fairly large family of badgers. I was going to ask if you would allow Timmy to come out with me one night for a badger watch. It would only be until about half past nine, if that. They tend to come out as night falls and there's a full moon the week after next which means that we might get a better chance to see them. They don't stay by the entrance to their set for long before they trundle off searching for food and so on."

"Ooh… can I Mum?"

"I should think you can."

"I'll get in touch nearer the time and arrange it all."

Their food came and all talk of foxes and badgers stopped as they tucked in and enjoyed their meal. Jacqui wondered if Mick cooked much for himself and if so what sort of a cook he was. She knew that some men living alone managed wonderfully well while others relied on take-aways and pre-cooked ready meals from the super-markets. Looking around she saw at the bar a couple of regulars were standing enjoying a drink while several of the tables were occupied with two or four diners happily chatting and enjoying their food. The evening sun had finally set and it was just getting fully dark outside, background music was softly playing and the whole atmosphere in the pub was relaxed and quietly happy.

Mick watched Timmy eating his steak, obviously enjoying his first experience of grown up dining out. It brought a smile to his face and it struck him that in the short time that he had known the boy he had watched him grow up enormously. Not just in stature, though he was still a bit skinny, but in his knowledge of the countryside and the wild life there. It seemed a huge leap from the tearful lad who had fallen and twisted his ankle to the confident young man that he was now growing into.

The time had come for dessert. A waiter took away their plates and gave them menus. After considerable mind changes, the choices were made and Timmy once more went up to the bar with their order. Jacqui and Mick were sitting quietly when the background music changed to Robbie Williams singing 'Angels'. Jacqui happened to glance over at Mick and noticed a change come over him. A look of great sadness took over his face like a dark cloud and she saw the muscles of his jaw working as he rhythmically clenched his teeth. He looked up towards the far corner of the room as if gazing into space and she saw light reflected in the teardrops in his eyes.

Something, probably the music and that tune in particular, had touched a chord; some sad memory maybe, or a memory of happier times from his past. She could see that he was far away, lost in his thoughts, and she wondered if she should say something. Could she in any way help or comfort him? At first she felt that now might be the opportunity to discover just what it was that caused him to put up the strange defensive wall around himself. The wall that he only came out from behind when he was talking to, or was spending time with Timmy. But she realized that he would probably not thank her for intruding into his personal life. She didn't know him well enough and in any case now was not the time, it was a birthday party. Also did she really want to get involved with this or any man at this stage in her life? She had just come out of a very unsatisfactory marriage, luckily without too much hassle, and was doing alright as a single person for the time being.

He looked towards the bar and seeing Timmy returning his mood lifted and he turned, smiled at Jacqui said

"Here comes Timmy, our desserts will soon be here."

The dark moment had passed and they laughed and joked as they ate the rest of their meal. When they finally got up to leave Mick said

"Thank you both very much for inviting me to join you tonight, I enjoyed it very much. I had almost forgotten what it was like to go out for a meal of an evening."

"Not at all" said Jacqui "It's your birthday tomorrow and it seemed only right to ask you along, especially as you've been so good to Timmy. We should thank you for coming."

TWENTY SIX

Sidney woke early; he had been waking early for the last few days. Since his relationship with Marilyn had started, he had been sleeping better, sounder but waking earlier. Part of this was no doubt due to the fact that she had been accepted so well by his gran, acceptance that he hadn't really expected. He had been fairly sure that his mother would like her, after all she had worked for several years in the pub, meeting and socialising with all sorts of people. But that was a few years ago now, and since she had been looking after his gran she seemed to have become somewhat nervous, withdrawn and almost afraid at the thought of going out.

He had also felt that his confidence had grown enormously since he had been with Marilyn. He wasn't quite sure exactly what had caused this. It wasn't any thing that she had said as far as he could remember. Just the fact that she was with him gave him a lift, a lift that he was able to carry with him even when he was away from her. Walking with her, talking about this and that, all made him feel good. It was almost as though he was a new man.

He kicked off the bed clothes and after a quick wash got dressed and went down to make the family's early morning tea. He took a mug up to his mum and then went in to his gran's room with a mug for her. She was lying with her back towards him, half out from under the bed clothes on the pillows. It looked as though she was trying to get something off the bedside table.

"You all right Gran?" he asked as he walked around the bed "Can I get you something?" And then he saw only too well that she was far from all right. She was moaning slightly and her face was all lop-sided as though her mouth had pulled down on one side. He quickly lifted her into a straighter, and he thought more comfortable, position on the pillows and then ran out into the living room.

"Mum" he shouted up the stairs "Gran's had another stroke, a pretty bad one I should think, she doesn't seem to be able to talk. I'm ringing for the ambulance, you'd better get dressed."

He added the latter because she was in the habit of coming down in her dressing gown and slippers for the first half hour or so of the day. Then he was on the phone explaining to the emergency services about his gran's stroke and her previous medical history. Once he had done that he went in to sit with her till his mother came down. There was nothing he could do, just wait and hope that the ambulance would arrive soon. He had no idea how long ago his gran had had her stroke. It could have been minutes or hours before he went in to her, and he knew only too well that time was of the essence. She seemed comfortable enough, but she still couldn't speak, just a sort of grunt and moan. He held her hand, for all the good that did, because it seemed to be floppy, almost lifeless.

His mother came bustling into the room, she had dressed but had not done her hair as well as she would normally have done, and had put on no makeup. Greatly agitated she asked Sidney if her mother was still breathing, then went straight over to the bed and putting a hand on her shoulder said

"It's all right Mother, Sidney's called the ambulance, they'll soon be here. Are you all right, no I know that's stupid of me, what I mean is... are you comfortable?"

A slight nod of the head and a grunt was all the reply that she got, so daughter and grandson had to resign themselves to the fact that there was nothing that they could do but wait. It was difficult; the frustration of sitting beside their ailing relative and being unable to do anything to help was unbearable.

"Where's that ambulance got to, how long ago was it that you phoned Sidney?" said Hilda, bursting into tears.

"I don't remember Mum, about ten minutes I should think. There's nothing we can do, we've done all we can, Gran seems to be in no pain."

"How long before the ambulance gets here... did they say?"

"'Twill be about twenty minutes, just calm yourself, there's nothing more we can do. Getting in a state won't help anyone, least of all Gran."

"When did it happen, d'you know?"

"I've no idea; she was like it when I came in. It looked like she'd been trying to sit up."

" Don't worry Mum, the ambulance will soon be here and then you'll be in the best of hands. You'll be all right then you'll see."

Moments later they heard the siren and then saw the blue light flashing on the curtain.

"Go and show them in Sidney" said Hilda standing up, her hands clasped in front of her and looking around the room anxiously, as if to see if it was all right to receive guests. The paramedics came in with their stretcher and took charge of the situation. While one checked on the patient the other asked Sidney what had happened. He told them as best he could, but he stressed that he had no idea when it had all started. They soon had her on the stretcher and into the ambulance.

"Would either of you want to ride in with us?" asked one of the paramedics.

"No" said Sidney, "we'll follow in our car, thanks all the same."

Hilda grabbed her handbag and followed him out to the car saying

"Did we ought to bring something with us for her, a change of clothes or something?"

"Let's see how long she has to stay Mum, it might not be for very long."

Sidney didn't like to say that she might very well never come out of hospital; his mother was upset enough as it was. In fact, he expected Gran to be dead before they even arrived at the hospital. Her breathing had been very shallow and there had been something about the look the paramedic had given him as they carried her out. That was the very reason why he had thought that it would be best if they didn't ride in the ambulance. He felt that the trauma of seeing her mum pass away would be too much for Hilda.

As they drove along she said

"Why didn't she ring her bell? I'd have been down here like a shot if I'd heard her bell." She sobbed into her handkerchief, racked with guilt at the thought of her mother lying helpless and alone while she was asleep upstairs."

"Maybe she couldn't get to it in time, maybe she wasn't properly awake. Apparently a person can have a stroke, or a heart attack, in their sleep. Don't go blaming yourself Mum, it's not your fault, you've always done every thing you could for her, you've been doing so for the last ten years. You gave up work to care for her when her arthritis got so bad she could hardly walk, and you've been waiting on her hand and foot ever since. She hasn't exactly made life easy for you either."

"I know, but you know what the doctor said after that last little stroke she had, the next time we might not be so lucky. And he said that time was the most important thing."

He parked at the hospital, at that hour of the morning there was plenty of space, and then they ran in to find out where Gran had gone and how she was. A nurse sat them down in a small waiting area and after what seemed like an age a young lady doctor came out.

"Mrs Turner? I'm sorry to have to tell you, but your mother passed away in the ambulance. I am

161

so sorry. We think she must have had a severe stroke, the paramedics did all they could."

"We didn't know, she didn't ring her bell, she could have been lying there for hours. If only we had got to her earlier she would have been all right."

"No, you mustn't think like that Mrs Turner, you mustn't blame yourself. She was a very frail old lady and she had had a TIA recently hadn't she? I don't honestly think that it would have made any difference even if you had found her earlier and called us then."

She sat down beside Hilda and took her hand in an attempt to console her. Her words seemed to help for Hilda stopped crying and thanked her for her kindness.

"I'm afraid there will have to be a post mortem."

"So what will that involve" asked Sidney "does that mean that we won't get Gran back for a few days?"

"The undertaker will collect her and take her to the chapel of rest, I think that's what happens these days" said Hilda.

"I expect that you would like to see her once more before you go. I'll get a nurse to call you when they are ready for you."

Mother and son sat holding hands in that hot little waiting room, though they didn't feel the heat, if anything they felt cold and numb. Neither knew what to say, it had all been so sudden. They both had known for a long while that she could die at any time, and yet when it happened it seemed to be a shock, a total surprise.

After another long wait a male nurse came in and asked them if they were ready, would they like to follow him. She looked at peace, although her face was still a little lop-sided. Hilda kissed her on the forehead and stayed looking down at her for a while. Then Sidney gave her a kiss on the cheek saying

"Bye Gran, thanks for every thing."

He turned, and taking his mother by the arm said

"Come on Mum, time to go home."

TWENTY SEVEN

Sidney was awake; in fact he hadn't slept at all well and had woken several times during the night. He lay looking at the ceiling, looking at the light brown stain by the chimney breast. It had always been there, several attempts to cover it with emulsion paint had failed. Each time he thought he had at last succeeded only to find after a few weeks the stain had reappeared. From a certain angle it looked like a rabbit and he remembered how as a small boy he had lain in bed looking at it and felt sure that he had seen it move.

His inability to sleep he put down to the fact that today they were going to bury his grandmother. Why he should be nervous at the thought of her impending funeral he couldn't understand. But he felt uneasy, felt somehow that she was there watching him. She had always felt strongly about doing things right, particularly in public. So he knew that this day every thing had to go smoothly. He racked his brain to think if there was any aspect that he had neglected to cover. He had had a long talk with The Reverend Quentin Russell about the service and chosen the hymns and the lesson. The undertaker had every thing under control, service sheets had been printed and his grandfather's grave, in which she was to be interred, had been opened so that they could be re-united. He and his mother would walk to the church behind the hearse, it was no great distance. After the service refreshments, tea and sandwiches etcetera, were going to be served in the village hall. Walter Blackmore from the café next door had agreed to provide this service for a modest charge.

He got out of bed and went downstairs to get an early morning cup of tea. He took one up to his mother and sat on the edge of her bed while they both drank. Like him she had not slept too well, but her worries were for a totally different reason. When he asked her if she was alright she said

"No, I'm not. I'm worried, worried sick. What am I going to do now? For the past ten years I've looked after her, waited on her hand and foot, hardly been out of the house. So what am I going to do now? I've got no purpose in life any more."

"Of course you have Mum, look at it this way, you're free now to do what ever you want. You could go out and get a job again, you know how much you used to love working in the pub."

"That was years ago, who would want to employ me now, eh? They'd want a young, pretty girl to work behind the bar, draw the customers in. They wouldn't want an old woman like me."

"You're not old Mum, and besides you've got experience, that's something the youngsters haven't got."

"My experience is probably way out of date. No, my main worry is, I've been cooped up in here for so long, hardly been out to the shops or anything, I'm not sure if I could go out."

She lay back on the pillows, turned her head away from Sidney and started crying. He put his hand on her shoulder, not really sure what to do or say.

"And if you and Marilyn get married" she said between sobs "What's going to happen to me then, all alone here in this house. How could I ever get a job that would pay enough money for to keep this place and me in food and all that?"

"Oh, don't worry about that Mum, I don't think that Marilyn and I are going to get married for a long time yet. We've only just started going out together. I'd like to think that she might want to marry me one day, but I don't know if she feels that way. And even if she did and we got married, we wouldn't move that far away, we'd be near enough to stay in touch with you."

He had had to think quickly then, he had nearly said that they would stay and live with her. But after all the years living in a house with three generations, one of them his grandmother, he knew it would never work. He had loved his gran, loved her deeply, but if he was honest with himself he hadn't always liked her. It was she that had brought him up, instilled in him a set of standards and moral values. Although he realised it was often a case of 'do as I tell you, not as I do'. She could be bossy and dictatorial, berating him for some minor offence one minute and then calling him her 'little beauty' the next. If and when she praised him it was always because he took after her; after all, wasn't she his wonderful gran?

"Don't try looking too far ahead Mum, let's concentrate on today, and don't worry. Now, I'm going to get us a good breakfast and you are going to eat it, alright? I doubt if we'll want any lunch, the service is at two o'clock and the bun fight after it will be at about three. So we need to have a good meal now."

He leant over and kissed her on the cheek, then he got up off the bed, opened the curtains and left the room.

As the day went on the weather became hot and sultry, heavy dark clouds built up and it felt as though the stifling hot air was squeezing them. Sidney had the front door open, partly to let in some air and also to see when the undertakers arrived. When they did he put on the jacket of his dark suit and taking Hilda's arm led her out into the lane. They walked slowly to the church, two solitary figures in black behind the equally black shiny hearse.

As he walked up the aisle behind the coffin, eyes straight ahead, he realised with some surprise that there were quite a number of people in the church, more than he had expected. He had had no idea as to how many would be there. His gran was of a generation and age group most of whom had already passed on. She had lived almost as a recluse for many years, because she couldn't get out and about with any ease she had chosen to stay at home. Many of the newcomers to the area would never have seen her or known of her existence and nor would those of his age group.

One person who was not there was Marilyn. She had been offered the chance to go on a course and had said that she would stay to be with him but he had insisted that she go. To miss the opportunity might have meant a long wait before such another chance arose. He was also acutely aware that their relationship was too new for her to have walked with him. Yet he wouldn't have wanted her sitting in the rear of the church as just another member of the congregation. Still, he missed her. She had changed him, emboldened him, lifted him out of his box of shyness and self doubt. Yet he was really only at his best when she was at his side.

The service was not a long one, with only two hymns and one short lesson. Quentin Russell read a eulogy; a job he didn't particularly enjoy. He hardly knew the deceased, he had visited her less frequently than he should have done, often leaving that role to his wife Grace. He had had a long talk with Hilda and Sidney and from what they had said he had gained several ideas on which to base his brief complimentary description of Alice May Turner.

After the last hymn, 'Abide with me' and the committal, all crossed slowly over the green in two's and three's to the village hall. A few went with Hilda and Sidney to the grave for the interment. Sal and Edna had gone ahead of the rest to get the kettle boiling for the cups of tea.

"Lovely service wasn't it Sal?"

"Yes, and a good crowd to see her off too; more'n I expected."

"The vicar gave her a good send off."

"Yes, though for a minute I wasn't quite sure who he was telling about. Didn't sound like the Alice I knew."

"No, still t'wouldn't do to speak ill an all that" said Edna with a smile. With that she saw the first of the mourners entering the hall.

"They'm coming in now... are we offering coffee or is it just tea?"

"Both... I'll take the covers off these sandwiches....'tis a good spread, Walter has done her proud sure enough."

"'Twasn't Walter, 'twas his daughter Jacqui done all this."

The sombre crowd came in and helped themselves to the refreshments on offer, all in turn making a point of talking to Hilda and Sidney. As the afternoon progressed the mood lifted and became, as it should, more a celebration of the life of the departed. For Hilda, still worried about her ability to cope when out in company, this lightening of mood was a great help to her morale. By the time she and Sidney left for home she was able to say

"Well, that wasn't so bad after all".

TWENTY EIGHT

The small crowd hadn't lingered long after Alice Turner's funeral tea. Jacqui went over and washed up the cups and plates and then tidied and swept the hall ready for who ever would be using it next. Then, taking the few large plates that Walter had supplied, she returned to the café. She had been thinking. The germ of an idea had come to her, as to what she might be able to do on a more permanent basis. Working for her dad would soon come to an end, she realized that. It was inevitable when the summer busy season tailed off. Back in the café kitchen she said to her dad

"I have been thinking Dad, d'you suppose there's any demand for outside catering around here? You know the sort of thing, providing and cooking the food for private dinner parties in people's homes."

"What exactly were you proposing to do?"

"Well, I would put on a three or four course meal in the customer's house, buy all the ingredients do the cooking and serve it all. And then maybe do the washing up afterwards."

"Why would any body want that in preference to going out for a meal in the pub, for instance?"

"Well I should think it would be a lot cheaper, for one thing, and also more homely. Also the host would be able to drink. I just thought that it might appeal to those who would like to entertain friends in their own home, but don't feel very confident in their cooking ability."

"It could work. You'd have to travel quite a bit, I don't think that there would be a lot of take up in this village. When were you thinking of starting this venture?"

"I thought that this autumn would be a good time, when things here started to quieten down and you weren't so busy."

"Yes, it might work; it would certainly be worth giving it a try."

They carried on discussing the idea and going into a few more details when the phone rang. It was Mick, wanting to speak to Jacqui

"I was hoping to come over and pick up Timmy tonight to go badger watching. The weather seems set dry, there's a few high clouds but they won't matter much, the moon is nearly full. If it's alright with you I would be over at half past seven."

"Yes, that sounds alright. What time would you be back?"

"Oh, not very late, before nine I reckon."

"I'll tell Timmy to expect you."

"He'll need warm clothes and a torch. It's mostly sitting and waiting and there's no guarantee that we'll see anything. Don't want him to build up his hopes too much and then be disappointed."

So at half past seven Timmy was waiting, watching out of the window ready to be picked up. Jacqui and her parents were watching television when Mick arrived in his van. Timmy jumped up and with a cheerful

"Bye Mum" was off and out of the door.

Mick drove out of the village, past the entrance to his lane and on for about half a mile until they came to an old gravel pit at the side of the road. Gravel for roads was no longer dug there and it now made a useful lay-by. There was a pair of mountain ash trees with their smooth, pale grey trunks on the lip of the pit. Their leaves were beginning to turn brown and the clusters of bright orange berries looked almost red in the evening light. Mick and Timmy got out and walked along a well trodden grassy path that ran slightly uphill between the bracken, now turning reddish brown, and the occasional gorse bush.

"Where does this path go?" asked Timmy.

"It doesn't really go anywhere now, just up onto the moor. I suppose years ago it was used by tin miners going to work."

"Is it far up here, to the badgers' sett I mean?"

Mick smiled to himself, hearing in his mind the age old almost inevitable question all kids ask 'Are we nearly there?' but turning to Timmy he said

"It's not very far, just a few hundred yards. We have to get there early, so that we can settle down and wait before they come out; and it may be a long wait. The wind is in the right place for where we are going to sit so hopefully when they do come out they won't smell us."

Soon they arrived at a point where there was an old hawthorn tree, twisted and misshapen by years of Dartmoor's winds and weather. Its trunk was smoothed and greasy from being rubbed on by generations of ponies and sheep. Beside it was a large flat rock a yard or two below the path. It looked as though it had been part of an old, now disused, wall that ran across the hillside.

"This is where we sit and wait, on this reave."

"What's a reave?"

"A wall or bank, they are centuries old. Some of them are miles long, running across the moor. They are thought to be ancient boundaries, maybe three thousand years old."

"Wow!"

"Just down below can you see in that short grass soil and gravel that has been dug out of the side of the slope?

"Yes"

"Well, that's one of the entrances to the badger's sett. We'll have to sit here quietly and wait till it gets nearly dark."

So sit and wait they did, as the day's light faded and the moon, by now well up in the sky, grew brighter. The flat rock that they were sitting on had a light covering of moss but it was not as soft as Timmy would have liked and he wished that he had brought a cushion of some sort. He found it hard to sit still and Mick scowled at him each time he wriggled. Timmy wondered how he managed to sit so still for so long. He thought that his friend must be some sort of Red Indian to be able to wait motionless as he did.

Eventually, in the half light they heard a slight grunting and snuffling. Mick nudged Timmy and pointed to a spot a little way away from them. In the dim light, amongst the bracken the grey body with the familiar black and white striped head was almost impossible to see. Then it moved out into the more open ground and the moonlight. As Timmy watched it, holding his breath lest he made any noise and disturbed it, another two appeared from the hole nearer to the watchers. They moved around, sniffing and snuffling as though checking to see if all was OK, then one by one they lumbered off into the gloom and the cover of the bracken and gorse. Timmy was about to jump up, but Mick put his hand out as yet another two badgers came out. These soon ran off, grey bundles, seemingly hurrying to catch up with their relatives. The watchers waited for a few more minutes, then Mick said

"I think that's all we're going to see tonight. Could you see them well enough? Can you remember enough to do one of your drawings?"

"Yeah, that was brill" said Timmy, his eyes wide and shining with excitement. "Did you see the way that big one looked up at us, d'you think he saw us?"

"I don't know if he saw us, they haven't got particularly good eyesight, but he knew we were here, smelled us I reckon."

"If I had brought my mobile I might have been able to take a photo."

"Has your mobile got a flash?"

"No, you only get that on some of the more expensive ones."

"Well, perhaps we can come another day and you may be able to get a photo then."

"Can we come tomorrow?" asked Timmy eagerly.

"No,'fraid not, I've got to go out tomorrow, I shan't be back till late. It'll have to be another night, don't worry, the badgers will still be here."

'But I'll be back at school next week and then that only leaves the weekends', thought Timmy.

They stood up and stretched, cramped after the long wait sitting in the same position. Looking around Timmy could see a lighted window across the valley below them. Not entirely sure of his bearings and wanting to check he asked

"Is that light from East Furzes?"

"Yeah, that's right."

Nearer to them, down the slope, he could make out the roofs of West Furzes, the slates shining in the moonlight. They looked quite eerie, the dark shadows cast by the buildings, black pools in the greys and silvers around them. A cloud passed over the moon and suddenly it all changed. Dark and light became grey as the brightness of the moonlight faded.

"What's that on the roof of that big building?" asked Timmy, pointing to what looked like a series of thin bright strips of light along the ridge of the barn roof.

"I've no idea. I've never seen any lights there before; they seem to be coming from vents in the roof. They'm a funny lot there, don't seem to live there, but every now and then I've seen a horse box outside that big barn. Enough of that Timmy, it's time we were going home. I promised your mum I'd have you back by nine."

They set off back down the path. Mick strode along, the bright moonlight clearly showing him the way, while Timmy, almost having to trot to keep up, used his torch from time to time.

"What do badgers eat?" he asked.

"They're omnivorous, they'll eat insects and worms and grubs. They particularly like leather jackets, the grub of the daddy long legs. You'll often see where they have been digging for them, particularly in areas of short grass, like beside the roads. But they also like roots and berries. The odd rogue badger will take lambs and chickens, which is another reason why farmers aren't that fond of them."

"Are they a danger to humans?"

"Not really, but they are very brave and if cornered they would put up a fight. They have a jaw that can lock shut, so when they catch hold of something or someone it's almost impossible to get away."

Once back at the van they jumped in and drove off towards the village. To Timmy's delight the headlights picked up another badger that ran along the road for several yards before scrambling up through the hedge on his side of the road. Mick stopped the van and turning it so that the lights lit up the hedge said

"D'you see that run, that little path going up and over the hedge? That's a badger run. To a badger that's like a main road. They use them all the time, year after year. They reckon some badger runs have been in use for centuries."

"Is there another going up over the hedge on the other side of the road?"

"Yes, it may not be right opposite but it's there alright."

"And that run could have been there before the road was built?" Timmy asked.

"Yes, and in some places where man has built a major road they have built tunnels under the road so that the badgers can cross safely."

Timmy was fascinated by all this information and the events of the evening that he had just had. When Mick dropped him at his home he ran indoors, bursting with excitement and wanting to tell his mum and grandparents about all the things that he had witnessed. They listened patiently, pleased and amused at his enthusiasm.

"And next time we go, I'm going to take my mobile."

"What, to talk to the badgers?" said Walter, eyebrows raised in mock surprise.

"No Granddad, to take a photo of them."

They all had a good laugh at this but finally Jacqui said it was time for bed. So a very happy boy kissed them all goodnight and went off up the stairs to his room.

TWENTY NINE

The next evening Timmy was up at the badger sett again. He had asked Jacqui if it would be alright to go and she had assumed that he would again be going with Mick. She and her mother had left before him; they were going to a meeting of the village ladies group, but not before she had reminded him to take his bag with extra warm clothes in it.

However, Timmy didn't bother with his rucksack, preferring at the last minute to wear an extra layer of clothes and so he set off with his phone in one pocket and his torch in another.

When he arrived at the flat rock everything was as before and he sat on the thickest patch of moss with his torch and phone in his hands and waited. It seemed to take an eternity for the twilight to fade, much longer than it had been the night before. One by one the birds ceased singing and all he could hear was the breeze in the gorse bushes and the occasional car passing along the road far below him. Eventually he heard the snuffling and grunting and occasional squeaking and finally in the gloom he could just see two badgers sniffing around outside their sett.

Cautiously he lifted up his mobile, set on camera mode, and with his torch in the other hand was about to switch on the torch and take a photo when another two badgers appeared. He waited a moment and then, trying hard not to let his hand shake in his excitement, he switched on his torch and took as many photos as he could in a few seconds. To his surprise and delight the badgers didn't run away immediately, and he felt sure that he had managed to get one or two good pictures. He switched off the torch and sat watching as the badgers trundled away into the bracken. Then he looked at the photos he had taken and was pleased to see that most of them did show the group of badgers, though perhaps not as clearly as he would have liked. However he thought it was definitely a good evening's work so he stood up and stretched ready to set off for home.

By this time it was fully night, clouds had covered the moon again and although not pitch dark he needed his torch to see his way along the path. As he turned to go he saw the headlights of a vehicle approaching West Furzes. It seemed to stop by the big barn, so he paused to watch. Mick had said that nobody lived there, so why was somebody stopping there and at this time of night? Soon after, a large rectangle of bright light appeared as the big doors were opened. From where he stood it looked to Timmy as though the vehicle moved into the barn. With the typical curiosity of a young boy he turned off the path and made his way down the slope, picking his way carefully towards the light. He took his time, remembering his fall and how he had twisted his ankle. Not that that had been all bad, after all it had brought him into contact with Mick and all the good times that had arisen from that friendship.

He had difficulty finding a path running down the hillside. Most of the animal tracks seemed to run across the slope but eventually he came across a reave that ran in the right direction and there was a sort of track at its base that he was able to follow. In places water draining off the moor in wet times, together with the hoofs of animals, had broken the turf and he had to walk on black peaty soil or gravel and the odd rough stones, uncovered by erosion.

Finally he arrived at the road and walked towards the barn. The doors were closed, though not so tightly that he couldn't see a chink of light coming from them. With his eyes concentrating in the pool of light from his torch in front of him, all around was in darkness. The moorland night seemed to wrap around him like a velvet blanket and there was not a sound to be heard except the scuffing of his boots on the gravel at the side of the road. As he approached the barn he had expected to hear some voices or some noise made by the men who had arrived earlier in the vehicle whose lights he had seen. He was about to touch the doors when he felt an almighty bang on the side of his head. For a split second it seemed as though his head exploded in a painful mass of bright lights as he reeled sideways, falling towards the ground. Then all went black.

The two men by the barn had been standing in the shadows watching Timmy coming down the slope toward them. They had no idea as to who or what was behind the torch, bobbing down the hill.

"I don't like it" said the younger one, "Don't want any body seein' us now, not now that we're almost finished 'ere."

"'Ee's probably going to the farm up the road, no need to worry. Once ee's passed we can get on and clear up everyfink 'ere and be gone."

"Yeah, tha's what I want, an' the sooner the better. The owners are moving in soon. They want the barn cleared by tomorrow to put their furniture in."

"Sh…ee's getting closer."

They waited in the darkness, watching the light coming along the road. Then when it was opposite the pathway leading up to the barn instead of going on down the road it turned in towards the doors. As the figure drew level with them the young man stepped behind him and hit Timmy on the side of his head with the large wrench that he was carrying. With barely a sound he fell to the ground.

"What the 'ell 'ave you done now… Gawd, 'ave you killed 'im?"

They both bent down over the prone figure.

"No, 'ee's all right…'ee's still breavin'….'ee's out cold, tha's all. Go an' get that duck tape out of the truck, I'll put a bit on 'is mouf and round 'is wrists. Then we'll put 'im in the shed an' we can get on wivout 'im bovverin' us."

When he returned with the tape and with the light from the open barn door falling on Timmy the older man said

"I don't like it, 'ee's only a young lad by ve looks of 'im."

"'Ee'll be all right, besides it's us you got to worry about not 'im. We got to get away from 'ere sharpish, before any one sees us, right? We been lucky up to now."

"Yeah, I s'pose you're right. I don't like leaving 'im 'ere. What if nobody finds 'im?"

"Stop worrying … you're worse than an old woman."

And with that the two men carried Timmy's unconscious body into the lean-to shed adjoining the barn, closed the door and went back into the barn to continue their work.

Some two hours later Jacqui and her mother returned home from the village hall. Walter had gone to bed early; he always did during the season. They walked in to the kitchen and Jacqui said

"Oh, I see Timmy's home, left his bag on the table again. Will he ever learn to put things away for himself instead of always leaving it out for me to do?"

THIRTY

It was six thirty in the morning, In the East the sky was just beginning to lighten. Pc's Stuart and Hudgell, known to each other and their work colleagues as Starsky and Hutch, were patrolling along the A360 from Devizes towards Stonehenge. They passed to the north of the famous ancient monument and tucked in behind a lorry coming up the A303. It seemed to be travelling rather fast and the offside rear light and the light over the number plate were not working. They followed it along the dual carriageway for several miles keeping about fifty yards behind.

"If that vehicle is carrying horses I'd be very surprised or sorry for the horses" said Starsky as the lorry swayed from left to right as it went around a roundabout.

"Let's just follow it a bit further" said Hutch "We can pull it over after we cross the A338."

"Call in its number and see if there's any thing on the system, it may be wanted."

After a few moments the message came back that there was no mention of the vehicle, so they carried on behind it, noting that whoever was driving it was obviously unaware of their presence.

Eventually they passed it before they got to Thruxton and pulled it over into a lay-by.

Starsky got out and approached the lorry, a pale blue horse box. There were two people inside, a young, dark haired man who was on the passenger side and an older man in the driver's seat. Starsky made a downward motion with his hand at the driver, who wound down his window.

"Are you aware that you have defective lights at the rear of this vehicle?"

"No, vey was alright when I left 'ome."

"May I see your driving licence and your papers, please?"

"Yeah, just a minute" he said as he made to reach into a shelf under the dash-board.

"So where are you headed for?"

"Lambourn."

"Really, why didn't you turn off at the last roundabout onto the A338?"

"Oh...er...it's quicker this way...better road."

"And, what are you travelling with? Not horses surely. I'd like to see your load, if I may."

At that the younger man opened his door, jumped out of the lorry, ran to the hedge, pushed through it into the field beyond and disappeared into the gloom. Hutch saw this and was quickly out of his seat to give chase. In the half light it was impossible to see just where the fugitive was and, thinking that half a loaf would be better than none, rejoined his partner.

"Take a look inside will you Hutch, I've got a feeling that you won't be finding any gee-gees."

He opened the small inspection door and shouted

"Wow, you're right, no gee-gees....but if they fed their nags on the stuff they've got in here they'd probably win all their races."

He laughed as he shut the door and came around to the front to join Starsky.

"It's full to the roof with what looks and smells like cannabis."

"Out you get, sunshine, you're coming with me. You'd better radio in, Hutch and tell 'em what's happened. They'll have to send somebody out to drive the truck back, and also there's one fellow out there somewhere on the loose, don't forget."

THIRTY ONE

"Timmy, breakfast's ready" Jacqui shouted up the stairs.

"I don't know what's up with him" she said to Jessica, "He's usually up long before me."

"Perhaps he was a bit late home from his badger watching last night and decided to have a lie-in for once."

"Timmy doesn't do lie-ins Mum. Dad, did you hear him come in last night, was he very late?"

"I couldn't tell you, I watched a bit of telly and went to bed early, like I usually do. But I doubt if I would have heard him if I had been downstairs."

"Oh, I suppose I shall have to go up and wake him."

Jacqui left the room and came down shortly after saying

"He's not in his room, perhaps he went out earlier."

"He'll be back soon, when he gets hungry" said Walter, as he helped himself to another round of toast. They all got on with their meal and then, when she had finished, Jessica said

"I'll go and get the paper." She got up and went to leave the house. When she got to the front door she stopped.

"This door's locked. You said he's not in his room Jacqui, did you check to see if his bed's been slept in?"

"No, d'you think…?" She left the table and ran up the stairs. She came back down with a puzzled frown on her face.

"Little monkey, I bet he's stayed over with Mick. That's not on, I wouldn't have minded too much if he'd asked, but to …wait till I see him."

"What are you going to do?" asked Jessica.

"First of all I'm going to ring Mick. If he has stayed the night there, then Mr Cribbett will have some answering to do. He's just as much to blame."

She strode over to the phone and spent a few moments looking up the number. While she was doing that Walter said calmly

"Timmy may not be there, don't jump too quickly to a conclusion and bite Mick's head off before he has a chance to speak. I know you Jacqui; you can be a bit hasty at times."

"Alright Dad." She dialled and waited for several rings before Mick, sounding somewhat breathless answered.

"Hello Mick, its Jacqui, is Timmy with you?"

"No"

"Well he was with you last night badger watching, wasn't he?"

"No, not last night…the night before, but not last night. I was out all day and didn't get back till late."

"But Timmy said he was going badger watching again, wasn't it with you?"

"No, he asked if we could go again last night, and I told him that I would be away. If he went out last night it wasn't with me."

"Well he went out last night and his bed hasn't been slept in. Where is this place where you watch badgers? I want to go there now. He might have slipped again and hurt himself. Perhaps he can't walk home."

Mick gave her directions and then said

"I'll see you there, I'll take Meg and walk over the hill from here. He might have tried to come this way, though there's no clear path. If he did I'm sure Meg will find him."

With that he hung up and Jacqui went and got her coat saying

"Mick says he hasn't been there, I'm off to meet him by the badger sett. Oh I hope he's alright."

"I'm sure he is" said Jessica "Don't worry love."

But Jacqui was gone almost before she had finished speaking, out in her car and speeding away up the road. She parked where Mick had parked in the old gravel pit and half walking half running made her way up the path to the big flat rock. She didn't know where to look and Mick wasn't there so she just stood on the rock looking all around and calling Timmy's name.

Meg was the first to arrive, running up to her and sniffing all around as she wagged her tail and looked up at Jacqui. Then Mick appeared looking very sombre.

"Well I've not seen him as I came up, and I'm sure that Meg would have done if I had missed him. Did you see any sign of him on your way here?"

"No, I wasn't really looking, I thought he would be here so I didn't look much as I came along, not to the side of the path that is."

"Have you rung any of his other friends? He might not have come up here at all."

"That's possible, he didn't have his bag with him. It was on the kitchen table when we came home from the village hall last night. That's what made me think that he was home and safely tucked up in bed."

"Well I think the best thing to do is for you to go back home. Look carefully all around as you go, just in case."

He didn't like to say 'in case he was hit by a car and is lying in a ditch beside the road', but the thought had passed through his mind.

"Ring any of his friends with whom you think he might have stayed the night, and meanwhile Meg and I will have a good look around here. You'll probably find he's at home sitting in the armchair watching telly when you get back."

"If he is I'll skin him alive" said Jacqui, forcing a grin as she turned and set off for home. Mick stood for a while on the flat rock scanning the surroundings through his field glasses. The whole thing seemed wrong to him; Timmy was a sensible boy, he wasn't the sort to do anything that would worry his mum. If he had been out there watching the badgers he would have gone home by half past nine at the latest. The fact that he hadn't slept in his bed meant that something had stopped him, maybe an accident. Meg had been sniffing around but was now sitting at his feet. He swept his glasses over the buildings at West Furzes and then back again. Something was different, what was it? He scanned all the buildings again and then he saw it. The doors to the big barn were no longer locked, in fact one of them was partly open.

"I wonder" he said to Meg, "Let's go and see if an inquisitive lad has gone down there. He was only asking about the place the other night when he saw that thin strip of light."

They set off down the slope, eyes darting from left to right all the way, taking it slowly so as not to miss anything. After a while he came across a patch of black soft earth and saw a footprint. He realised then that he was probably following the same path that Timmy had taken beside the reave, though he was still not sure if he was doing the right thing. Then

"I think we're on the right track Meg old gal, looks like he came this way."

They carried on down the path, a little quicker now that Mick felt that they were going the right way. Once on the road he walked straight to the barn. As he turned towards the doors he saw, lying in the grass a little to one side of the path, a torch.

"He's been here alright Meg, that's his torch. See if you can find him."

He went through the door and looked in the big barn calling out for Timmy as he did so. There were lots of grow bags in rows with the stalks of some plant, now cut off, sticking out. There were also a few star shaped leaves on the ground but no sign of the boy he so badly wanted to find. He went out again and found Meg by the door to the lean-to shed behind the barn sniffing and doing a little squeaky sort of bark. The door was bolted but Mick slid it back and opened it saying

"What is it Meg, is he in here?"

It took him a moment for his eyes to get accustomed to the dark, but Meg had run forward and was standing over a heap of something at the far end of the long narrow shed. Mick ran forward, his heart beating faster now, his face pale and cold as he feared what he would find. What he saw in the dim light that came in from the open door filled him with dread. Timmy was lying on the dirty straw and leaves that covered the floor, his hands bound behind his back and a length of wide sticky tape over his mouth.

"Oh my God Timmy; what have they done to you?"

Mick crouched down beside him and gently took off the tape that was across his mouth. Timmy let out a slight moan and Mick, taking out his lambsfoot pocket knife, cut the tape that bound his wrists. Then he was about to pick up Timmy and carry him out, but he hesitated, fearing that by doing so he might make matters worse. He was getting a little more used to the light now and could see a little dried blood above Timmy's ear. That side of his head looked to be swollen. He put his hand on it gently, it felt hot. Timmy moaned again and mumbled something incoherent. He could make out something that sounded like 'bright lights' and 'mobile' but it made no sense to Mick. 'Concussion' he thought, 'some bastard has hit the poor lad on the head, knocked him out and he's now suffering from concussion'. Mick had seen more than one case of people who had fallen off a horse, landed on their head and been concussed. He still was a little unsure as to whether he should move Timmy. Then he heard a car coming and ran to the door and out onto the road. It was George, the postman, in the mail van. He waved him down and said

"Thank God you've come along. Have you got a phone with you?"

"Yes, why?"

"Dial nine nine nine and get an ambulance here as quick as possible. Young Timmy's in here hurt bad, concussed I think. It looks like some devil hit him over the head and then tied him up and gagged him."

By this time George was on the phone

"Ambulance please, and police" he said, looking at Mick who nodded at this. He then gave the name and post code of the destination and a brief description in layman's terms of what had happened to Timmy. When he was finished Mick said

"Can you go back to the café and tell Jacqui what's happened. Don't frighten her too much for God's sake. She'll want to come down here and probably ride in to the hospital in the ambulance with young Timmy. I'll stay here with him."

"Yeah, sure I can" said George, "what was the boy doing here to get hit on the head and tied up like that?"

"Dunno, I'll tell you all I know later."

With that George went over to his red van, turned and went back up the road towards the village. The other houses on his round would have to wait a little longer today for their mail. An emergency like this took precedence.

THIRTY TWO

Jacqui arrived at the same time as the air ambulance. She had been delayed for several minutes. Firstly she couldn't find her car keys, as is so often the way when in a hurry. Eventually she found them under a newspaper on the table in the hall. Then as she was driving out of the village she got behind a tractor with a huge dung spreader that kept her behind it for what seemed like an eternity.

Mick had heard the helicopter, whirring and chattering as it approached, the noise getting louder and louder. Then the clouds of dust as it landed on a small area of nearly level grassy ground by the road.

"You'll be alright now Timmy, the air ambulance has come to take you off to hospital."

He didn't know if Timmy could hear or understand what he was saying, but in case he could he wanted to comfort him. He had been talking to him all the while since George had gone, hoping that he was doing some good. Timmy had said nothing in return just the odd moan.

Jacqui came running into the shed and was down on her knees beside him just as the paramedics came in with their equipment and a stretcher. They moved her to one side and speaking calmly to Jacqui asked what had happened.

"I don't exactly know" she said "Mick here found him.

"I found him here about an hour ago, I've no idea what happened. His wrists were bound with wide tape and there was a piece of the same tape over his mouth. My guess is that he disturbed somebody who then hit him on the head and knocked him out before tying him up. I'm no expert, but it looks like concussion to me."

"You could be right; we'll get him to hospital as soon as we can".

Then, after what to Jacqui seemed a very long time while they did various tests, the paramedics put Timmy on the stretcher and loaded him into the helicopter.

"Where are you going to take him?" shouted Jacqui over the noise of the engine.

"Derriford hospital, Plymouth."

The door slid shut and the engine note rose, roaring as the helicopter lifted off the ground, dust and debris flying every where. Jacqui turned away, shutting her eyes and putting her hands over her ears. As the noise died away she said to Mick

"Can you tell Mum and Dad what has happened and where I've gone? I'll ring them later".

She brushed the bits of straw off her knees and some of the dust off her clothes that the helicopter had blown everywhere. Then she was gone, a worried and more than somewhat frightened mum.

She drove around the hospital car park several times before she managed to find a parking space. Then she rushed to the accident and emergency department, went up to the desk and gave her name and her reason for being there. The receptionist asked her to sit and wait while she found out what was happening. Jacqui found sitting doing nothing very hard and kept getting up and pacing up and down the room. She knew that it would achieve nothing but sitting still was even worse and she felt that she had to do something. She realized also that it would do no good to keep asking at the desk, though the temptation to do so was very great.

Finally a nurse came and called her into a small side room.

"Your son has had a bad knock on the head and is concussed. He is being examined at this moment by the doctor and is in the intensive care unit".

"Is he going to be alright, can I see him?"

"As soon as the doctor has finished his examination, we will know better exactly what his condition is. And then yes, you will be able to see him. Meanwhile, I'm afraid you'll have to wait here a little longer. I'll come and get you as soon as we are ready for you".

More waiting, thought Jacqui, looking around her. It was a small room with a table of light coloured wood a chair behind it and two others in front, all in the same light wood, with blue material covered seats. There were a few old magazines, the sort that were full of pictures of so-called celebrities.

There was no point in ringing home until she had some news. Through the small square window in the upper part of the door she could see the head and shoulders of people going up and down the corridor about their business. She stood up and watched them, anything to pass the time and hopefully take her mind of her reason for being there, if only for a minute. Two orderlies pushing a stretcher with a young man on it passed by, a large blood-soaked bandage around his head. 'Poor devil' thought Jacqui, 'I wonder what happened to him, a car accident perhaps?' Then an old man came down the corridor the other way in a wheelchair with his leg in plaster, smiling and joking with the person pushing him. 'He seems to have recovered. I pray that it won't be long before I'm taking Timmy home'.

She stepped back from the door and sat down in floods of tears as the enormity of the situation hit her and the adrenaline that had so far kept her going faded. The door opened and a young man in a check shirt and brown moleskin trousers entered.

"I'm Doctor Pritchard" he said "I've been looking at your son Timmy. He's gone to have an x-ray of his head, we think that there is probably a small fracture to the skull. He has had a serious knock on the head and is concussed. Though conscious, his speech is slurred and he doesn't make a lot of sense when he talks. I very much doubt if he will remember anything that happened, either for a few hours before or after the incident. We will have to keep him here under observation for a day or two, or until we feel that it is safe for him to go home"

"Will he be alright then? What I mean is, will there be any lasting damage?"

Jacqui had fears that her beloved son might end up brain damaged, a vegetable, unable to do anything for himself for the rest of his life.

"It is too early to say yet, I'm afraid, but early indications are fairly favourable. As soon as he's back from x-ray you will be able to see him in the ward. Someone will come and get you then".

THIRTY THREE

The helicopter had barely passed over the hill and out of sight when the police car, with two uniformed officers in it, arrived. They climbed out and walked over to Mick, who was standing by the shed door talking to George. Introductions were made and then Mick told them that Timmy had been taken off to Derriford hospital. Then he explained how Jacqui had rung him that morning because Timmy was missing and she thought that he might have been badger watching with him that night.

"I arranged to meet her by the badger sett and we had a good look around. It was not possible to see if Timmy had been there last night, but I suggested that she go home and I would look around on the moor as I went home. Looking through my field glasses I noticed that this barn door was open, and I wondered if Timmy had come down here,"

"Why would you think that?" asked one of the policemen, while his partner looked around and in the big barn.

"Well, the night before when we were up on the hillside by the badger sett, we noticed a series of thin strips of light on the roof of the big barn here."

"So what was special about that?"

"Well, this farm was sold several months ago. The new owners haven't moved in, in fact I don't know if anyone has seen them. A while ago new doors were put on the barn and a big padlock. People don't put big padlocks on barn doors as a rule. It all seemed a bit mysterious and the lights last night made us both curious. Another thing, I have seen a light blue horse box here from time to time."

"Yes, so have I" said George.

"The last time I saw the horse box here, there was a man standing beside it. He turned his back to me as I went by, which I thought was a bit odd."

"Why did you think that?"

"Well, I was on Osprey, my grey horse. Any horse owner would look to see who it was that was riding by and what sort of horse they had. It's only natural; if you keep horses you can't help but be curious as to what other people are riding. And another thing, I don't think that there had ever been horses in that horse box. Osprey didn't sniff at it or show any interest in it at all."

"So what has that got to do with the lad, Timmy?"

"Well, he's a lad of thirteen, with a natural curiosity. If he had seen something down here last night he might well have come down to see what it was. Perhaps he disturbed who ever it was and they clocked him one on the head and tied him up…I dunno."

"You say that they tied him up?"

"Yes, I found him at the back of the shed here, with his hands behind his back and a bit of duck tape around his wrists. He had another bit of tape over his mouth too, it's a wonder he was still able to breathe."

"We had better get the crime scene boys over here. Where is this tape?" Asked one of the policemen, the other officer was back at their car talking on his radio.

"In the back of the shed where I found Timmy; I took it off his mouth first and then cut off what was round his wrists. It's probably lying on the ground in there somewhere."

"You'll have to come down the station later and make a formal statement." Then turning to George he said

"How did you come to be involved in all this?"

"Mick stopped me as I drove down here, I called the ambulance and you lot. Then I went and told the boy's mum. Now if I may I ought to get on with my round, I've been delayed long enough already."

"Sure, but you will have to come in and make a statement too. Did either of you by any chance get the number of the horse box?"

Mick thought he could remember it and George had an idea as well so between them they were fairly sure of the number. With that George drove off and Mick asked if it would be alright if he went as well.

"Yeah, just show me exactly where you found Timmy. The sergeant will want to see you, no doubt, for a few more details when you come in to make your statement."

After Mick had gone the officer who had been looking around said

"It's pretty obvious what's been going on here, this barn has been used for growing cannabis. There's hundreds of grow-bags with those thin watering pipes, like people use for hanging baskets, from a tap in the corner. And there's a few tell-tale leaves on the floor if any more proof were needed. They'd have had high powered lights here an' all. There's a row of ventilation slits near the ridge of the roof. Maybe from up on the hill strips of light could be seen, and that's what they saw last night. It looks like a really professional set up to me. No wonder if he came snooping around they didn't want the boy to see what they were up to. Let's just hope to God that he's alright and not too badly hurt."

Mick, with Meg trotting beside him, walked back over the hill to Braggator. His mood was dark, not solely because of what had been done to Timmy. He kept thinking that he could have prevented it from happening. When, the night before, Timmy had been curious about the place, he should have warned him not to poke his nose in. But then, he thought, that would only have made the boy more inquisitive than ever, more likely to explore. Tell a youngster that something was out of bounds and that would be the first place he would go. If only he hadn't said 'no' to a second night of badger watching. But it had never occurred to him that Timmy would go there without him.

So he had done as he had previously arranged. He had been out all day, a part business part social call. He could have driven straight home and gone out with Timmy. But he chose to stay late with his friends and then he had stopped in a pub on the way home and had a meal. What made it worse was the realization that this wasn't the first time that a tragedy had occurred when he had stayed out late instead of coming straight home. His guilt and self-recrimination had played on him and kept him shut in his private world for the past six years. Now this terrible business had brought it all back two-fold.

Once home he got into his van and drove over to the café. He was dreading having to tell Jessica and Walter. They were full of questions as to how and what, but the one question that they wanted an answer to, 'How is Timmy?' he was unable to give them. He naturally wanted to go off and drive down to the hospital; he wanted to see how Timmy was and to support Jacqui. Instead, he said to Walter

"You and Jessica will want to go down to be with your daughter and grandson. Is there anything that I can do here to help?"

"Thank you" said Walter "Jess will go and I'll stay here and open up. I reckon I can manage on my own today".

"Can I drive Jessica down, would that be any help?"

"No thanks, she will no doubt want to come home before Jacqui does, so she'll be better with her own car. Then I'll go in and see Timmy tonight perhaps. He'll want to see you as well, maybe we'll go in together".

"Well, just let me know if there's anything I can do to help, any thing at any time".

"Sure" said Walter "now… have you had any breakfast, can I get you something to eat, a cup of tea, anything?"

"No thanks, I'm fine" said Mick

'Such kind people' he thought, 'why is it that it always seems to be the nice people that get the hard knocks?'

THIRTY FOUR

Phil came out of the shop and stood for a moment looking across the green. He was hoping to catch Frank as he passed through. Earlier that morning he had had a disturbing phone call from the vicar's wife, Grace. She told him that his old friend, Jane Wilcox had four of her lambs stolen during the night. Jane lived all alone and kept a small flock of Jacob sheep, more as pets than as a commercial project. What made it worse, as far as Grace was concerned, was the fact that this was not the first time. The previous year, when there had been a spate of burglaries in the neighbourhood, Jane had been the first to have been targeted. The trauma that Jane had suffered then had been significant, and Grace was naturally concerned for her.

Phil hadn't told her about the other thefts of livestock in the area. He wanted to have a chat with Frank first. He had seen the air ambulance passing overhead as he stood waiting, but had no idea as to where it was going or who it was that was in trouble. After another five minutes he was about to leave for home when Frank drove into the village green and stopped beside him.

"I'm glad I caught you, Frank. There's been another case of sheep stealing in the parish."

"What, some of your lambs?"

"No, Mrs Wilcox had four of her Jacob lambs stolen last night. Grace Russell phoned me this morning in some state. It's not so much the loss of the lambs that worries her; it's the fact that poor Mrs Wilcox lives on her own and is terrified in case whoever it is that is doing this might attack her."

"Has she got any one who can come and stay with her for a while?"

"Yes, she's got a daughter over Crediton way who came over last time. But of course she's got her own life to lead and can't stay for ever."

"And still no idea as to who might be behind all these thefts?"

"No, not a clue. I've told the police and I've asked Jay Bee to keep a look out for anything suspicious. The police seem to be more interested in the cases of large sheep rustling on the moor, like where flocks of fifty or more have been taken. In fact I hear one farmer has taken to dying his sheep a bright orange, dips them in a bath of dye I believe. It makes them more easy to trace and rather obviously stolen."

"But whoever is stealing our sheep is only taking a small number. It has to be somebody local who knows exactly where the sheep are and somebody who has an outlet for a few lambs" said Frank. "Either he is selling them to a butcher who doesn't mind where they are coming from, or he's killing them himself and selling the carcasses to a restaurant."

"I'm inclined to think it's the latter. A butcher these days has too many rules and regulations; lots of paper work and ear tags and so on to keep track of and record."

"But an individual killing them himself would need somewhere to dispose of the waste, the offal and skins etcetera. That would mean somewhere to bury the stuff or burn it. And, let's face it, four or five lambs as black market meat isn't going to make this person very rich, is it?"

"No, I agree. I don't understand it at all. If I see Jay Bee I'll have another word with him. He may have some ideas. He shoots a lot and knows where to sell his rabbits and the odd deer. Meanwhile I believe that Grace has gone over to spend a bit of time with Mrs Wilcox. What a cruel and despicable thing to do to that poor old lady."

"Have there been other cases in the neighbouring parishes?"

"Yes, I understand that one farmer has had four fat lambs taken and there was another case of six from a farm just outside Ashburton. There may have been more that I haven't heard of."

"And maybe some that haven't been noticed. Some of these hobby farmers hardly know what they've got, wouldn't miss the odd lamb." said Frank. "Well I must be going, keep me informed if there's any news. I'll see you around." And with that he was gone.

THIRTY FIVE

Somehow bad news in the country travels faster than good news and by the early afternoon Timmy's attack was the main topic on everybody's lips.

"Poor little fella, what a thing to do to a young boy like that. I mean, he's only twelve isn't he."

"No Sal, he's thirteen, had his birthday last month I believe."

"Well, twelve or thirteen he's still only a child."

"Whatever was he doing over to West Furzes, that's what I'd like to know? His mum thought he had gone out badger watching with that blacksmith fella, Mick Cribbett. Instead it seems he was out on his own, little monkey."

"I know Edna, and I hear that the police found a drugs factory there in that big barn. George told me that he probably saw lights down there and went to have a look. Got hit on the head and then trussed up like a chicken. An' he said that they had put a piece of wide sticky tape over his mouth so as he couldn't be heard. Could have suffocated the poor boy; might have killed him."

"This is the trouble Sal; these folks buy up these places and move in, we don't know who or what they are or what they are up to. And then they often only stay here for four or five years."

"But I understand that the new people haven't moved in yet. Charlie told me that he's seen them once. They didn't want to say much though. An oldish couple he said they were. He reckons that the barn was let out or used by these rogues, whoever they are. They've been using the place to grow cannabis in."

"What is the world coming to? I never thought to see drugs in our village. Has anybody heard how the boy is now? Is he still unconscious? Is he going to be alright?"

"I've no idea, I haven't seen either Walter or Jessica today. Jacqui went down behind the ambulance and I reckon she'll stay down there."

"Yes, I 'spect she will, they let mothers stay with their children these days" said Edna, sighing deeply as she thought of the worry and fear for her son's future that Jacqui must be feeling. Any time anybody had a head injury as bad as Timmy's it was only natural to be afraid that he might be brain damaged, end up as a vegetable for the rest of his life.

They both stood silent for a while, deep in thought, then changing the subject Sal asked

"Have you seen Hilda lately?"

"No I haven't; she seems to have shut herself in more than ever since her mother died."

"She needs to get out and about, get a job or something."

"She'll have to. She had her mother's pension and that there carer's allowance. That'll be stopped now, and if Sidney were to get married and move out....well...."

"Is he likely to do that? I know he's got that girl friend of his, but he's never going to get married just yet is he? They've only known each other a matter of weeks."

"Seems like that's all they need these days" said Edna. "My man was courting me for two and a half years, and then he was so slow, I pretty nigh had to propose to him."

"I'm glad to say that my Charlie was a bit quicker off the mark"

They both had a good laugh at this and carried on reminiscing about their courting days before going back into their homes.

THIRTY SIX

At half past five Mick pulled up outside the café in his van. Walter came out and climbed in.

"This is very good of you Mick, to take me down to Derriford."

"It's no trouble; I was going there anyway. Have you heard from Jacqui or Jessica? Any news as to how Timmy is?"

"No, well Jess phoned but there's no more news. Timmy is conscious, like he was when he went off in the ambulance, but he's still very confused. His speech is sort of garbled; doesn't make a lot of sense. He certainly doesn't remember anything that happened."

"I don't suppose he will. I remember a case of a girl who fell off her horse and was concussed. She doesn't remember to this day what happened for about two hours before and for several days after. I suppose it's the body's way of shutting out the memory of a bad event."

They drove on in silence over the moor. Autumn was coming, several of the sycamore trees that they passed had lost their leaves and on those that hadn't the leaves were brown or yellow. The gorse was still in bloom on the hillsides but the heather was over, no longer a blaze of purple, now a greyish brown.

Several cars passed them, coming home from work out of Plymouth. There were grey clouds above and a slight damp feeling in the air, but not enough for Mick to have to use the windscreen wipers. Once in the hospital car park they were lucky and found a space in which to park almost immediately. Then it was into the maze of corridors and passages, lifts and staircases, until they reached the ward.

They waited outside, looking through the glass of the doors until they caught Jacqui's eye. She came out and hugged her dad

"How's Timmy?" he asked

"Much the same, they keep doing tests on him. They come round every half hour, open his eyes and shine a torch in to test for something. Poor boy, he hates it. All he wants to do is sleep but I suppose they are afraid to let him."

"Has he said anything about what happened, anything that makes sense?"

"No. You go in Dad, Mum's in there with him at the moment. I'm not sure if they allow more than two by the bed."

She smiled at him, a weak forced smile that was her attempt at looking brave. Walter smiled back and gave her a further hug, then he pushed open the swing doors to the ward and made his way past the nurses' station and to the bay where Timmy was. He looked so small and fragile lying there in bed. His face, though tanned with his life in the outdoors all summer, looked pale and strained. Jessica was sitting beside the bed and got up to greet him. They smiled at each other and on a signal from Walter moved away from the bed out of Timmy's earshot. Walter anxiously said

"How's Jacqui bearing up?"

"Not too bad really, it's the strain of not knowing and having to wait for answers from the doctors that is the worst part."

"So they still don't know if or how Timmy will be affected?"

"No; it seems that it's a matter of wait and see. But they are fairly confident that he should be alright, I think that they are just afraid to commit themselves too soon."

"For fear of being sued if they get it wrong, I suppose. Cor, what has this country come to? Sue for this and sue for that, get a lawyer and he'll get you compensation. It's all wrong."

Out in the hallway Jacqui was saying to Mick

"Why on earth did you let him go out last night on his own?"

"I didn't, I told him the night before that I would be away and that we couldn't go last night. I said that we could go another time but he said something about school term starting."

"Well he told me that you were going badger watching, he never told me that he was going alone. Mum and I went off to the meeting in the hall, when we got back his bag was on the table, so I assumed that he had come home and was in bed."

"I'm sorry"

"Yes, so am I, and I'm worried sick. Timmy may never be the same again and all because you encouraged him to take part in all these ideas of yours. You encouraged him to go horse riding and walking on the moor, living the country life. He's a town boy, he doesn't understand all the dangers. You were supposed to be looking after him, and now this has happened."

Mick said nothing. There was nothing that he could say. He understood how Jacqui was feeling, her anger and frustration, her fear of the as yet unknown future. He desperately wanted to comfort her, put his arms around her and hold her in an effort to reassure her. But he knew that he couldn't. He was the last person who could do that at the moment, the way she was feeling. In her eyes he was the enemy, the bad guy, and she needed a bad guy to blame; some one on whom she could vent all her fear and frightened feelings. She was crying now, crying with anger and fear and Mick knew that nothing he could say or do at the moment would help.

"I didn't realise…" he began to say

"No, that's the trouble with you, you didn't realise. It's not surprising really is it? It was all just a big game to you, playing together like a pair of kids. Maybe if you'd had kids of your own you might have realised. Then maybe this wouldn't have happened."

Mick looked her straight in the eye, raised one eyebrow as if to ask if she had really meant what she had just said and then turned on his heel and walked out, down the corridors and into the car park. For several minutes he sat in the van. He was hurt but not angry, just very sad. Was he jinxed? Was his relationship with this boy going to be like the last time and end in disaster? Would he be able to continue his friendship with Timmy, or would Jacqui put an end to that? He had found that his feelings for her had grown stronger of late, which caused him to wonder somewhat. She was no longer just Timmy's mum, she was Jacqui, and it surprised him to realise that he felt that way. He had never expected to feel anything for a woman ever again. The pain of the past he had tried to bury, and along with it all hope of a relationship with someone like Jacqui. Now that he was beginning to feel the old stirring once again, it seemed that he was also jinxed to lose her.

A car behind was looking for a place to park, so he started up and pulled out of the car park. Although he had brought Walter down with him he knew that it would be alright for him to leave on his own. Walter would be wanting to stay as long as he could and then he would be going back home with Jessica. So he drove out of Plymouth and home across the moor in the fading light.

"What a bloody mess" he said to himself "I thought things were getting better; I thought at last my life was beginning again. Ah well ..."

THIRTY SEVEN

The next morning George was delivering the post again. He was running a bit late because nearly everybody on his round wanted to hear from him at first hand all about Timmy and the part that Mick and he had played in his rescue. It was a dirty drizzly day with a light wind, the sort of day that said that summer was really over. A few leaves were falling and getting stuck on the road with the wet.

At half past ten he knocked at Hilda's door. He had a packet for Sidney, something that he had ordered off the internet, and it required a signature. He hadn't seen Hilda for some time, possibly because she didn't get many packets that needed to be signed for, so he was shocked when she opened the door. She was wearing a pair of jeans, an old navy blue jumper and a pair of slippers on her feet; but it wasn't the clothes, it was the look on her face that worried him. She had dark rings under her eyes, her cheeks were sunken and she had obviously been crying. Her whole demeanour was of a sad, probably depressed, woman.

"Sorry to disturb you Hilda, I've got a packet to be signed for." He waited while she put a scribble on the little glass window on his machine.

"I also want to say how sorry I was to hear of your mother's passing. I would have come to the funeral but I was on the wrong shift."

He paused for a minute, watching her face carefully. She nodded but said nothing and he continued

"It would be wrong of me to say that I know how you are feeling, because obviously I don't. But I do know how I felt when I lost my wife, and I hated it when people ignored me, or were afraid to approach me and talk to me, probably because they didn't know what to say."

She started crying softly, dabbing her eyes with an already wet tissue. George gently stepped in through the door and putting an arm around her shoulders led her into the living room.

"Sit down Hilda, I'll make us a cup of tea. We've known each other a long time, after all we went to school together. I know we haven't seen a lot of each other socially, but I like to think we're old friends. We'll have a drink and then if you want to you can tell me just what it is that's upsetting you."

He went through into the kitchen, found the kettle and put it on to boil. Then he searched for mugs and the tea, saying over his shoulder

"D'you take milk and sugar?"

"Just milk thank you." She said in a weak plaintive voice, the first words she had spoken. He brought out their tea and sat down opposite her.

"What's up maid? You can tell me."

"I just don't know what to do" she sobbed and pulled another tissue from the box beside her. "It's like I'm lost, it's like my life has no purpose any more. For the last ten years I've been looking after Mum. I've been at her beck and call morning, noon and night. Oh, don't get me wrong, I loved her, but she could be very demanding. Every thing had to be done her way, and she was always right, you know. So I didn't have much of a life of my own, but I suppose I mustn't grumble, she did give me and Sidney a home."

"But you earned it" said George "you earned it because you looked after her so well and for so long."

"Yes, maybe so; but now I don't know what to do. I've got nothing to do. I'm here all day on my own. All I have to do is get a meal for Sidney in the evening. Life is just empty and meaningless."

"Have you thought of getting a job?" asked George, thinking to himself that she would probably need to, from a financial point of view if nothing else.

"Yes, I've thought of it, but who would want me? I haven't worked for years, ten years it must be."

"You used to work in the pub here, if I remember rightly. You were always smiling and laughing, made everybody feel welcome. You're great with people, I'm sure you'd have no trouble getting a job."

"I wouldn't know what to do in a pub now, every thing has changed so. Beside they've probably got all the staff they need."

"Would you like me to ask around, see if there's any jobs going? I expect you'd prefer a part time one to start off with wouldn't you?"

"Oh I don't know, you mustn't trouble yourself on my account, you've been very kind just listening to my woes."

"It's no trouble, no trouble at all. And I'll look in later on today, if it's alright with you."

"Thank you, thank you very much George. That would be nice."

He stood up to leave, and she looked up at him with a faint smile on her sad face. He bent down and putting his hands on her shoulders said

"You're a young woman Hilda, a young woman with a lot of living to do. I know when my missus died I thought that the world had come to an end. I felt totally lost like you do. There didn't seem any point to life, no reason to do anything. But I went back to work, and slowly but surely things got better. You'll find the same, and you'll find there are a lot of good nice people out there, helpful people who want you to be happy, like I do."

She stood up and walked with him to the door.

"Thanks George, you're a tonic and no mistake."

He waved and gave her a big smile as he went away on his round. Ten minutes later he walked into the café where Walter was working in the kitchen.

"How's Timmy getting on Walter, any more news?"

"Not really, he's still much the same, no better no worse."

"Has Jacqui gone down there again?"

"She stayed there overnight. She'll probably come back tonight, just for the night and get a bath and a change of clothes."

"It must be a bit difficult here for you without her, I daresay you could do with a pair of hands."

"It's not so bad in the mornings, it's the lunch time and the afternoons where I could do with some help. Especially as Jess wants to go down and be with Jacqui and Timmy."

"I've just been speaking to Hilda. She's very low, feels that there's not much point to life now that her mother's gone. What she needs is a purpose in life, a job. Trouble is, she's afraid to ask, she thinks she's too old and nobody would want her."

"D'you think she would like a few hours a week here?"

"Yes, I'm sure she would, but you would have to go and ask her. I think she would be too afraid to come and ask you. She used to work in the pub years ago, both behind the bar and waiting on. She might be a bit rusty but I reckon she'd soon pick it up."

"Well thanks George, thanks for telling me. I'll go and see her as soon as I close here this afternoon."

George went out into the drizzle again, totally unconcerned about the weather. He was feeling good, he had probably helped two people and that wasn't bad for a morning's work. If Hilda were to take up Walter's offer of a job it could be a very satisfactory outcome. Sometimes, he thought, things did fit together like the pieces of a jigsaw.

THIRTY EIGHT

Sidney had a number of customers who worked all week, so he sometimes had to help them with their home computers at the weekend. This meant that he would take an odd day off during the week as he was doing this day. He had collected off the internet a treasure hunt of Paignton. He had followed one or two of these treasure hunts before and enjoyed finding out about the towns near his home. Often the trail would take him up little side alleys and into corners that he would never have known existed. Sometimes the clues were a little hard to work out and he would be stuck for a while. If he was in real difficulty there was a number that he could ring for help, but he considered this to be cheating.

Marilyn was with him today which made it a lot more fun and together they had driven to Paignton, parked in the suggested car park and followed the clues. It had been fun and fascinating and they had laughed and joked a lot, especially at some of the silly mistakes they made.

When they had finished and done a bit of shopping they went into the big cinema complex and watched a film. The story was all about a young girl who suffered a tragic accident and was left badly disabled. She struggled to cope with her disability, at first not very successfully. Eventually she learned how to live a new sort of life and found a man to share her life with. It was a bit of a tear-jerker, not the sort of film that Sidney would normally watch but it got him thinking about his own situation.

There was no doubt that Marilyn had helped him to find himself. He had been like a snail; if anyone had got too close to him socially he had drawn back into his shell. It was his sort of protective safe place. But since he had been spending time with her his confidence had grown and he didn't feel the need to hide away so much. Also since his gran had died he felt somehow more free. He no longer felt the need to watch every thing he said and did. Though he had loved her dearly he had somehow felt that he never quite managed to live up to her expectations.

Now he found himself wondering just where his relationship with Marilyn was going, and where he wanted it to go. He had never thought of himself as the sort of man to get married. Marriage had never been a part of his life plan, not that he had really had a life plan come to think of it. She was a very nice girl, there was no doubt about that, and very pretty too. He had often wondered what she had seen in him, the quiet shy computer geek that he knew himself to be in most people's eyes.

Did she want their friendship to go further, was she thinking of marriage? That would be a bit scary if she was, he certainly wasn't ready to make that sort of commitment.

They came out of the cinema into the bright lights of a town at night.

"Do you fancy something to eat? I'm starving" said Marilyn, breaking into his reverie.

"Yes, we haven't had anything to eat all day, apart from some popcorn and you could hardly call that food. Where do you want to eat?"

"D'you fancy an Indian, I've always liked curries. There's a restaurant over there, on the other side of the street."

"That sounds good. I don't know much about curries, I probably will want a fairly mild one. You will have to help me choose."

She took his hand and they ran across the street together. Once inside she helped him to order and they sat back with a drink while they waited for their meal.

"How is your mother now, since your gran died? Is she taking it OK?"

"Not really, she's very sad. I don't know how to help her. She needs a good friend to confide in, someone who will listen and not tell her what to do. She's had enough of that from Gran over the past ten years. But she could do with someone who will coax her, suggest things that might help her."

"Do you think that I could help, I'd be very glad to."

"Well, you certainly helped me. I have become more confident since I met you. If you wouldn't mind trying it would be great, but I don't think we ought to tell her what we're up to. She might not like it if she thought that we had been discussing her behind her back."

"No, that might undermine her even more, I see what you mean. Perhaps I could call in tomorrow say, and just spend a bit of time with both of you to start with, just to see how we get on."

"That's a good idea…Yes… that could probably work."

The meal came and Marilyn explained the various dishes to him. She laughed at the faces he pulled, but it was mostly acting on his part. He found the whole experience very enjoyable. When they left the restaurant they turned down a dimly lit alley beside it that led to the car park. It was a short cut that they would not have taken normally, but with their new found knowledge of the town, gained from doing the treasure hunt, it would save them quite a walk. As they passed the back of the restaurant they saw a man delivering what looked like carcasses of meat. He was unloading them from a rather dirty truck, a four wheeled drive vehicle that looked as though it would be more at home on a farm. It wasn't easy to see clearly in the dim light of the back yard, but then a door at the back of the building opened and a beam of light spilled out. For an instant it lit up the man and they were able to see his face. When they had got to the car, Marilyn said

"I'm not sure that I liked the look of that man delivering to the restaurant. That was meat, wasn't it? If so, his van looked a bit scruffy and dirty, in fact he did too. I hope we don't go down with some tummy bug or something. D'you think it was dodgy meat, have we disturbed a black market ring?"

She laughed excitedly at the thought of having witnessed some clandestine illegal operation.

"Yes, it certainly did look a bit odd."

"They always used to say about Chinese restaurants that they weren't too fussy where their meat came from; cats, dogs even rats."

She laughed again and couldn't stop giggling at the thoughts running through her head. Sidney meanwhile was deep in thought. It had only been a glimpse, but there was something familiar about the man unloading the meat. Did he know him from somewhere? He certainly wasn't one of his customers. Then of course, he could have looked like an actor off the telly or some such, and that was what made him think he recognised him. Then again, he realised that he had often not recognised a person that he knew, because he was seeing them out of context, wearing the wrong clothes or in the wrong place. But it still puzzled him and he was still thinking about it when he fell asleep that night.

The next morning he was surprised to find his mother up and about before him. She had been in bed when he had arrived home rather late the night before. He assumed that she was asleep, as there was no light showing under her door, so he hadn't gone in and said goodnight to her. It was his usual practice in the mornings to make the early morning cup of tea and take one up to her. He had heard some movement downstairs and thought that he must have

227

overslept or some such thing; maybe his bedside clock had stopped. Then when he walked into the kitchen he found his mother fully dressed sitting at the table drinking a cup of tea.

"Mum" he said "what on earth are you doing up at this time? It's only half past seven. And why are you dressed up like that? You look very smart, are you going somewhere?"

She smiled at him, almost shyly and said

"I've been offered a job. I'm excited and terrified at the same time. I couldn't sleep, so I got up and got myself ready."

"A job? That's great Mum, where?"

"At The Old Smithy Café. Mr Blackmore came and asked me yesterday if I could give him a few hours."

"But I thought that his daughter Jacqui worked there."

"She does, but at the moment she's busy at the hospital. She has gone down there to sit with young Timmy. At the moment nobody knows how long he'll be there."

"Of course, I hadn't thought of that. When do you have to go in? Not this early in the morning, surely."

"No, not until eleven, and then it's just to get some idea of what the job entails. I understand that most days he'll only want me from twelve o'clock until about five."

"Well, good for you Mum, it's probably just what you need to cheer you up. You've been a bit down lately, not surprisingly, and I must admit I have been a bit worried about you."

"Don't get too excited Sidney, the job may not last, I may not be any good at it. After all, its years since I waited table or did anything like that."

"You'll be alright Mum, it's like riding a bike, once learned you never forget."

"Yes, but I never learned to ride a bike" she said and they both laughed at this silly bit of humour. Sidney went over and put his arm around her thin shoulders.

"You'll be fine Mum, you always used to love meeting people. I remember the tales you used to tell us when you came home from the pub. You made me and Gran laugh so, especially at the antics that you said some of the customers got up to."

"Yes, they were good days" she said "and then your gran got crippled up with arthritis and I had to stop work and look after her."

"Did you mind, having to stop work I mean?"

"Not at the time I didn't. There was a new boss at the pub and he wasn't very nice. Couldn't keep his hands to himself, seemed to think that just because I was an un-married mum I was 'easy'."

"I never knew that Mum, how awful. No wonder you weren't sorry to leave."

She looked at her son and thought. 'I can't tell him, he worshiped his gran. How can I say that it was like jumping from the frying pan into the fire? All I did was to change one bad boss for another.

Only difference was that the second job was twenty four hours a day, seven days a week.'

"I was wondering if I could bring Marilyn home here for supper, but if you're going to work perhaps not."

He could see by the slightly worried look on her face that he had probably suggested the wrong thing so he said

"I know what; why don't we celebrate your new job? Why don't the three of us go to the pub for a meal instead? Would you like that?"

"Oh, I don't know about that. That would be too much excitement in one day. No, you go with Marilyn, you don't want me there playing gooseberry".

"It's not like that Mum, Marilyn and I are just good friends, there aren't any wedding bells on the horizon, leastways, not as far as I'm concerned. So please do come Mum, it would be fun and Marilyn was only asking after you yesterday, she was saying that she would like to come and see you."

"Oh, alright then, that would be nice. I haven't been in that pub for ten years or more. I expect it's changed a lot since I was last there."

So it was that at half past seven that evening Sidney, with Marilyn on one side and Hilda on the other, walked into The New Inn.

"My word" said Hilda "this has changed and no mistake."

They went and sat at a table by the fire, cheerfully blazing away and warming the cool autumn evening. Hilda kept looking around her, noting the changes and trying to work out how it had been when she had worked there. Sidney went up to the bar to get their drinks and some menus. While he was gone Hilda leaned towards Marilyn and almost whispered to her

"Do I look alright? I hadn't got anything new to wear, only this black dress that I bought for the funeral."

"You look lovely, you've got a great figure and it shows it off beautifully."

"Thank you, I can't help feeling a bit awkward, it has been so long since I went out."

"Would you like to come back here to work?" asked Marilyn.

"It's nice, very different from when I was here. I don't know…."

They ate their meal, talking about Hilda's new job and how it had felt to go back to work after so many years. Then Marilyn said

"I've been offered a new job, it was only confirmed today."

"Really?" said Sidney, somewhat surprised.

"Yes, it's on a cruise ship. I'm due to join the ship next month. I'm still not sure whether I'm doing the right thing."

"Why ever not, it sounds great to me. Is this something you've always wanted to do? It will certainly give you a chance to see the world."

"It wasn't something I had ever thought of doing, I didn't expect to get the job. That's why I haven't mentioned it before."

"It sounds very exciting, much more exciting than me working at the café" said Hilda. "How long is it for?"

"I think it lasts all winter, I go on several cruises on the same ship."

"You'll have to send us lots of postcards" said Sidney. "Then we can follow your progress on the map. I'm really happy for you, it sounds as though it will be a fantastic opportunity. You've got to go for it. "

"Yes, and when you get back, we can have another meal together in here" said Hilda, looking at Sidney and smiling. He smiled back at her; he knew that she would be relieved at this unexpected bit of news. What she probably didn't realize was that he was equally relieved.

THIRTY NINE

Jacqui came home after the second day sitting beside Timmy's bed. The doctor had told her that he was improving, that he was certainly out of danger and that there was really nothing to be gained by staying. Most of the time all he wanted to do was sleep. The nurses still had to disturb him from time to time doing their tests, which made him irritable, but these tests were less frequent now which Jacqui saw as a good sign.

She was glad to be home, away from the almost unreal atmosphere of the hospital. She could see that several of the children in the ward were suffering from complaints that were far more serious than Timmy's, whilst others seemed to have nothing wrong with them at all. It was a strange situation, but the staff were wonderful, doing everything they could with their cheerful manner to speed the children's recovery. Happy patients recover more quickly. She was also amazed at the bravery of the children, their fortitude probably enhanced by the attitude of the nurses and doctors.

She went upstairs to her room and then spent half an hour in a hot bath, luxuriating and relaxing her tired body. Once dressed and before she went down to join her parents, she felt she ought to ring Alan. It was only right that he should know. Even though they were divorced, he was still Timmy's father. She had thought about it before, while she was sitting at Timmy's bedside, worrying and wondering, but she had no idea of Alan's phone number. The only way she knew of contacting him would be through his new girl friend.

She went to the dressing table; somewhere in there was the mobile phone of Alan's that had given away his sordid secret. Several times she had thought to throw it away, but something had made her keep it and now she was glad that she had. She hunted through the drawers and finally found it under a pile of jumpers that she hadn't worn since the spring.

With some trepidation she dialled the number of Alan's girl friend. Would he answer or would she? Would they even be at home? And why was her heart beating faster and her stomach churning? After what seemed like a long time the phone was finally answered.

"Hello" said Jacqui "I'm sorry to bother you at this time of night, is Alan there?"

"No, he's not, why, who wants to know?"

"This is Jacqui his ex, our son Timmy has been in an accident and I thought that Alan ought to know."

"Well, he's not here, he's left me. Well, that's not quite true. I told him to leave."

"Why was that?" asked Jacqui, more than a little intrigued. "I do apologise, it's no business of mine, I shouldn't have asked."

"That's quite alright, I don't mind telling you; in fact I don't care who knows. I couldn't stand his jealousy and his stupid tantrums. Then, when he got violent....well ....that was it. I didn't want anything more to do with him. He left about a month ago."

"So he hasn't changed then" Jacqui said, feeling somewhat selfishly, rather glad and yet sorry for this woman, whose name she didn't even know, just her initial S.

"Sorry to have bothered you, I'll try and contact him through his place of work, bye."

She sat for a while just thinking. How come she had stayed so long with a man who had no idea how to treat a woman right? It was quite obvious from what she had just heard that Alan's behaviour was no better and maybe even worse. Did she really want to get in touch with him? Would Timmy want to see him? After all he was off the danger list now, although he was far from totally alright.

She picked up the phone again and rang the coach firm that Alan worked for. It was probably too late in the evening for anybody to be there working. But she had sometimes rung at this sort of time in the past and got an answer. After three rings a woman's voice came on the line

"Hello" said Jacqui "Is Alan Thompson still working for you?"

"Yes, just one moment, let me see now....yes, he's still with us, though if you wanted to speak to him I'm afraid you're out of luck."

"Oh, why is that?"

"He's on tour in Italy at the moment; he's due back later this week."

"Thank you, I'll catch him then."

"Do you want to leave a message for him?"

"No thank you, that won't be necessary."

Well, she thought, that might make life easier for me. Timmy may be home by then and I can ask him if he wants his dad to visit him. After all, if he's well he may not want to see him. Coward, she thought, I'm passing the buck to Timmy and it's not really fair of me to ask him to make the decision. No matter what, he is still Timmy's dad.

The next day Timmy asked her to bring in his drawing things. He was sitting up now and taking a bit more interest in what was going on around him. Jacqui was delighted and hoped that this was a further sign that he was getting better. His speech was a lot better too, more fluent and coherent. But it was abundantly clear that he hated being in hospital and was desperately wanting to go home. He kept asking what was happening in the village, and if she had seen Mick recently. To the latter she was able, quite truthfully, to say no she hadn't and then she would steer the conversation away from that subject.

The police came in the afternoon, two plain clothes officers, a sergeant and a woman police officer. They were told by the doctor that Timmy had no recollection of anything that had happened that evening, but still, they had to ask. It was their job after all. They were very kind and made Timmy feel very important but as the doctor had said, he remembered nothing. He couldn't remember going out in the evening, watching badgers and taking photos of them on his mobile. In fact he could remember nothing that had happened until they arrived to see him. They said they would come back to see Timmy if he did remember anything at a later date.

Jacqui walked with them to the passage outside the ward and asked them if they had any idea as to who were the villains that hit Timmy. Unfortunately they had no idea, but they were following several leads and if anything came of it they would let her know.

'In other words' thought Jacqui 'you haven't a clue, have you?'

FORTY

"Is there anything that you need to take in with you?" asked Walter. They were sitting around the breakfast table, seemingly very quiet without Timmy chattering away as he usually did.

"He asked me to bring in his sketch pad and drawing things, though I don't know what he intends to draw in a hospital ward. Probably the other kids, or maybe the nurses."

"Didn't he say something about taking photos of the badgers, with his mobile? I seem to remember something about it. Cor; it seems such a long time ago now, was it only three days?"

"Yes, you're right Walter" said Jessica. "Where's the coat he was wearing that night? Did you bring it back from the hospital Jacqui?"

"Yes, it's hung up in the hall. I'll go and get it." With that she left the room and came back moments later with Timmy's mobile phone in her hand.

"Here it is" she said, switching it on. "I'll see if I can bring up the pictures, I'm not very good at this." She pressed a few buttons and after a brief pause shouted excitedly

"Great, I've got them, and they're not bad. There's one that isn't particularly good, but he ought to be able to do some good pictures using these. You have a look."

She passed the phone to her mother who leaned over to share it with Walter.

"What time are you going in today?" he asked.

"I'll leave here at about eleven. By the way, how did Hilda get on yesterday?"

"Very well, a bit nervous at first, but that's to be expected. After all, she hasn't done anything like it for years."

"Good, I'll give Mum a hand with these dishes and then I'll get ready. I don't think I will be staying so late tonight."

In the children's ward Timmy was sitting up waiting for her. He was still suffering from pains in the head but that was only to be expected. She gave him his sketching things and the mobile phone. He was delighted with the pictures of the badgers in it and, without asking how they came to be there, started drawing immediately. Jacqui was amazed that he hadn't asked, but pleased to see him so much happier

The doctor came later on his rounds and told Jacqui and Timmy that because results of the ex-rays had shown that he had a hairline fracture of the skull it meant that he would have to stay in hospital for a few more days at least, and that when he came out he would have to be very careful not to knock his head again. No sports or anything like that until

Easter at the earliest. He had been very lucky; there should be no lasting damage.

"Does that include horse riding?" asked Timmy.

"Yes I'm afraid that it does, I'm sorry but riding would probably be about the worst thing you could do. You've had a very nasty bump on the head and you have to be very careful while it heals."

Jacqui felt relieved, not just because Timmy's injury was no worse and should leave him with no lasting ill effects, but also if he wasn't allowed to go riding perhaps he wouldn't be visiting Mick so much.

She went to get herself a bite to eat at the small canteen at half past one. There was not a great deal of room and she took her sandwich and a cup of coffee and sat at a table with a young man who had already got his meal. He was busy reading, and when he turned the page she saw to her horror the headlines on the front page of the red top newspaper that had grabbed his attention.

CANNABIS FARM ON DARTMOOR THIRTEEN-YEAR-OLD BOY IN HOSPITAL

She sat transfixed, her heart pounding like a trip hammer and her mouth dry. Where had they got their information from, who could possibly have told them? Not anyone in her family, that was certain.

'I suppose I've got Mick to thank for that. Glory hunting, because he was the one who had found Timmy.'

She sat for a while, unable to continue her snack. At length the man put down his paper and looked over at her. He smiled and she said

"D'you think I could have a look at your paper a minute?"

"Sure, I've finished with it, you're welcome to keep it. There's nothing much in it."

"Thank you" she said, taking it and immediately turning to the front page as if her life depended on it. The article told how a young thirteen year old boy, fortunately his name wasn't mentioned, had disturbed a gang of thugs who were growing cannabis in a large barn on Dartmoor. One of them had hit the boy on the head knocking him out before making off with their crop of 'weed' in a horse box. However, their luck ran out on Salisbury Plain, when sharp eyed police patrolmen, PC's Stuart and Hudgell stopped their get-away and found the lorry packed with several thousand's of pounds worth of the drug. One man was detained immediately, the other escaped across the fields in the early morning mist. He was later apprehended and police sources stated that 'two men were helping them with their enquiries'.

She sat looking through the article for a second time. Well, thank God they hadn't given his name. There was no mention of how Timmy had been found, but it would no doubt come out very soon. She got up and went back into the ward, unsure as to whether she should mention it to Timmy. If the press knew the story, as they obviously did even though their report wasn't entirely factual, they knew his name. Would telling him at this stage be damaging? He still had no recollection of the events of that night, and probably never would have.

She went over to the nurses' station and showed the paper to the nurse on duty there. She read it quickly and then Jacqui said

"What should I do? Do I try to keep this from Timmy? Will it harm him to know?"

"He will have to know eventually, the best thing would be to answer his questions when he asks them. Wait until then."

"But what if it's on television, on the news?"

"He won't see any telly for a day or two; he's not up and walking yet and he won't go to the day room until then."

"Thank you. I'll wait 'til he asks." But she didn't have to wait long. She had been sitting at his bedside for another hour or so when he put down his pencil and sketch pad and said

"Mum, the doctor said that I got a nasty bump on the head, what exactly did he mean? What sort of a bump and how did I get it?"

"Do you remember going out badger watching with Mick?"

"Yes, I've got the photos here that you brought in for me to draw."

"No, you didn't take your mobile that night; it was the next night when you went on your own, d'you remember?"

"No, I don't think I can remember anything until today; not clearly that is."

So she went on to tell him the events of that fatal evening as far as she knew them, and how Mick had found him and George had called the air ambulance.

"Has Mick been in to see me?"

"No, not since you came in. Perhaps he's waiting until you come home."

"I would like to see him, if he's not too busy."

"If I see him I'll tell him" she said, almost relenting when she saw the sad look on his face. Perhaps seeing Mick might help speed his recovery.

FORTY ONE

Having one's village put on the map because it has won the 'Britain in Bloom' contest, or some such accolade, is one thing. To have journalists from all the London newspapers swarming all over the place, trying to interview people because of a crime, is a totally different thing. The incident at West Furzes and Timmy's injury was a local matter, almost a private matter for the village alone. It was by no means something to be proud of and bragged about. It had been the news three days ago, so by the time the national press got hold of it, it was old hat. Besides, they resurrected it in such a sensational way, exaggerating and distorting the facts to the point where the story in the papers bore little or no resemblance to the truth.

Phil came out of the shop that evening, having seen the headlines, in a none too happy mood. He felt for Jacqui and her parents, he understood the anguish that they must be suffering, not knowing just how well Timmy would recover. The articles in the papers would do nothing to help. He thought about going over to the café to have a word with Walter when he saw Jay Bee drive into the green and walked over to talk with him instead. He stood by the truck and Jay Bee opened his window.

"Hi, I don't suppose you have any more ideas as to who is stealing lambs around here, have you?"

"No Phil, no idea at all and I haven't seen any sign or clue any where. It's a complete mystery to me. At first I thought that it might be that blacksmith chap down to Braggator."

"No, he's as straight as a gun barrel is Mick."

"So I gather, but a new chap, living on his own, you can't blame me for wondering. Then I saw that horse box at West Furzes on more than one occasion, usually at night. But it seems that they had other and bigger fish to fry."

"It's a pity you didn't say something about them before; young Timmy might have been spared his head injury and a lot of pain and worry."

"Yeah, perhaps I should have done, I was sort of looking the other way, if you know what I mean. It's hardly fair to blame me Phil" he said, somewhat defensively.

"No, I know I shouldn't, it's not your fault at all. I got a bit riled seeing the headlines in the paper when I was in the shop just now; load of sensational rubbish. It makes me wicked the way they can get away with printing so many lies. Any way, keep looking, our sheep stealer will slip up one day, just like those two that hurt young Timmy."

"Have they charged them? Are they sure that it was they as hit him?"

"Oh yes, apparently it was the younger one who hit Timmy and tied him up. The older one thought that he had gone too far and when they were

245

caught he split on his mate, totally spilled the beans. Talk about 'honour among thieves', there wasn't much love lost between they two when they got caught. Anyway, I must get on, I'll see you around."

Phil stepped away and at that moment Sidney and Marilyn drove through the village. She turned her head looking at the truck as they drove through, with a puzzled expression on her face.

"Who's that in that truck Sidney?"

"Who, that scruffy looking man talking to Phil?"

"Yes."

"I can't say as I know him, I've seen him around I think; why d'you ask?"

"I recognise him from somewhere, at the moment I can't think where. Never mind, it will come to me later."

They drove on to have supper with Hilda. Sidney was pleased at the way his mother and Marilyn were getting on so well together. After their meal they moved into the sitting room. Sidney had restored it to its former use. He had taken out the bed and brought back the armchairs so that it was no longer his gran's bedroom. Hilda sat in the recliner chair, tipping it back and sighing as if glad to have the chance to relax. Seeing her in that position Sidney said to Marilyn

"Why don't you give Mum a Reiki session?"

"No no, I don't think I want that."

"Go on, it would do you good Mum. I've got some things to do on my computer" he said as he left the room.

Marilyn smiled at Hilda and explained to her what she could expect, so after a while Hilda decided to give it a try. Then some forty five minutes later Marilyn said

"Don't rush to get up, take your time, you might feel a little strange after sitting so long."

Hilda opened her eyes and looked around.

"I'll get you a drink of water, you might be glad of one. You may even feel that you need the toilet, it's quite normal."

"Wow, is that the time" said Hilda looking at the clock, "I didn't realise we had taken that long."

"How are you feeling now?"

"Fine, I did have some unusual feelings in my legs, like sort of muscle spasms."

"That's quite normal too. Often it's just getting rid of the toxins, moving things a bit."

"Thank you very much, but now I think I'd better get off to bed, I'm working again tomorrow, and I'm feeling relaxed, like I will get a good night's sleep for a change."

"Well I do hope so, I hope I've been able to help."

Marilyn was also feeling a little tired and called to Sidney, saying that she felt it was time she was off. As Sidney was driving her home he asked how the session had gone.

"Very well, I think I might have helped your mum a little."

They drove on in silence for a while and suddenly Marilyn said

"I remember, it was in Paignton"

"What was, what on earth are you talking about?"

"That man, in the truck talking to Mr German earlier. I remember where I saw him before. It was after we had had that Indian meal. You remember, we took a short cut down that alley and saw somebody unloading meat into the back of the restaurant. I'm sure that's who it was"

"I think you could be right. Mmm…interesting…very interesting."

School had started again after the long summer holidays and Sidney was back driving the bus. He couldn't help hearing the children's conversations going on behind him. Most of the time the subject matter that they chattered about was to do with so called celebrities, pop stars and soap stars. Recently the main topic had been 'Timmy and the Drug Farm', as they called it. This had led to some of the older children discussing more seriously the problem of crime in the country. Thefts from cars parked while their owners went for a walk, and the spate of farm burglaries of fuel oil. Then Helen and Margaret, Phil's grandchildren, had brought up the subject of the theft of lambs in the neighbourhood. That was something that Sidney hadn't heard about before, something that made him think of what Marilyn had said the other night.

FORTY TWO

Timmy seemed to be a lot better when Jacqui went in to see him next day. Whether it was the drawing that had helped brighten him and lift his spirits or just the natural healing progression didn't really matter. What mattered to Jacqui was that he was improving. He even walked the length of the ward down to the toilet with her, although he still needed her arm to steady him.

He hadn't seen the newspaper and the nurses had done their best to keep all the papers out of his sight. Unfortunately this didn't stop a determined young man from approaching the ward with the intention of interviewing Timmy or somebody on the staff. He wanted to get a scoop for his paper. He got as far as the nurses' station and almost got away with it, posing as a concerned friend. Luckily Jacqui had already spoken to the nursing team on this matter after she had seen the headlines in the paper the day before. So the nurse on duty politely but very firmly told him to leave.

But if Jacqui had thought that that would be the end of it she was mistaken. When she got home her mother told her that several news people had been around the village that day, trying to get a story. The villagers had closed ranks and had said very little, despite the lure of having their faces shown on television. As Walter said

"I don't understand them. Don't they realise that they don't have to go asking questions and upsetting people. All an intelligent reporter needs to do, is to go to the pub, sit in a corner quietly and listen. He'll get all the news he wants that way."

"I wouldn't mind betting that it was Mick who blabbed to them, wanting praise and glory for rescuing Timmy."

"D'you really think so!" said Jessica "it seems very out of character for the man to behave like that. He's such a secretive sort as a rule. I would be more inclined to think that the police were the ones that told the press. They may have thought that it would help them to catch the villains."

"But they've already got them haven't they? I read that they are holding two men who are 'helping them with their enquiries'. Do they think there are more of them?"

"The police may well think that there are" said Walter "perhaps they think that these two are just the workers and there are big bosses still to catch."

Jacqui went up to her room and her parents continued their conversation. Jessica was worried and not just because of Timmy's state of health

"I'm none too happy at the way Jacqui wants to blame Mick for Timmy's injury. It seems that she thinks he encouraged Timmy to go out on his own that night."

"I agree, she may well do more harm than good by her attitude."

"Yes, and I don't think Mick has been in to see Timmy yet. I believe that's because Jacqui said something to him." Jessica stood up and walked over to the window, unable to keep still. She turned and went on to say

"Timmy worships that man, he looks up to him. I think he almost sees him as a father figure. And compared to his real dad Alan, he's a saint. If Jacqui stops Mick from seeing him she may well turn Timmy against her. That would be a tragedy. It's almost as though she's jealous of Mick because he is such an important person in Timmy's life."

"And Timmy has seen enough of jealousy and the damage it can do. You're right about Mick. He's a very quiet and almost secretive man, but he obviously loves children. Charlie tells me that he's done a lot for the children's' pony club. And that lad at Larchcombe, the one with learning difficulties, he got him a pony."

"You mean he paid for it?" asked Jessica.

"Yes, so I understand, and he shoes it every six weeks or so, free of charge. It has helped the lad enormously. He's a good man is Mick, I can't understand what's got in to our Jacqui, to be so against him all of a sudden."

"I wonder" said Jessica, sitting down again and looking thoughtfully at a picture of their daughter that was on the mantelpiece.

"I wonder if she is trying to cover up her feelings for Mick. Perhaps she feels more for him

251

than she cares to admit; may even be somewhat afraid of the way she feels. After her disastrous marriage to Alan, she probably doesn't want to get involved in another relationship."

"D'you mean to say that you think she might be falling for Mick?"

"Why not, he's a very attractive man. More to the point he is obviously fond of her child; that's often the first obstacle to a successful second marriage."

There was a knock on the door and Walter went to answer it. A smart looking young woman was standing outside, gazing across the green at the sunset. She turned as Walter opened the door saying

"Is Mrs Jacqui Thompson here, I wonder if I might have a quick word with her?"

"Jacqui, someone to see you." Walter shouted up the stairs.

Jacqui came down and went to the door, her eyebrows raised

"Yes, I'm Jacqui Thompson, may I ask who you are."

"I'm Jenny Sandhurst, a free lance writer, I have articles printed in the local paper and before you throw me out, as I'm sure you feel like doing, I hope that you will listen to what I have to say. First of all I want to say I feel for you and your family. I have a son who was injured in a motorcycle accident, and I know how worrying it can be, waiting to find out if he will be alright or not. "

Jacqui stood saying nothing, just looking with a stony face at the woman in front of her.

"I don't want to interview you or do a piece for the paper like the reporters that have been all over the place today. I want to do a sympathetic article, written from your point of view. I realise that it can't be written yet, it would have to be after Timmy gets out of hospital and you are happy that he is better. As I say, I have been in a similar situation, and though I can't possibly know what you are feeling, I do have some idea. It can be horrible, the intrusive way reporters work, they have no respect for the feelings of their victims. And when they are asked to leave you alone, they seem to poke and pry even more. So if you want to set the record straight, when Timmy is better, please give me a call and together we can write a mother's version of the events."

She took a card out of her handbag and offered it to Jacqui.

"I don't think I'll be interested, but I'll take your card and if I should change my mind I'll know where to contact you."

"I quite understand, thank you for your time and good luck to both you and Timmy."

FORTY THREE

It was eleven o'clock and Jessica was arranging the cake stand in the café. Jacqui had gone into the hospital again and Hilda wasn't due to start for another hour. The door opened and a couple walked in. The man was tall and slightly stooping, as is so often the case with those over six foot, hair thinning on top but an unlined and pleasant looking face. Jessica put him at about forty five.

"Are we too early?" He said, "I wasn't sure if you were open or not."

"Please come in, yes we are open" said Jessica, smiling and handing the woman a menu. She was slightly shorter than her companion, with light brown hair tied back in a pony tail. Both were smartly dressed in expensive looking casual clothes. They ordered coffees and went and sat at a table in the window. Some twenty minutes later Jessica returned to the table to see if they needed anything more. Looking at Jessica in an enquiring way the man said

"Nothing more to eat or drink thank you, but maybe you could give me a little information regarding the man called Mick Cribbett."

Jessica frowned but didn't answer, at which the man with a slight laugh said

"It's alright, I'm not the press. I imagine that you've had a belly full of reporters hassling you. By the way, how is your grandson, Timmy isn't it?"

"He's still in hospital."

"I do hope he pulls through alright. I know that you must think this a terrible intrusion and I apologise and understand if you don't want to talk to me. It's just that we were passing through on our way to the Scilly Isles. We stopped in the next village for bed and breakfast and read in a newspaper about the incident here. What intrigued us was the name of the man who found your grandson."

"Oh" said Jessica, a little relieved that he didn't want to question her about Timmy or Jacqui.

"We were puzzled that there was no photograph of him. There was one of the postman who called the police and the ambulance but none of Mick. We are interested because we used to know a man by that name in Cheshire. Lovely chap, always smiling and joking, do anything to help anyone."

"That doesn't sound much like the Mick Cribbett that lives here. He's very quiet, keeps very much to himself."

"Really? Our man was a huntsman, master of our local pack, that's where we met him. Wonderful man with horses, has a natural way with them, and dogs too. He was also a farrier, which was very handy for a lot of the members of the hunt. He'd often get called out at the last minute to see to some horse that had lost a shoe, but he never complained, always happy and smiling."

In some ways it was beginning to sound more like the Mick she knew but Jessica didn't want to say too much just yet. After all, Mick might not want to see these people, they seemed very nice… but you never could tell…

"I have to admit I was one of those who abused his kindness in that way" continued the man. "Sometimes he would be called out after dark on the evening before a meet. I believe that was his downfall so to speak; the cause of his tragedy."

"What tragedy was that?" said Jessica, finding herself becoming more interested in the man's tale.

"We never really knew the details, we were out of the country for over a year at the time, and he had disappeared by the time we got home."

"But the tragedy…?"

"Oh that was awful! He lost his wife and six year old son in a fire. By the time we came back into this country he had gone, taken his two horses and just disappeared into thin air. Mind you, I would have been very surprised if he hadn't taken his horses, they were like family to him, all the family he had left. What were they called Sue?" he said turning to his wife.

"That beautiful dappled grey of his was called Osprey, I'm not sure of the name of the other; I think it also was the name of a bird, sorry I don't remember."

"Never mind dear, it sounds like the Mick Cribbett here is probably not the one we knew. Any way, we must be getting along, got a plane to catch.

If we are talking about the same man, tell him that Sue and Dennis were asking after him. "

They got up, and after shaking hands with Jessica Sue said

"I do hope all goes well for young Timmy; and for you all in fact."

"Thank you" said Jessica, her head in a whirl. So much of what Dennis had said about Mick was nothing like the man she knew. Yet there were similarities, especially the horses, she felt sure that she had heard Timmy talking about a grey called Osprey, and another called Ptarmigan. She had remembered the names because she thought they sounded funny names for a horse. And this tale about an accident, losing his wife and son in a fire; she would have to tell Jacqui when she got back home tonight.

FORTY FOUR

Sidney had almost forgotten about the man that they had seen talking to Phil, the man that Marilyn thought they had seen delivering meat to the back of the restaurant in Paignton. Then something one of the children had said on the school bus had reminded him. So as soon as he had returned home from work he decided to walk down to Home Farm and see Phil. It was a mild evening with little or no breeze. Swallows lined up on the telephone wires, ready for their amazing long flight to the south of Africa. They twittered away and jostled for position on the best bit of the wire. 'Just like the kids in my bus' he thought 'arguing over who should sit where'.

He walked through the village, quiet at this time of day, and down the road to Manor Farm. There were two houses, the original farm house, where Phil's workman lived; and above it the newer larger house that had been built and the farm yard. He rang the old brass bell that hung in the granite porch and waited. He was about to ring again when Elaine, Phil's wife answered it.

"Is Phil in, Mrs German?"

"Yes, he's doing some paper work, he'll be glad to see you, any excuse to get away from the dreaded forms."

She led him into the sitting room, a lovely bright comfortable room.

"Can I get you a cup of tea?"

"No thank you" said Sidney "I've not long had one."

Phil came in to the room, walked up to him and said

"What can I do for you Sidney?"

"Well it's a long story and I'm not altogether sure that I've got it right."

"Well let's hear it then" said Phil as he slumped down into a comfortable armchair.

"Marilyn and I were I Paignton a week or so ago. We had a meal at an Indian restaurant and on leaving we passed by the back of the place. We saw a man delivering what looked like carcasses of meat. To be honest it was dark and it was not easy to make out for sure but then a door opened and the light fell on his face; scruffy looking bloke with a beard.

Anyway, a couple of days ago we were driving through the village and saw you talking to this same man. He was in one of those big pick up trucks. I've seen him around occasionally, but I don't know his name."

"He's called John Badcock, or more usually Jay Bee" said Phil, with a puzzled look on his face.

"Well, I hear things on the school bus, and I've heard about these lambs that have been stolen. I understand you've had some pinched. So I thought I ought to tell you, in fact I didn't know what else to do. I may have got it all wrong and the man we saw in Paignton isn't the man we saw talking to you. What d'you think?"

"I'm very glad you told me before you said anything to anybody else. I'll look into it, you were right to come to me Sidney, thank you."

"Well, I'll be getting on."

"Are you sure you won't have a drink before you go?"

"No, no thanks, Mum will have got supper ready."

With that he walked home in the twilight, still unsure if he had done the right thing but glad that he had passed on the information to Phil. But he couldn't help feeling as though he had passed the buck, or as his gran would have said; 'he had loaded the gun for someone else to pull the trigger'.

FORTY FIVE

Jacqui was driving across the moor after spending another day at Timmy's bedside. He was certainly getting better; his walking was a lot more steady and his headaches less. However, his mood swings had become worse, a symptom that worried Jacqui. He had always been a very easy going boy, placid and unlikely to seek out or get into an argument. Now, by comparison, he was almost aggressive. Was this as a result of his injury or was it just that he had finally grown into a teenager, with all the tantrums and moodiness associated with that age group?

He was particularly upset by the fact that he hadn't had a visit from Mick, which might have accounted for his bad temper. Jacqui realised that if this was the case then it was she that was responsible. Her anger at Mick she knew had been misplaced and brought about by her anxiety. But like any mum she found it hard to admit that her beloved son could possibly do wrong or behave badly. When Timmy had been admitted to hospital, in what appeared to be a very critical condition, she had felt the need to lash out at somebody, anybody on whom she could lay the blame. In her attempt to punish Mick for being the cause of Timmy's injury she had really only succeeded in hurting Timmy more.

In a way she should be glad that Timmy was inquisitive and resourceful. It meant that he had learned a lot about the countryside, an area of which he had previously had no knowledge at all. It had given him an interest and had no doubt helped him to settle into his new home. There was no doubt that he had grown up a lot during the summer. His friendship with Mick; which had started when he fell and hurt his ankle, had grown into a relationship that could only be good. Where this recent episode was concerned, he had gone out with Mick on the first night, and learned enough to feel confident to go out alone on a second night and take some photographs. These were clear enough to act as a basis for him to draw some good pictures of the badgers, something which he had wanted to do and which had probably helped his recovery. His natural curiosity had led him to explore what was going on at West Furzes. If the goings on there had been legitimate he would not have been in any trouble or danger.

As for Mick's involvement, he had found Timmy and, with George's help, got him to hospital as quickly as possible. If he hadn't spotted the changes at West Furzes, changes to a state of affairs there that had seemed curious and unusual, he might not have gone down to investigate. Timmy could have been left there, bound and gagged for days. She really should apologise to Mick, thank him for the part he had played in his rescue and tell him that Timmy wanted to see him.

'It's not going to be easy' she thought 'it'll be very embarrassing but I must do it for Timmy's sake. I'll go down first thing in the morning and then I'll have something to tell Timmy that may cheer him up.'

She drove on through the darkening drizzle of a typical Dartmoor autumn evening. A pair of ponies stood with their backs to a stunted hawthorn tree, sheltering as best they could from the weather. The tree itself had grown in a lopsided fashion, leaning to the east due to the prevailing winds and looking like a one sided umbrella. Cars coming towards her had their lights on, as much to warn oncoming motorists as to light their way, and on the wet road they were already beginning to dazzle.

'I shall be glad to get home and out of this' she said to herself 'It's more like winter than autumn.'

Once indoors Jessica greeted her with a smile and a hug and asked after Timmy.

"He's certainly improving, the doctor said that if he goes on this way he could come home in two or three days." She didn't mention his bad mood or the fact that he wanted to see Mick. She was well aware that her parents considered her to have been more than a little hasty in her recent dealings with Mick

"Dad's gone in to the wholesalers, he had an early supper so it's just the two of us. I expect you're starving aren't you?"

"Yes, thanks Mum. I'll get washed and changed first, get the hospital smell off me."

Later, when they were sitting down to their meal Jessica said

"We had an interesting couple in this morning. They had stopped for bed and breakfast in the next village while on their way to the Scillies. They called in here for coffee, but the real reason for stopping here was because they had read in the paper about Timmy's incident."

"Oh no, not another lot of newspaper people. I had hoped we had seen the last of them."

"No, these two, man and wife, were nothing to do with the press. They live in Cheshire and they used to know a man there called Mick Cribbett. Unfortunately there was no photo of Mick in the paper, so they wondered if it was the same man. At first I thought that it wasn't because the man they described didn't sound a bit like the Mick that we know. But then they said that he left the area suddenly, taking his two horses with him. One of which was a grey called Osprey and the other had the name of some bird which they couldn't remember. I didn't say anything, I just kept listening, but it did sound as though the Mick they knew and the one who live here could be one and the same man."

"You say he had to leave suddenly Mum, why was that?" asked Jacqui, who had always felt that there was something in Mick's past that he was trying to hide or escape from.

"Oh, I don't think he had to leave, I think it was more that he wanted to leave. Apparently he lost his wife and six year old son in a fire.

These people were out of the country at the time and when they returned Mick had gone and the whole story had died down. The more I think about it the more I feel that it must be the same man. What do you think?"

"Yes, it does sound like it. Oh God, what have I done? Not only have I not thanked him properly for saving Timmy, I've as good as accused him of leading him in to danger. But worst of all, I said that he had no idea of how to look after kids 'cos he had never had any of his own. I had been thinking as I drove home that I ought to tell him that Timmy wanted him to visit, but now….."

"You can't say anything about his dead wife and child….."

"No I know that, I know I can't, but I can and must apologise for being short with him and not letting him visit Timmy. In fact" she said, getting up "I think I'll go now, otherwise I'll be worrying about it all night and I'll never get any sleep."

"You can't go now Jacqui, look at the time. You'll just have to leave it 'til the morning, sleep or no sleep."

So it was that after a sleepless night tossing and turning and worrying as to what to say when she met Mick, Jacqui finally got up and went downstairs. She made herself a mug of tea and then before having anything to eat she set off to see Mick. She had decided to walk, the rain of the day before had passed and the morning was clear and bright, if a trifle cold.

She had just reached the gate at the top of the drive leading to Braggator when she heard his van coming up the lane towards her. She waited by the gate, ready to open it for him, her heart beating a little faster than usual and what felt like a swarm of butterflies dancing in her stomach. All her anxieties of the previous night flooded into her mind. Before opening the gate she walked over to him and he wound down his window.

"I'm glad I caught you" and hoping to lighten the mood and sound cheerful she said "You've saved me a walk."

He looked up at her, his grey eyes cold and expressionless.

"I owe you an apology. I spoke hastily and unkindly in the hospital. I was upset and worried. I should have thanked you for all you did to save Timmy."

"It's alright, I understand. How is Timmy?"

"He's a lot better, he would like to see you."

"Good, so he can have visitors now can he?"

"Oh...yes" she said, grateful that he had given her a way out. "Yes he's much better and ready to see his friends."

"I'll pop in this evening then, if that's alright."

"That'll be fine, I'll see you down there then."

She opened the gate and waved him through, glad to have managed the encounter without as much difficulty as she had anticipated.

FORTY SIX

Jacqui had not been the only person in the village to have suffered a restless night. Phil was used to waking at about five o'clock in the morning; many years of milking cows had meant that his morning routine started early. Although he no longer had a milking herd, having converted to beef production instead, he still woke early. Quite often he was able to go back to sleep again, but this particular morning he had found his mind working overtime and sleep eluded him.

Sidney's story about a man who looked like Jay Bee delivering meat to the back of an Indian restaurant late at night had worried him. The inference that Phil drew was that he was not just delivering meat, but sourcing it as well. That could mean that Jay Bee was the man that was stealing the lambs. Phil would have sworn that it was somebody else that Sidney had seen; after all it was dark and he could have made a mistake. Jay Bee would never do anything like that, he was a friend and neighbour. They had known each other for years. He trusted him, allowed him access to any and all of his fields to shoot. Part of Phil's reason for doing this was because he knew that if Jay Bee were to see anything wrong with any of the animals, he would not only spot the trouble but report back. The thought of him stealing just didn't make sense. It wasn't what a man like Jay Bee would do.

But what if Sidney were right and it had been Jay Bee that he had seen? What had gone wrong, what had turned the man to crime? It didn't seem possible, Jay Bee was a friend, he wouldn't do that would he? Would he betray a friend? Not that it was such a big crime; a few lambs here and there weren't likely to make a man a fortune. It just didn't seem plausible. Jay Bee had never seemed to be particularly short of money. He always seemed to have work. Nor did he appear to have a lot of money and what he had he didn't splash around a lot, wasn't in the pub every night. The truck that he drove wasn't old and falling to bits, his clothes were working clothes, a bit dirty maybe, but not full of holes and ragged. So if he had turned to stealing the question was, why? What did he need the money for?

It was typical of Phil that he tried to find a reason, an excuse for a man straying from the straight and narrow, rather than condemning him outright. He decided to have a word with Frank; he'd go over there after breakfast and have a chat. Frank might well have some ideas, might know something or have heard something that would throw some light on the matter.

"Two heads are better than one, even if they're only sheep's heads" he thought, smiling at his use of an old expression.

So it was that after he had had his breakfast Phil drove through the village and out on the moorland road. He crossed the Redacre Brook and turned right up the small lane towards Wistworthy, the farm where Frank lived. The lane ran up the valley beside the brook, on the other side of which was Brown Tor, covered in a mixture of gorse and heather with clear patches where swaling had burned off all but the grass. To his left was the rock strewn Wistworthy Tor; bracken, gorse and scrub thorn grew through the clitter of granite boulders that lay all over the slope, as though scattered there by some giant hand. After a few hundred yards the terrain changed dramatically. The ground became less steep and was enclosed in the tidy cultivated fields of Wistworthy Farm. A rough path coming down from Brown Tor crossed the brook on a clapper bridge; two huge flat rocks resting on stone pillars at either bank and on a large square boulder set in the middle of the stream. It was an old bridge, almost as old as time, built high enough to be above the water even when in flood. Opposite was a small disused quarry where gravel had been dug to surface the roads before the advent of tarmac. Nowadays it was orten used as a place to park a car by the people who came to picnic by the stream and have their photo taken on the little bridge.

On the corner of the field wall was a damson tree with a few fruit on its branches. Not such a good year for fruit this year thought Phil. On its trunk were several marks and clearly carved were the initials RB = SW. Phil smiled to himself; fifty years ago he had carved them. As children in the village primary school they had always had nick-names.

Because his surname was German he had been called Red Barron and Blanche Leaman was Snow White. They had been childhood sweethearts, but as so often happens, that romance hadn't lasted and she had married Stan Narraway. Phil and Stan had grown up together, were close friends and routinely helped one another on their farms. When Stan died suddenly Frank had come home to help his mother. The farm was small, only sixty five acres, and though productive was too small to be a viable source of income on its own. Frank had served fifteen years in the REME as a mechanic. He had brought his skills home and in addition to farming had set up a useful business looking after the vehicles in the area.

As he drove up the lane towards the farm he met Frank's pretty wife Linda, out for a walk with their eighteen month old girl Jasmine in her push chair. He looked up at her out of the car window and couldn't help thinking how good she looked. Her long black wavy hair fell thickly to her shoulders and she had a smile that would melt ice. Motherhood had if anything enhanced her beauty.

"Good to see you Linda, you look lovely as ever. And little Jasmine is growing to be as beautiful as her mum by the looks of it."

"Oh go on with you Phil, you old flirt. You always were an old tease."

"Seriously though, Jasmine is growing up fast, last time I saw her she was just a baby, now she's a little girl and no mistake."

"Yes, they don't stay babies very long. If it's Phil you've come to see he's in his workshop."

Phil found him, busy servicing a car. They exchanged greetings, talked about the weather and its effect, as all country folk do, and then Frank asked

"What brings you over here?"

Phil proceeded to tell him what Sidney had seen Jay Bee doing in Paignton and its implications.

"D'you think he could steal like that? I find it very hard to believe, is he that short of money that he's got to sink that low?"

"It doesn't seem like the Jay Bee we know."

"I might understand it if he had some reason to need money desperately, like a sick relative or something."

"Or if he was on drugs…."

"Jay Bee wouldn't take drugs….would he?"

"I don't know Phil; I learned in the forces that a man can do the most unexpected things. I have heard that Jay Bee likes a bet on the horses now and again, if that got out of hand…."

"I'm thinking of going over to see him. I think that's the best thing to do, what d'you reckon? I still find it difficult to believe, I still think there's probably a perfectly normal explanation for all this."

"Would you like me to come with you?"

"Yes, if you wouldn't mind."

"Right, I'll pick you up this evening at five o'clock."

271

It was gone half past five when Frank and Phil stopped outside the gate to Jay Bee's field. As they drove over they had discussed their reason for going and what exactly they would say to Jay Bee. Obviously they couldn't go in accusing him of stealing, saying that they were looking for evidence. And if they said that they had heard that he was seen delivering lamb carcasses to an Indian restaurant that would be as good as accusing him. They had to have a plausible reason for visiting him, if he was there.

"Why don't we say that as these thefts are still going on, could we lay a trap for the thief? Would he be prepared to help us do so? Then perhaps we might be able to say something about a man being seen delivering stuff to that restaurant in Paignton."

"Yes Frank, but I'm not too sure about mentioning the Paignton business."

"What ever we say, we must keep our eyes open and not just for what we might see at his place, watch him like a hawk for any sign of guilt."

"You still prefer to think of him as guilty, don't you?"

"Yes Phil, I'm afraid I do. For your sake I'd be glad to be proved wrong, he's a friend of yours and I realise what it means to you. But guilty or not, it would be good to bring this whole matter to a close."

They got out and walked towards the caravan that was his home. It was a fairly large type of mobile home, though this one hadn't moved for several years and was unlikely to do so ever again.

The door was open and Phil put his head in and called out to Jay Bee. There was no answer and no dogs came rushing out to greet them.

"He must be hereabouts somewhere, he wouldn't go away and leave the place open like this" said Frank.

"We'll have a look around, he could be in one of his sheds working on something."

They moved around to the back of the caravan to the row of assorted sheds. The first one was a simple wooden structure, its door open and with a number of tools in it. They moved along the line, checking in all the buildings and calling out for Jay Bee as they went. The last building was a more elaborate affair, timber framed with corrugated iron exterior and plywood interior.

"I'm not sure that I like snooping around like this" said Phil.

"I agree with you, but why would he have a set up like this? This isn't a shed or workshop; it's too clean, too clinical for Jay Bee. I know I like to keep my workshop tidy but it's never this clean."

The floor was scrubbed concrete with a tap in the corner. There was a bench or rough wooden table along one side. Beyond it was a large white metal cupboard. Frank walked over and opened it to find to his surprise that it was a large fridge. It wasn't switched on and there was nothing inside it, no shelves just a bar across the top with some hooks on.

"I think that we need to find him and ask him a few questions. In view of what Sidney told you and what we've seen here it all looks as though Jay Bee may well have been up to no good. This place looks like it's been used as a small abattoir" said Frank.

"There could be a perfectly rational explanation" said Phil, still hoping to find that his friend was innocent. So saying they went and stood outside and called again for Jay Bee. Beyond the line of sheds was his truck, half loaded with logs and beside it stood his tractor with a saw bench and a pile of logs. It looked as though Jay Bee had been interrupted while loading them into his truck. On the far side of the tractor was a tall neat wigwam shaped stack of timber, ready to be sawn. A white electric fence separated the whole of this area from the rest of the field, in which were two horses and several hens, happily scratching around. In the far corner, beyond the wood stack, was a small mechanical digger.

"Well, he doesn't seem to be here" said Phil, calling out once more.

"I think the best thing for you to do now Phil, is to report this to the local police. You told them about the theft of the lambs, this is a follow up that they need to investigate. We can't poke about here any more, we don't have the authority."

"I know that you're right, but I wish that we could have spoken to Jay Bee first, I'd have liked to have given him the chance to explain all this, wouldn't you?"

"I can't see as there's very much to explain. In fact I reckon that somewhere in this field, maybe right where that digger is parked, you'll find a pit full of feet and skins; covered over now, no doubt."

They turned and walked away from the caravan, Phil shaking his head and saying

"I still can't believe it. If he is involved I just can't think why. If he were that short of money, the sale of a few lambs wouldn't make such a difference, would it?"

Frank didn't answer; he had already found the man guilty. Besides; there could have been many more cases of lamb stealing that he and Phil hadn't heard about. They went out through the gate and turned to look back over the place before getting into the car and driving off. It all looked so peaceful and normal, a typical pastoral scene, with horses grazing and hens scratching. The whole surrounded by hedges and trees, several of which were beginning to show the russet hues of autumn. What they didn't see was the figure standing behind the wood stack, a figure that had heard almost every word that they had spoken.

FORTY SEVEN

When Mick arrived at the children's ward he found Jacqui outside in the corridor. She was talking to a smart looking middle aged woman in a dark suit.

"This is Detective Sergeant Allen" said Jacqui "she has been here before to see Timmy, hoping that he might remember something, though unfortunately so far his memory of that night is absolutely blank. She wondered if, when talking to Timmy, you told him how you had found him it might just bring some of the lost memory to the surface again."

"I don't know, is it alright with you? I don't want to upset him, I haven't seen him since that morning. How is he, is he well enough for questioning?"

"I was thinking of sitting with you and just listening" said the sergeant "I wouldn't expect you to ask questions though maybe your presence might help him to remember. I understand from his mother that you are a particular friend of his whom he trusts."

"Well if it's OK with his mother and the doctor I'd be happy to help. But I thought that you had the devils that did this to him. I understood that they had confessed or something."

"Yes, one of them has admitted to the drugs charge and has implicated the other in the charge of the assault. It could help to have Timmy's version if possible."

Would he have to go to court and give evidence? I wouldn't want that," said Jacqui. "That would only bring it all back and probably do more harm than good."

"I doubt if he would have to go to court, but I must confess I don't really expect him to remember any more than he has already."

So the three of them entered the ward and, after a brief word with the nurse, went over to Timmy. He was clearly delighted to see Mick, sitting up and smiling broadly as they approached his bed.

"Hi Mick, it's great to see you at last. How is everything, how're Meg and Floss? And Osprey and Ptarmigan and Dillon? I can't wait to get out of here and come home and see them all."

"They're all fine; I expect that they are looking forward to seeing you too. But you have to be properly fit and well first. You had a nasty bump on the head. The doctor won't let you go home until he's sure that you're ready. If you come home too soon you might have a relapse and have to come back again and that would never do, would it?"

"Mum said that you found me in a shed at West Furzes."

"Yes, that's right; you were in the shed beside that big barn."

"The one with the funny strips of light along the roof?"

"That's right, you remember that then"

"Yes, we saw them when we went badger watching. It was as we were leaving. You said that they were a funny lot down there, bit of a mystery."

"Yeah, I wondered how you came to be there and how you got the bump on your head."

"I haven't a clue" said Timmy smiling at his friend and his mum. The police sergeant looked on, disappointed but resigned to what she had expected his answer to be.

"Mum tells me that you have been drawing pictures of the badgers, can I see them?"

"Course you can" and with that Timmy turned and pulled his sketch pad out from the shelf in his bed-side locker.

"Here you are, they're not very good, some of the photos were a bit blurry."

"I think they're excellent, especially that one on the right. He looks like he's just caught wind of you and has looked up to see who and where you are. What do you think Sergeant?"

"I think that you have a real talent Timmy, but I must be getting on. I hope you get well and can soon go home."

She got up and left them, realising that Timmy would never recall the events of that night. It was nature's way of blocking out the unpleasant. Mick and Jacqui stayed until visiting time was over. Timmy showed Mick the other drawings that he had done of some of the nurses and the other patients.

They all had a good laugh at them and as they were leaving Jacqui said to Mick

"Thank you for coming down, your visit has been like a tonic to him, he's so much brighter. You must come again, and certainly when he gets home, which could be in a day or two"

"It's been a pleasure; I always look forward to seeing him anytime."

FORTY EIGHT

Timmy was coming home. The doctor had told Jacqui when she was in the hospital the day before that she should bring in some clothes for him to wear.

"Does that mean that he'll be spending more time in the day room?" she said.

"No, it means that he'll be going home" said the doctor with a smile. "There's no reason to keep him here any longer, we think that he will probably improve quicker in his home environment. He knows that he must be careful, not take part in any sport or games until Easter."

"And that includes horse riding?"

"Yes, most certainly it does. Is that something that Timmy likes to do?"

"Yes, he loves it. It's a pity, because he's only just started riding. Perhaps with winter and colder, wetter weather coming he will find it easier to accept."

So Jacqui spent the morning tidying Timmy's room and collecting a bag of clothes for him to wear for his return home. The doctor would have to see him one last time before he discharged him and his round seemed to be late in the morning as a rule.

When she arrived at the ward she was amazed to find Alan, her ex-husband in earnest consultation with one of the nurses. When she approached he turned to her and angrily said

"Why didn't you tell me that Timmy was hurt? I had to read about it in the paper, if I hadn't seen that I wouldn't have known anything about it. He's still my son, even though we are divorced. I have a right to see him."

"I tried to contact you; I rang your girl friend and she told me that she had finished with you. I wasn't surprised. Then I rang your coach company and they said that you were out of the country. So I was going to wait until Timmy came home and then ask him if he wanted to see you."

"And if he hadn't....?"

"I wouldn't have told you, provided that he was fit and well, there would have been no point in telling you."

"As his father I do have rights, you know."

"Yes, but not the right to make a scene here in this hospital."

Jacqui was surprised at how calm she was feeling; Alan was in a foul mood and trying his usual bullying tactics and yet she was almost unmoved by it. She smiled, not so much at him, though he took it to be a sign of friendship, but more at the fact that she had found the strength to deal with him. She was no longer afraid of him, subservient to him as she used to be.

"If you haven't already spoken to Timmy you had better have a quick word with him now;

that's if he wants to see you. He's due to come home today."

"So the nurse was telling me."

It was at that moment that Mick came into the ward, nodded and smiled to Jacqui and went over to Timmy's bedside.

"And who's that fella, may I ask? Your new boy friend I suppose."

"No, that is the man who found Timmy and if he hadn't it might well have been ten times worse. Instead of trying to find fault with everybody it would be better if you were to go up to that man and thank him for saving our son."

Alan made his way over to the bed and introduced himself. He smiled at Timmy and said

"How are you feeling son, you've had a rough time of it I hear. Still, that's what comes of mixing it with the big boys, I always told you you had to be a real man if you wanted to do things like that. But the nurse tells me that you are going out today, that's good isn't it?"

Timmy just looked at him briefly with an almost scared expression on his face. He shrank back under the bedclothes then he turned to Mick and in a small voice said

"Can I come down and see you tomorrow? I'm dying to see Floss and all the others."

Before Mick could answer, Alan said

"I'll be looking in to see you tomorrow."

"Does he have to come and see me Mum? I don't want to see him, not ever" said Timmy, without taking his pleading eyes off Mick who calmly said

"I'll be glad to see you whenever you feel well enough Timmy, you can be sure of that. Now I must be getting on. I don't want to get in the way, you will want to get ready."

He nodded to Alan as he stood up and left Timmy's bedside, glad to get away from the awkward atmosphere. Jacqui had been standing at the foot of the bed watching this exchange and then took the seat that Mick had left. In that moment she had witnessed the vast difference between the two men, Alan and Mick, and the effect that they had on Timmy. One was arrogant and bullying, the other calm and kind. It didn't take a genius to work out which of the two Timmy wanted as a father, or a father figure. The poor boy looked terrified and almost in tears. By his mere presence Alan had managed to undo all the good that had happened to Timmy since they had left London. Like Timmy she didn't look at Alan, hoping that by ignoring him he might leave them alone, but spoke only to Timmy, telling him what clothes she had brought for him to wear and how his grandad was preparing a special meal for him. Then she asked if the doctor had been round. Timmy told her that he had, and that he had said that there was no reason why he shouldn't go home.

"Right then, let's get you up and dressed, I'll just pull the curtains around."

She stood up and drew the curtains around his bed, moving Alan away from the bed in the process. He stood for a while grumbling that no one was taking any notice of him. Jacqui had heard enough, she turned on him and in a quiet voice full of venom said

"You come here, expecting to be treated like some long lost hero, when all you've ever given Timmy is grief and fear. After all you've done to him in the past; you constantly belittled him and called him a wimp. You as good as told him just a few minutes ago that it was his own fault for mixing it with the big boys and that that had caused his injury. What do you think that has done to his self esteem? Do you think that approach will help his recovery? You come here wanting him to welcome you with open arms, and yet you couldn't even remember his birthday, you've got no idea, have you, no idea of how to be a dad."

"I'm sorry son, I was out of the country at the time.

"That's a lame excuse and you know it. Timmy like me doesn't want anything to do with you. So stop trying to put yourself first all the time, stop making this silly scene and go…. out of our lives forever."

"But I wanted to help, I wanted to see my son, don't you understand?"

"As I told you before, if and when Timmy wants to see you at some time in the future I won't stand in his way. Right now we both want you to go and the best way you can help is to leave us alone. Do you understand?"

She went back in behind the curtain where Timmy, now fully dressed threw his arms around her and whispered

"Thanks Mum."

They stayed hugging each other, waiting as the emotions of the past few minutes died away and by the time that she and Timmy came out Alan had gone.

FORTY NINE

George had not been delivering to the village; instead he had been on another round that morning. So after he finished work in the afternoon he called in at the café to see Hilda. She was excited because Timmy was on his way home and everybody was so pleased that his recovery had been so quick. Walter had planned and even started preparing a special meal for him.

"I'm delighted to hear the news" said George, "give my regards to all the family will you. What I came to see you about" he paused and looked at the floor, slightly embarrassed and then continued, "would you like to come out for a meal with me tonight?"

"Why…yes….is there something special…" Hilda was a little flustered, but happy to be asked. It had been a long time since she had been asked out on a date.

"I just thought that it would be nice to celebrate your first week back at work."

"Well thank you, yes I'd love to. Gosh, that's twice now, first with Sidney and Marilyn and now with you. I feel proper spoiled."

"Then I'll pick you up at seven, is that OK?"

He left the café a happy man, happy not just because she had agreed to come out for a meal with him, but also because he had managed to ask her. It had been a long time since he had asked anyone out on a date and he had not been too sure if he had the courage to do so. He had been thinking about it all morning as he delivered the post. They were friends weren't they? She wouldn't take offence would she? He tried to convince himself that it wouldn't matter if she said no, but he knew that it would. It wasn't just that he feared rejection, he wanted to take her out; he liked her and he wanted to tell her that he liked her.

"So where are you taking me George?" said Hilda as she slid into the passenger seat of his car. It was funny, she thought, she had somehow never imagined George with a car, he always drove a red Royal Mail van. And he wasn't in uniform; he was wearing a smart pair of light brown trousers, a pale pink shirt and a dark brown jumper. She was glad that she had spent time and trouble getting ready. Since the funeral she had been working and hadn't made the time to go into town and add to her wardrobe. So once again she was wearing her little black dress, but she had added a small white fitted jacket, one that she had worn many years ago. She had smiled as she put it on thinking 'if you keep things for long enough they come back into fashion'.

"You look absolutely lovely Hilda, I'm taking you first for a drive over to Holne; the autumn colours along the road on the way there are fantastic."

"What a nice idea."

"Then I thought we could eat in the Church House Inn."

"That'll be nice, I've never been there."

He drove on over the moor and eventually through the wooded area that surrounded Holne. As he had said, the colours were spectacular, the different species of trees all having different shades of russet and gold.

"Oh, you are right about these colours, they're wonderful."

She chatted excitedly, mostly about Timmy coming home and how well he seemed. Walter was going to do him fillet steak with all the trimmings and his favourite pudding to follow.

George looked across, amazed at the change in her. The sad nervous woman of a few days ago was gone. Where before she had been withdrawn and anxious, now she was bubbly and joyful. He couldn't help wondering if it was just the new job that did it. She was obviously enjoying their outing together and hoped that some of it could be attributed to him. Or could it be that since her mother had died the release from all the years of caring for an oppressive and domineering woman had finally allowed her to be herself again? And she looked so attractive, it wasn't just her attitude. Every time she looked at him she smiled and her face seemed to light up.

"Where is Sidney tonight, out with Marilyn?" asked George. They were sitting side by side on an old settle at a table by the fire. The meal had gone well, good food in comfortable surroundings. Now as they drank their coffee they relaxed even more, warming to each other.

"Yes, I expect they want to make the most of their time together. She starts her new job on the cruise ship soon, won't be back for six months."

"I don't think I could wait six months before I saw you again. In fact I hope that we can do this sort of thing on a regular basis, what d'you think?"

"If you like George" she said with an almost coquettish smile, "if you like."

FIFTY

Timmy woke with a start. He had been dreaming that he and his mum had been out watching a litter of foxes. Every thing had been going well, the cubs were playing outside their den and the vixen had brought them some food to eat. Then out of a clump of bushes beside them a man had jumped with a large club in his hand and started beating the cubs. Timmy had leaped to his feet and ran over to protect them only to find that the man was his dad. Timmy had tried to stop him but it had been no good. His dad had pushed him aside saying

"You've got to watch that head of yours, no sport or fighting."

Then his mother had grabbed him by the arm to pull him away, saying

"Timmy, Timmy…."

He opened his eyes, bemused at first, not really sure as to where he was. Was he out on the moor…..? In the hospital….? No, he was at home in his own bed at last. He smiled up at Jacqui, happy that her face was the first one he saw when he opened his eyes.

"Hi Mum, what is it?"

"Are you well enough to get out for your breakfast, or do you want it up here?"

"I'll get up Mum…just give me a minute or two."

"That's alright, there's no rush. You may get several visitors today, that's all."

"What day is it?"

"Saturday, so some of your friends from school may call in."

He got up and found that he was still a bit weak and woozy. Still, the doctor had warned him that he would be for a while yet. He sat in the comfortable sitting room after he had eaten his breakfast. To his surprise he felt happy just sitting and doing nothing. His energy level was certainly low.

Grace Russell, the vicar's wife, was the first to visit him. He felt rather awkward when she came in. He had never been a church goer and he wondered why she was there.

"I'm so pleased that you are back home again, and so soon… such a good recovery. Yes…well… I found this little book in a charity shop the other day, thought it would be right for you."

She handed Timmy a small volume entitled 'Birds of the British Isles'. The pictures inside were beautiful, all hand painted not photographs. Timmy's mouth fell open at the sight of the pictures

"These are brill, absolutely fantastic, if only I could draw and paint like this. Wow, thank you….."

"I'm so glad you like it, I'm told that you are a good artist and I'm sure that you will be able to paint like that in time. Now I'll leave you to it, you don't want to be talking to an old fuddy duddy like me, you've got plenty of young friends to talk to. In fact, I think I can see two of them coming across the green right now."

She got up and trotted out of the room like a little robin. Timmy heard her talking to his mum in the passage saying goodbye. Then the front door was opened and he heard the voices of Helen and Margaret. They came in all quiet, not sure how much of an invalid he was and how he should be treated. As soon as they found out that he wasn't at death's door they were laughing and joking and telling him all the goings on at school and on the school bus; all the wonderful rumours that had been spread about his injuries. One was that he'd lost an ear; another was that his head was bashed in, leaving a great hole the size of a tennis ball above his ear. And there were at least six men, all in balaclavas and armed to the teeth with baseball bats. The papers hadn't managed to get all the gory details.

"The trouble is" said Timmy, "I can't remember a thing that happened that night, not one single solitary thing. I seem to have lost about three days. Mum said that a lot of what was in the papers wasn't true, and several things that could have been put in weren't. And they didn't have a picture of Mick, and he was the one that saved me."

"I doubt if anybody has got a picture of Mick. He's such an odd chap, a right mystery man" said Helen.

"P'raps the reason he doesn't want his picture in the paper is because he would be

292

recognised as being on crime watch" said Margaret, laughing.

"That's not funny" said Timmy, trying hard not to laugh. "Who's starting rumours now, eh? Anyway, you're glad to have him come and shoe your ponies, aren't you?" He had hoped that Mick would have been in to see him before now, but he knew he was probably busy and that he would have to be patient and wait.

After the girls had gone he went for a little walk in the garden, glad to be out in the fresh air. He felt that he had had enough of the indoor life, what with the hospital ward and now the sitting room. He longed to go and see all the animals at Braggator. When he got back indoors again Sidney was there with a get well card signed by all the kids off the school bus. He thought that it was a very nice gesture and wondered why the girls hadn't said anything about it.

Then George came. He had delivered the post two hours earlier, but when he knocked off he had found that he had a letter in the van that had somehow been overlooked. He felt so bad about it that he had made a special journey to bring it to Timmy. It was a long illustrated letter from Jacko, telling him all about his new life in America. They had been sending one another the odd text, but of course there was a lot more news now that Timmy needed to pass on. Perhaps he ought to send Jacko an illustrated letter, done on his granddad's computer. He might be able to include some of his own pictures.

FIFTY ONE

The next morning Timmy was up and out of bed before his mum. She had promised him that if he were strong enough they would go and see Mick. Walter had cooked him a Dundee cake for them to take, but Jacqui was thinking that she ought to give him something a little more personal. She still felt the need to apologise and to show her thanks for all he had done. Maybe some day she would find something more suitable.

She told Timmy that they would go down in the car, it was too far for him to be walking yet. The doctor had suggested that he should miss school for a week, to allow him to get a bit stronger. The pushing and shoving as pupils went from one classroom to another at the change of lessons could be a hazard.

It was just as well that they did, it was dark and threatening rain as they left. Even so Jacqui thought that the homestead at Braggator Mine looked warm and welcoming despite the dark brooding look of the moor all around. She stopped the car and had to tell Timmy to slow down as he almost threw himself out. Mick came around from behind one of the buildings with his two dogs. Timmy crouched down and held out his arms towards his canine friends. Mick tried to keep them from rushing over to greet Timmy, but had only partial success. Meg stayed to heel but Floss, a typical pup, bounded forward and almost climbed on top of Timmy, licking his face all over.

"I don't know who missed who the most" said Jacqui, "but I couldn't have kept Timmy at home much longer, unless I tied him to the bed."

"It's good to see him out and about at last."

Timmy got up and walked over to the gate into the field where the horses were. He called to them and after the third call Ptarmigan turned and ambled towards him closely followed by the other two. They stood with their heads over the gate and Timmy patted them and rubbed behind their ears.

"Careful Timmy" said Mick, "they can easily swing their heads up and catch you a nasty crack on yours. That's something we don't want, do we?"

Timmy grinned and after a few more words with the horses turned and rejoined Jacqui. She reached inside the car and taking out the cake said

"We've brought you a small present; you give it to him Timmy."

"Well, thank you very much, that looks like quite a big preset to me."

At that moment it started to rain again and quite hard. Mick took the cake from Timmy and walked towards the house door saying

"You'd better come in, I'll make us a cup of tea, or would you prefer coffee?"

"Tea would be lovely" said Jacqui, surprised and delighted at the unusual invitation into Mick's house. Up until then Timmy was the only person who had seen inside and the only time that that had happened was when he had sprained his ankle. Mick opened the door and led them into the hall. It was wide, with a flag-stoned floor. A staircase in front of them went up eight steps and then turned at a half landing to come back towards them. Beside it was a door that Jacqui later found out led to the downstairs toilet. Mick ushered them into the large kitchen/living room on the right, put the cake on the table and asked them to sit while he made the tea.

Jacqui looked around her. Timmy had described the room after his first encounter with Mick, but his description, as seen through the eyes of a boy, wasn't much like the room that Jacqui was looking at. She felt that it was a bit cold looking, too plain and stark. She watched as Mick lifted the big round lid and slid the kettle onto the hotplate. There was a hiss and splutter as a drop or two of water got caught beneath the kettle. Then she looked across at the pictures on the opposite wall, pictures that Timmy had failed to mention. It seemed that her heart missed a beat when she saw the face of the beautiful woman in one and the same woman with the child on a pony in another. These must be the wife and child that Mick had lost. She couldn't say anything, she was not supposed to know anything about them. She had to wait until Mick chose to tell her, if he ever would.

The tea made he joined them and sat at the table with plates for the cake. They ate in silence apart from the odd *mmm* of satisfaction. After they had finished Mick said

"That was lovely. Now I'm glad you came this morning, Jacqui. I've got something to ask you, it may sound a bit odd."

"Ask away."

"Do you know yet if you intend to stay here?"

"Yes, you're right, it does sound a bit odd. Why d'you ask?"

"Well, Dillon's owners rang me this morning."

"Do they want him back|?" asked Timmy anxiously.

"No, just the opposite in fact, they offered him to me. I'd be happy to keep him if Timmy is going to be here to ride him. I appreciate that he can't ride until Easter, and I don't want to seem to be trying to put pressure on you. Take your time, but if you don't want me to keep him I know of a place where he would be welcome."

"Mum…." Timmy's tone of voice said it all.

"D'you mind if I don't answer right away. I have been thinking a lot about what I'm going to do now that the season is over and there's less work at the café. I've had several ideas, some better than others."

"We've just settled in here Mum, it's a lovely place, you can't want to leave, please…"

"Believe me Timmy, I don't want to leave here either. But there are certain things that have got to be sorted out first. Granddad said this morning that he wants to have a word with me tonight. I don't

297

know what it's about but I may be able to find a way to sort things after I've spoken with him. OK?"

"Sorry, I shouldn't have said anything about the horse, I've put you in a difficult spot."

"Nonsense Mick, it's not your fault. In fact it's probably a good thing to have brought the matter up, otherwise I could have been putting it off for days. And now Timmy, I think it's time we were going home. You'll be able to come again, don't worry, in fact you'll soon be well enough to walk over here on your own."

She stood up and taking Mick's hand, thanked him once again. Was he beginning to thaw a little towards her? She looked over his shoulder at the pictures on the wall, thinking

'One day, if you won't tell me I'll ask.'

FIFTY TWO

Sidney had had an urgent phone call from his friend Terry. In fact, almost all the phone calls that Sidney received were urgent. When anybody had a problem with their computer, getting it fixed was a priority, a matter of great urgency. It seemed that people were so dependent on their new electronic machines that they could no longer survive without them, even for a few hours. Those few that hadn't succumbed to the digital age, wondered how people had ever managed before.

Sidney was, of course, delighted. It kept him in business, kept his wheels turning. So he re-arranged some of his appointments and was soon round sorting out the problem that Terry had. When he had finished and they were enjoying the essential cup of coffee Terry said

"So how's things going with you and Marilyn?"

"Fine....well no.... that's not quite right..."

"Why, what's up, you haven't had a row or something, have you?"

"No, no nothing like that. She's going away, she's joining a cruise ship, she'll be away for six months."

"Oh, that's a bit of a bummer. I'm sorry to hear that. You'll miss her. You were getting on so well I thought."

"Yeah, that's sort of the trouble. Mum seemed to be hearing wedding bells, which frightened her a bit. I think she was afraid that I was going to get married and move out and leave her all on her own."

"Had it got to that stage? Were you thinking that way yourself?"

"No, far from it. Oh I like Marilyn, sure enough, she's a lovely person and I enjoy being with her. But I'm certainly not ready to get married or move in with her. I need to get to know her a lot better first. I also need to get to know myself. I seem to have changed lately, I'm just not sure..."

"Yes, you have changed. Whether it's due to your relationship with Marilyn or because of the death of your gran I'm not sure. Both have made a deep impression on you."

"I'm not sure that I want her to go away" said Sidney, almost oblivious of what his friend had said "I know I shall miss her, but if she stays will I feel that I've got to take the relationship further?"

"Have you slept with her?"

"No" said Sidney defensively, painfully aware that where sexual relationships were concerned he was probably way behind most of the kids on the school bus that he drove.

"I didn't think that I was ready for that sort of commitment. I mean, that's like saying you want to get married, isn't it?"

"Well, I doubt if many young people see it that way, but I admire you for having that view point. I think that you're right; you're not yet ready to take that sort of step. D'you know what? You're a bit like a canary."

"How d'you mean, like a canary?"

"You're like a caged bird that has found the door open. You have flown out and had a little look around the room and you like what you've seen. You now have the chance to spread your wings and go for longer flights than you were able to go on before. But you still like to go back to the cage for food and the security of a peaceful night's sleep. Now a new event has occurred; the window to the room has been left open and you can fly out into the big wide world. It's exciting and tempting, but also a bit frightening. Should you stay or should you go?"

"Well tell me... that's what I want to know."

"I think that Marilyn going away for six months is exactly what you need. It will give you the chance to find out what your true feelings towards her are; and what her feelings are for you as well. They say 'Absence makes the heart grow fonder' and well it may. On the other hand, it may cause you to drift apart, who knows?"

"But I don't want to go looking for another girl."

"I'm not suggesting that you should. But you've become much more confident of late; you're not so shy or afraid to meet new people. I'm not saying that Marilyn is or isn't the one for you. All I'm saying is, she's not the only one."

"Yeah, I'm beginning to see what you mean. Thanks, thanks a lot Terry."

"Any time Mate, you've always helped me when I needed it."

"But that's different. I help you to sort out a bit of an electronic gismo. You help me to sort out my life!"

FIFTY THREE

Phil had waited until he had finished his supper before contacting his local policeman. Over the meal he had discussed the matter with his wife Elaine. She was pleased to hear his point of view. She admired the considerate nature that made up a large part of her husband's character, his ability to see good in all people until proved otherwise. But she felt that he needed to pass this matter on to the police. If Jay Bee was guilty, then it would only hurt Phil more if he let things go any further before he acted.

So it was with a good deal of hesitation that he picked up the phone and made the call. Having explained why he was calling he re-told Sidney's story and how he and Frank had decided to go and see Jay Bee.

"I wanted to give him a chance to tell us his side of the story. But what we saw there does seem to be pretty damning."

He went on to describe in detail all that they had seen and their thoughts on the matter. If the police could make some sort of a visit, they might see something...

"I can't go in there poking around without an official search warrant, you know that Phil."

"Yes, but surely you could pretend that you had to check on his gun licence or something, couldn't you?"

"Yes, I suppose I could. But this is a special, a one off favour for you. I'm not going in there poking and prying, looking for dead sheep, but if I do see anything suspicious I'll report it and let the law take its course."

Phil put down the phone, relieved to have put the matter in the hands of some body who was equally as fair as him.

The next day, while he was enjoying a solitary lunch there was a knock on the door. Elaine had gone shopping with a friend and Phil had come in a bit early for some bread and cheese. He went to the door to find his policeman friend standing there.

"Sorry to disturb you Phil, are you having your lunch?

"Just about finished, Elaine's away and I came in a bit early, why, what news have you for me?"

"I'm glad the good lady's not here, may I come in a minute?"

"Of course, come in, you'll join me in a cuppa won't you?"

Phil led the way into the large farm kitchen where the remains of his snack looked dwarfed on the huge kitchen table. He made them both a mug of tea and sat down, looking over expectantly.

"I went over to Jay Bee's place this morning and it's not good news I'm afraid."

"Oh, so he has been up to no good has he?"

"It's worse than that Phil. I found the place much as you described it, except that the caravan door was shut, though not locked. I called out to him and started looking in the sheds like you did. When I got to the big one on the end..."

"The one with the fridge in it, that Frank thought was an abattoir?"

"Well, it looked even more like an abattoir when I went in. There was a lot of blood on the floor and his two dogs were lying there, shot."

"Oh no..."

"That wasn't all; there was a bale of straw near the far wall, and I didn't see him at first."

"Who, Jay Bee?"

"He was behind the bale, see. He had obviously brought it in to sit on and I suppose the blast had knocked him off. He'd shot himself Phil, with his shotgun, shot his dogs first and then himself."

"Oh my God, how awful. The poor man, what could have been so bad that he felt he had to do that?"

"There was a note on the table, very brief. You were right, he had been stealing lambs, not just in this parish either. The CID boys are looking into it now, it seems that he had got himself into some kind of debt to one of those money lender types."

"Why would he do that, he wasn't ever that short of money was he?"

"I doubt if it was very much, but he wasn't the sort to understand debt, never been there I don't suppose. Probably was a bit frightened by the repayments or something. I'll see if I can get more details for you later. It may be some time though."

"All I can say is 'what a waste'. He was always a good kind man as far as I knew; a proper countryman who loved the land and everything on it. Well, thanks for telling me, like you said, probably best that Elaine wasn't here. I'll give Frank a ring d'reckly."

He watched as his uniformed friend got in his car and drove away, saying to himself

"I wouldn't have his job for all the tea in China."

FIFTY FOUR

Timmy didn't find it at all easy being at home, cooped up in his bedroom or the sitting room downstairs. He wanted to be out of doors enjoying what he referred to as 'His Dartmoor'. Jacqui understandably and protectively was afraid to let him go out on his own just yet, and she didn't have the time to go with him. Although the high season in the café was nearly over, there was still a lot of work to do. Walter had asked Hilda to continue for at least another two weeks and she and Jacqui were kept busy. This meant that she couldn't be out with Timmy. As a compromise, one which suited him very well, she took him over to see Mick in the afternoons of every other day and Mick would run him home in time for their evening meal.

"If he's in your way or becoming a nuisance, make sure you let me know" said Jacqui. "But if he can be of use, I'm very grateful to you for your help."

Walter had had a long chat with Jacqui as he had promised. She and her mother had sat and listened to all that he had to say. Afterwards Jacqui had gone out for a long walk on her own. She had a lot to think about and would need time, lots of time. She wished that she had a companion with whom to discuss the matter, someone off whom she could bounce ideas. That was where a good husband or partner would have come in very handy, she thought.

Then on the Wednesday evening when Mick brought Timmy home he asked if he could have a quiet word with her. Fearing that something had gone terribly wrong with Timmy, she nervously took him back out to his van and said

"What's up? Has Timmy been a trouble or hurt himself again? He seems to have been a bit accident prone since we came down here."

"No, Timmy's fine, no worries there, he's getting fitter by the day. He'll be off to school next week no bother. No, what I wanted to ask you is…." he paused, looking straight at her with his piercing grey eyes "Will you come out for a meal with me on Friday night? Timmy tells me that it's your birthday on Saturday, and I expect that you've got a party planned for that night. So I hoped that Friday…?"

"It's not my birthday on Saturday."

"Oh, well I'm sorry I got that wrong, but it doesn't alter the fact that I'd like you to come out for a meal with me on Friday."

"My birthday is on Saturday week, that knock on the head must have affected Timmy after all, it's not like him to get that wrong." It was her turn to pause, looking at Mick with questioning eyes. "Yes, I'd love to come out with you for a meal, where had you in mind?"

"I can't think of a better place than our own village pub, can you?"

"Fine by me."

"Well, I'm sure I'll see you again before then, but if not I'll pick you up here at seven, Friday evening."

"I look forward to it" she said and briefly touched his arm before she turned and went back into the house.

Jessica, who had been watching from the window said

"What was all that about?"

"He's just asked me to go out to dinner with him on Friday night. Mr Mick Cribbett, the silent man who keeps himself to himself, has actually asked me out to dinner at the New Inn."

"Well, aren't you pleased?"

"Yes, very pleased and more than a little surprised. I hope it's a sign that he's warming to me a bit. I know I made a mistake when I told him he didn't know how to look after kids, but I think he forgave me for that a week ago."

"He has become a very important part of Timmy's life, do you want him to be an equally important part of yours?"

"You asked me once before if I fancied him, Mum. My honest answer is…I don't know. If I did get the chance to know him better, then I might very well fancy him, and not just because he's good for Timmy. The trouble is, he's got baggage; we both have and although I know a bit about his, there's a lot more I need to know. Will we be able to live with each other's baggage? At our age we tend to be very set in our ways, will we be able to cope with that?"

"So you're going out to dinner with him in the hopes that it will be a nice night out and with luck, you may find out a good bit more about Mr Mick Cribbett. Well I don't blame you, you'd be fool not to in my opinion."

Jacqui wished her mother was not her mother right then. She wanted to confide in someone, she had always managed to confide in her mother up until then, but it was a bit different now, especially after what her dad had said that night. So after their evening meal and when Timmy had gone to bed, she rang Pippa and asked her if she could go over and have a chat, get a bit of girly advice if she didn't mind.

"Sure come on over, Jim's out to a meeting of some sort so we'll have the place to ourselves once the girls are in bed."

Half an hour later she pulled into the yard by the riding school and jumped out. The automatic light came on, almost dazzling her with its brightness. Anything to help deter burglars I suppose, she thought. The front door opened and Pippa greeted her with a huge smile

"How's Timmy getting on? No problem there I hope."

"No, he's fine, getting better every day."

"We're a threesome, I hope you don't mind. Linda has come to join us as Frank has gone with Jim. His mum's baby sitting for her, so it makes it possible for her to get out."

"No, I don't mind at all, she may be able to help."

"Good, come on in then, I've got a few nibbles and some wine on the go."

Jacqui went in and sat down in an easy chair opposite Linda, who straight way asked after Timmy. Then Pippa came and sat beside Linda on the settee.

"Have you heard about Jay Bee?" said Linda

"No, who's he?" asked Jacqui.

Linda proceeded to tell her all about the thefts of lambs and how Phil and Frank had been suspicious after what Sidney had seen.

"So what was the outcome?" asked Jacqui, who had not heard any of this saga of the lamb rustling before.

"Well, Phil reported it to the police; that's to say our local one whom he has known for years. He went around to see if there was anything to confirm their suspicions and he found Jay Bee dead."

"You mean, he had dropped dead, just like that?"

"No, he'd shot himself... and both his dogs too. Awful... must have been awful...the poor man... to be that desperate."

"Did he leave a note or anything?"

"I believe so, confessing to everything... so very, very sad."

"Well, after that my problems seem as nothing."

"Let's have another drink and then we'll try and help you with yours, Jacqui" said Pippa. Glasses were filled and after a little bit of mum's talk about children and babies Pippa said

"So what's this problem of yours then?"

"I don't know that it's that much of a problem really, I just need a bit of common sense advice from someone of my own age." She took another drink as the others looked on, waiting for her to continue.

"As you know I've been working in Dad's café since I came down here in the spring. When I was in London I worked in an estate agent's and before that a bank, so you can see, this work here was totally new to me. Last Sunday evening, after Timmy had gone to bed, Dad told me that he and Mum are going to retire this autumn."

"What, are they going to sell the place or something? Where would you go?" said Linda.

"No, they are not going to sell, they intend to stay living there. What they asked me…offered me…was the business. Would I like to take on the café business? They would let me have the whole lot; lock, stock and barrel for a peppercorn rent. Dad would be willing to give me guidance, he's taught me a lot this summer already. It seems a great opportunity but will it work? Will I be able to do the job? Will Dad be always looking over my shoulder? Can I forget that he's there, if he is always looking over my shoulder? Will he be able to leave me to it and not be forever looking over my shoulder?"

"I see your point and you are right to have concerns. I know that Frank could never have worked for his dad, that was one of the reasons for his leaving and going in to the Army all those years ago. And when he came back, after his dad died, he had to work out with his mum just who did what and who was responsible for what."

"Yes Linda, but that's a bit different" said Pippa "Jacqui isn't going to be working with her dad, her question is really 'will he be able to leave her alone to get on with the job, make her own mistakes if she has to, and learn from them?' Have you talked to your dad on those lines Jacqui?"

"No I haven't. I've thought about it, and then I thought that I'd rather have a chat with you first. It might be that there was something else that I had forgotten, something that I needed to bring up when I did finally have a chat with him."

"How separate is the business from the living quarters, their living quarters I mean?"

"They have a sort of separate wing, though we eat together and I would have thought that we'll continue to do so."

"Is your dad very domineering, does he have very fixed ideas as to how things should be done, or is he laid back, doesn't care too much so long as the job gets done?"

"Bit of both really."

"And have you got on well working together?"

"Yes, he's been fine. It has been fun, I've enjoyed myself immensely."

"Then" said Pippa, "the only thing I can say is....Go for it gal." and with that got up and went to the kitchen for another bottle. She came back with it and three fresh glasses in her hand saying

"I was given this bottle of fizz some time ago by a grateful customer, and I can't think of a better reason or occasion for opening it."

She eased out the cork and poured the pale sparkling champagne into their glasses.

"Here's to Jacqui and her new business venture!"

"Thanks" said Jacqui, "But I am relying on you both to keep this to yourselves until it's all signed and sealed".

It was nearly midnight when Jacqui finally returned home. Her worries about her future at the café had been dissipated, though whether that was due to her friends' advice or the effect of the champagne she didn't know.

Would the quandary regarding Mick be as easy to solve?

FIFTY FIVE

Mick rang the bell at Jacqui's door and stepped back. He hardly had time to adjust his tie before the door opened and Timmy was there in the open doorway.

"Come in, Mum won't be long."

"Thanks Timmy, how are you feeling today? Are you still getting those headaches?"

"No, I'm fine, I'm going to school on Monday."

"That's great, just remember to be careful, we don't want you back in hospital again."

"He knows what to do" said Jacqui, walking down the stairs with a smile on her face. She bowed slightly towards Mick

"Good evening, I hope I haven't kept you waiting."

"Not at all, Timmy was making sure that I was entertained."

He wanted to say that he thought that she looked lovely. Her hair was shining and bouncing with every step she took and her eyes, as she looked at Timmy, were full of the love and pride that a mother has for her child. Instead he said

"Shall we go?" as he turned and opened the door. They walked across the green together. A cold autumn wind was blowing, driving the fallen leaves that had come from the chestnut tree. Various shades of yellow and brown, they tumbled and twirled past their feet. Nearer the tree in the centre of the green the shells of the conkers littered the ground. Mick was reminded of his boyhood days and endless games of conkers played in the school playground. All manner of solutions and practices were tried to harden the nut to make it stronger and a winning champion. Some kids favoured soaking in vinegar, others thought that baking in the oven was the best way. None of these strange ideas really worked.

"Do kids still play conkers these days?" he asked

"I don't know, I suppose they do."

"Does Timmy?"

"Oh yes, he and his granddad have had a few games. It's the first time that he's lived as close to a chestnut tree as we do now, he's loving it."

"He certainly seems to love living down here, he's taken to country life like a duck to water."

"Yes" said Jacqui pensively. She would have to tell Mick about her plans for the future, after all he wanted to know whether to keep Dillon for Timmy or not. But she needed to know more about him and his past life. He had become an important part of Timmy's life and that meant that he was becoming a part of her life too. If there were any skeletons in his cupboard now was the time to get them out.

They walked into the pub and Mick led her to a table in the corner. The fire was burning, happily crackling away; little flames dancing on the split logs, reflected on the copper coal scuttle and the large copper jug that stood one on either side of the grate. It added not just warmth but cheer as well. They ordered their meal and as they were eating it Mick looked across at Jacqui and said

"Tell me about your early life. I know that you and your husband are divorced, Timmy has told me a little of that, and I realise that that was part of the reason for your coming down here this spring. But what about your childhood, where did you grow up and so on?"

Jacqui looked at him with wide eyes. It was hardly the question that she was expecting. Yet she thought 'If I tell him about my past it will be easier for me to ask him about his. In fact it will be alright for me to expect him to tell me.'

"I was born in north London. It was quite a nice area really; a leafy suburb is how I think the estate agents would describe it. I went to the local school, the primary school was fairly small and I made several friends there, some of whom stayed friends through secondary school. I enjoyed sports, swimming and netball in particular, though I was never especially good at either of them. I never managed to get into the first teams or anything like that."

"And after school?"

"What d'you mean? In the evenings, or when I left school and started work?"

"Both really."

"In the evenings I suppose I did what all kids did; we'd go out in groups of three or more and hang

317

around. Then at weekends we might go to a disco or perhaps the cinema. I remember one awful time when my mum was coming to pick me up after a disco. I was supposed to be outside waiting for her at a certain time, midnight I think it was. Well I wasn't there and she got worried and cross, like any mum would. She came in and got me out of the club, in front of all my mates. It was so embarrassing, I felt awful, mind you I never was late again."

They both laughed and felt themselves relaxing as a comfortable warmth was growing between them.

"When I left school I went to work in a bank. Dad was in the finance business and it seemed a natural thing to do. I met Alan at a friend's birthday party. He seemed a lot of fun and after a while we got together and finally married. When Timmy was born I changed to working in an estate agent's. The hours were more flexible."

Mick didn't ask what had gone wrong in the marriage, or why she and Timmy had left Alan. Instead he asked

"What made you come down here? What I should say is what made your parents come down here?"

"Oh, we used to come down on holiday. Not every year, stayed in a small caravan park on a farm in South Devon. I think it was called Lanscombe Farm. Mum and Dad realised that it would be easier for all if I had a friend come with me. So my school friend Charlotte, or Charlie as a called her came along too."

She paused and looked at Mick smiling, hardly seeing him as her mind went back to those summer days long ago.

"We used to go to the end of the farm lane where it joined the road. There were two boys who used to ride by from time to time. Charlie and I fancied them, sort of. One of them was the son of the local lord of the manor or something. The other, the one that I fancied, had a dad who worked on the estate. He was the better rider, looked like he was glued to the horse."

"And did you ever get to speak to these boys?"

"No, we were far too shy to do that. If they had spoken to us I'm sure we would have burst into fit of embarrassed giggles."

"Did you go back there again, for holidays?"

"No, we started going on package holidays after that, to the south of Spain and places like that. Bit like everybody else I suppose."

They had finished their first course and the waiter took away their plates. While they waited for the sweets to arrive Jacqui said

"Now it's my turn to ask. Where did you grow up and where were you before you came to live here? Dad tells me that you arrived at about the same time as he did."

"I was born down in the South Hams, my dad was a game keeper on a big estate. He taught me all I know about the country before I was six. I would go out with him and he would point out the plants and flowers, animals and birds. I didn't realise

I was learning, it all just went in as it can do when you're a kid. I learned about the seasons and how everything in nature has its place and its purpose, everything links in to each other so to speak, like the cogs in a clock."

"It sounds an idyllic childhood, living close to nature and all that. Which of the seasons did you like the best?"

"Oh Spring, without a doubt, the season of rebirth. I used to love walking through the woods and the fields with Dad, seeing the different flowers coming into bloom. The snowdrops came first, then the wood anemones and the celandines. Then came the bluebells and the wild garlic. And the first leaves on the trees, so soft and tender, almost fragile. I used to think the beech leaves were like green butterflies."

Jacqui was looking at him, she could see that he was miles away in his childhood reminiscing. His love of all things to do with the natural world was blatantly obvious.

"And the birds," he continued "all of the cock birds vying for the attention of the hen birds with their bright colours and their loud songs. Oh, I like all the seasons, and as they come around I'm ready for them, but I like the spring the best."

"So what did you do when you left school?"

"I went to work with the local blacksmith. I had been spending a lot of time with him in the school holidays. I always loved horses and being with them, I sort of drifted into it I suppose. When he retired a few years later I was able to take over from him. Then I got involved with the hunt, mostly as an unpaid helper, kennel work and stable work."

"Was that where you were working before you came here?"

"No, I was up in Cheshire, I had been there for …let me see…it must have been ten years."

"How did you come to go up there?" Jacqui was amazed at her boldness, asking all theses questions, but more amazed that he was seemingly happy to answer them.

"It was all rather odd, now I look back on it. At the end of the hunting season we had several members of a visiting hunt from Cheshire come to join with us for our last meet. One of them offered me a job, not as farrier but as whip. It was to be a proper paid job with a big hunt. I would still carry on with my shoeing work but that would be my secondary job. I was footloose and fancy free, it seemed like a good chance, too good to miss, so off I went and moved up to Cheshire. After three years the master retired and I was offered his job. I was in clover."

"Did you ever marry?" asked Jacqui, knowing that this might well be the one subject that he would be unwilling to talk about. At that moment there was a guffaw of laughter from a group of young men who were sitting around a table some feet away.

"I don't think that this is the time or the place to tell you any more. I hope you don't mind."

Whether it was the potential answer to her question or the raucous laughter from the other side of the room, but his mood had changed and he was no longer happy to talk. The dark look had come into his eyes again and he was politely telling her that that part of the evening's conversation was over. Jacqui knew that she had nearly gone too far. She reached across the table and put her small hand on top of his broad one. He looked into her eyes and she returned the look saying

"Of course I don't mind... but I'm a good listener so maybe some other time."

He smiled at her and after a long pause said

"Thank you.... Thank you for a lovely evening. I wasn't sure if I could enjoy an evening like this, just you and me. I haven't done anything like this for many years."

"It's been lovely" said Jacqui. She sensed that he had been unsure about being alone with her, that he felt safer when Timmy was with them.

"I hope we can do this again some time" she said

"So do I."

FIFTY SIX

Jacqui was very pleased with the way the evening meal with Mick had gone. He had opened up to a far greater degree than she had expected. He had told her more about his early life than she had hoped to hear. As a result she felt that a lot of her concerns regarding Timmy and his relationship with Mick were no longer justified. It was her relationship with Mick that could be a problem.

As long as she and Mick were just acquaintances Timmy should not suffer in any way. But if she and Mick became more than just friends there could be problems. If the relationship was good and long lasting it would be fine. In fact that was probably just what Timmy wanted. But as she knew only too well, things could go wrong, as they had with her and Alan. The damage that this had done to Timmy had been enormous. Not only had Alan's bullying had a very bad effect on him, but Timmy felt that he was in a large way responsible for his parents' separation and subsequent divorce. Jacqui and her parents had managed to persuade him that this was not so, but it had left a scar. If she and Mick were to become an item and then for some reason they split up, it would prove to be disastrous for Timmy. It could open an old wound that would be impossible to heal.

So on the Sunday after, she and Timmy went to visit Mick. Timmy was always happy to go, both to see Mick and also to see his many animals, the dogs and horses who had now become his friends too. She didn't really have an excuse for going except to say thank you for a nice evening, and she had said that already. When they arrived at the farm Mick was in the far field seeing to his sheep. The dogs were busy working, so to Timmy's disappointment, they didn't run up to greet him as they would normally have done if they were in the yard when he arrived. So mother and son stood and waited at the field gate until Mick had finished, and then he walked up to meet them.

"Morning Jacqui, hello Timmy."

"Morning" said Jacqui "as Timmy is starting school tomorrow and with the dark evenings, he won't be able to come and see you so often. So we hoped you wouldn't mind us coming to see you today."

"Not at all, come in the house and have a cup of coffee, this wind is a bit keen."

"Can I stay out here with the dogs Mick, or go over and talk to the horses? Can I stay out here with the dogs Mick, or go over and talk to the horses? I don't mind the wind, and I won't see them again for at least a week."

"Yes of course you can, but remember they are working dogs, don't fuss over them too much and don't encourage them to jump up. They aren't pets or performing animals."

He smiled and turned to Jacqui saying

"I don't like to keep on at him, but I feel I've got to make sure that he learns in the same way as I did from my dad. Only difference is, I was much younger when my dad started teaching me."

"You carry on" said Jacqui with a brief laugh as they walked towards the house. "He takes far more notice of you than he ever does of me."

Indoors Mick made them coffee and Jacqui sat at the table with her back to the door. She could see out of the window and watch Timmy and also look across the room at the three pictures on the wall. It's now or never, she thought, and looking straight at Mick she said

"I asked you the other night if you had ever married. I appreciate that at the time it was difficult for you to answer; now here in your own home I hope it might be different. I can't help but see those pictures on the wall, is that your wife in two of them?"

"Yes… that's Amanda." He came and sat beside her, looking at the pictures. After a long time he started talking in a soft, almost hushed voice.

"She was one of the reasons that I went to Cheshire. She had come down with the hunt that day and I was struck by her beauty."

Jacqui could understand why, the picture showed a very beautiful woman, but she kept quiet, not wishing to interrupt.

"We saw more and more of each other as the years went by and were married shortly after I got the job as master. It was a lovely day for the wedding and we had a wonderful marriage. Then our son Sam was born two years later and I think we were in heaven. He was a bright lad, learned fast and was interested in the countryside, like both his parents. We had hoped to have a brother or sister for him, but it wasn't to be unfortunately. I sometimes felt that life had dealt me such a good hand that my luck couldn't last and that something was bound to happen to spoil it all. How right it turned out that I was."

He paused for a moment and Jacqui reached over and took his hand.

"It was the night before the end of season meet. I had a call from an old gentleman who was a great supporter of the hunt. His horse had thrown a shoe and could I come and fix it; he didn't want to miss the last meet of the season. He was getting on and it was probably going to be his last season. Well, what could I do? I said goodnight to Amanda and Sam and off I went. It didn't take too long, but I had to go in and have a drink with the old gent. By the time I left it was nearly eleven o'clock.

As I approached the kennels I could see lights, flashing blue lights. I turned the final corner and found the way blocked by a police car. Ahead were two fire engines and an ambulance which was just leaving. There were men in day-glow jackets everywhere and lots of noise. To begin with the policeman wouldn't let my go by, he wasn't our local one, didn't know me. When he found out who I was he called to his superior who came over to talk to me. He told me that my house had been burned down."

He stopped again and Jacqui waited, just giving his hand a gentle squeeze. She watched his face, agony clearly showing in his grey eyes, his jaw muscles working rhythmically. Outside in the yard Timmy was happily talking to the three horses over the gate to their field.

"A neighbour had raised the alarm but, like so many rural areas, it was a long way for the fire brigade to come and by the time they arrived and it was safe for the firemen to go in, Sam was dead. Amanda died in the ambulance on the way to the hospital."

"Oh my god, how awful, you poor man."

He went quiet for a while, looking first at the pictures on the wall and then at his hands. Finally he looked up at Jacqui and continued

"There had been a lot of ill feeling towards the hunt. You have to remember that this was before the hunting ban. The anti's and the hunt saboteurs were very active. Lots of people would turn up at a meet and protest, making lots of noise, blowing hunting horns, anything to disrupt the hunt. Several of these so called protesters were students, paid to come and be a nuisance. Rent a mob we called them. On one occasion a girl got too close and was knocked down by a horse, it spooked the horse which stepped on her leg, injuring her badly.

It turned out that the fire had been an arson attack. Someone, we assumed one of these anti's, had pushed a large lighted firework through the le᾿ er box. The whole hall caught fire, staircase and a , but the worst part was the vinyl wallpaper. It burns giving of a horrible black smoke, an acrid, poisonous smoke that not only suffocates but kills."

Jacqui listened spellbound. What a terrible tale, what an awful end to the lives of Mick's wife and child! She could see he was having difficulty telling her and going on, but she said nothing, just waited.

"I was in shock as you can imagine. To this day I don't really know what I did for over a week after the fire. Then there was the funeral....but that didn't bring an end to it. The police did their best but they were up against a conspiracy of silence from the anti's, and who could blame them?"

"Did they ever find the culprit?"

"No, the police didn't, but his parents did. He was a nineteen year old student who had got roped into the movement. He thought that it would be a joke to put a firework through my letterbox. I don't suppose he had any idea just how much damage it would cause, he was most likely high on drugs of some sort at the time."

"You said his parents found out, what did you mean by that?"

"They came home from a dinner party and found him. He had hanged himself off the banisters of the landing. He was the first thing that they saw as they entered the house. He had left a note, well quite a long letter actually, saying how he couldn't live with what he had done and how sorry he was. I felt sorry for his parents, it must have been awful; enough to drive a man maize. So the lives of two families were ruined by one senseless act.

I left the area soon after; came down here and bought this place. All I wanted to do was to bury myself away from the rest of the world and everybody that knew me. It was awful for Amanda's parents as well. They had lost their beloved daughter. But I couldn't join with them and share our grief. I couldn't help but feel responsible. I kept thinking if only I had come home earlier instead of staying for that drink...."

"What about your parents...your brothers and sisters... was there no one you could turn to?"

"I was an only child, my parents had both died, so I was alone in the world. All I had were my two horses, Osprey and Ptarmigan and those three photographs. They had been in the office beside the tack room of the stables so fortunately they hadn't been destroyed by the fire."

"What age was Sam?"

"He was six, he would be twelve now, about the same age as Timmy. So you see I found it difficult at first,when I found Timmy up on the moor that day with his sprained ankle. Then later, as I watched him grow and learn about the country and his love for the animals I found that I couldn't help but love the boy. He reminded me so much of Sam."

He turned away and she could see his shoulders shaking as he cried, silent heartfelt sobs. She got up and put her arm around his broad shoulders

"Thank you for telling me, I realise how difficult it must have been."

At that moment Timmy came bursting into the room, saw his mother with her arm around Mick and just said

"Oh" before dashing out again.

Later, on the way home in the car, Timmy said

"What was up with Mick just now? He seemed upset."

"He was; he had just told me about the night his wife and son died. They were burned to death in a terrible fire; it must have been awful. He's never told anybody about it before, I don't think he wants it made public now, it's just between us....you understand?"

"Yes Mum. He was always very quiet, not so much with me but with people he worked for, shoeing and that. He'd talk to me... explain things to me... teaching me like. But sometimes I'd catch him looking at me in a sort of far away fashion with a bit of a smile. It was as though he was looking at me, but watching someone else...but he always had that sad look in his eyes."

"Maybe now that he's told me about it, he'll start to get over it."

"D'you think so... just by talking about it?"

"It can help; he's been living behind a protective wall that he built up around himself. Maybe by talking to me he has taken the first step towards breaking down that wall."

330

"I hope so. I think he's a nice kind man...I don't want him to be unhappy....I like him, don't you?"

"Yes Timmy, I'm beginning to like him a lot."

FIFTY SEVEN

It was a beautiful autumn morning. The wind of the past few days had dropped, the sun was shining and there was a crispness to the air, not exactly frosty, but cold and clear. Gossamer hung on the gorse bushes, sparkling in the bright sunshine, and in the stillness, sounds from afar could clearly be heard. All around the leaves on the trees were glorious shades of browns, orange and gold. With the sun low in the sky, sunlight shining through the beech trees made them look as though they were on fire.

Sal and Edna were standing outside the village shop, having their customary morning chat.

"I dunno what this place is coming to" said Edna "never used to have all this crime and violence."

"I know, 'tis terrible. Poor Jay Bee, who'd have thought it, he must have been desperate."

"Yes, and shot his dogs too."

"My Charlie said he was arse and ears in debt on account of his gambling, he'd got himself into some syndicate or summat. Got addicted to it...."

"That's the trouble with men living on their own, they'm not very good at it. Not like us women, we can manage. But men... seems like they can't help but get addicted to something or other when they'm on their own."

"And then there was that drugs factory over to West Furzes, there was thousands of pounds of cannabis growing there apparently."

"And that poor boy, his mum must have been out of her mind with worry."

"I think he's alright now Edna, he's been getting on the school bus all this week."

At that moment Walter came out of the shop with his morning paper.

"Morning Sal, morning Edna, lovely morning"

"Yes, 'tis beautiful" said Sal "I was just saying to Edna that I see young Timmy's going to school again. That's a good sign."

"Yes, he's a lot better now, thank God."

He nodded to them and walked on towards his home.

"Charlie tells me that Walter's giving up the café."

"What, is he moving away?"

"No, he's offered it to his maid Jacqui."

"Oh that's good, 'tis a nice little business, good to keep it in the family like. I wonder if that means Hilda will still be working there."

"I don't know, I hope so, tiv done Hilda a world of good, she's come out of herself a lot since she's been working there."

"Was it the working in the café" said Edna musing "or going out with George that has done it?"

"Whatever, she's a lot better for it. Poor maid, she hasn't had much of a life, lost her man just a few days before the wedding, and her pregnant at the time."

"I'll say she hasn't had much of a life, she hasn't had a man for over thirty years."

"Some might say she's lucky" said Sal, laughing. "Still George is a decent sort, probably just the thing for Hilda. He's been on his own for ten years or more. That hasn't affected him, being on his own like you said, he didn't get addicted to aught."

"Well no, but then he was meeting folks on his round every day. It wasn't like he was on his own really, was it?"

"That Mick Cribbett lives on his own and he's a bit of an odd one."

"True, he doesn't have a lot to say. He's been very good to young Timmy though, and don't forget 'twas he that found him all tied up and that."

"Talk of the devil, here he is now"

Mick had driven into the green and jumped out of his van. As he walked over to the shop he smiled at Sal and Edna saying

"Morning ladies, lovely morning today isn't it? Makes one feel glad to be alive on a morning like this, doesn't it? And it looks like it'll stay fine for the rest of the day." He ran into the shop almost jumping up the step.

"Morning" said Edna to his disappearing back, her mouth and eyes wide open in surprise.

"Well, whatever's got into him" said Sal who was equally as surprised as her friend. "He seems full of the joys of spring for some reason."

"There's only two things that can have that effect on a man; he's either come into a lot of money, or he's got himself a woman and has fallen in love."

"You don't think....Jacqui....?"

"Time will tell, or like they say these days, 'watch this space'. Now, are you coming in for a cuppa?"

"No, thanks all the same, I'd better get back to Charlie."

"He won't miss you; he'll be down in that shed of his at the bottom of the garden."

"I 'spect you're right" said Sal laughing "that's what he's addicted to... his shed."

Sidney meanwhile was helping Marilyn, loading her cases into his car. He was going to take her to Exeter Airport where they would have a last cup of coffee together. Then she would board her plane to Madeira where she was due to join her ship. The queue to go through the security check was long, so they sat and drank their coffee slowly. Finally the time came for Marilyn to go. All the self confidence that Sidney had gained over the past few weeks, weeks spent with her, had evaporated. He stood tongue tied, not knowing how to say what he felt.

Marilyn smiled at him, seeing his predicament, put her arms around him and gave him a big hug.

"Goodbye Sidney, thanks for every thing, it's been fun."

"Yeah, you will write, or an e-mail from time to time?"

"Of course I will, and say goodbye to your mum for me. Now I must go."

She kissed him, a long meaningful kiss on his lips and then she was gone. Sidney went up into the upstairs lounge and waited for her plane to go. It was a long wait but he didn't mind, there was nothing else that he wanted to do that day.

When he got home George and his mum were sitting watching telly. George got up saying

"I'll be going now."

"No, don't go on my account George. I'm off up to my room, got a few things to do…. No, you stay and keep Mum company."

FIFTY EIGHT

Walter had prepared a lovely birthday breakfast for Jacqui; smoked salmon with scrambled eggs washed down with freshly squeezed grapefruit juice followed by home-made tuff cakes with cream and honey. Half-way through the meal there was a knock on the door. The local florist from Bovey Tracey was there with a huge bouquet of flowers. There was a small card which read

HAPPY BIRTHDAY TO A GOOD LISTENER

"What a wonderful bouquet, who sent you those?" asked Jessica.

Jacqui looked at Timmy smiling knowingly and said

"I think I know. I believe it could have been Mick, I'll go and see him tomorrow. I've got something to tell him, an answer to a question of his. It's really the same answer as the one I've got to give to you Dad. You asked me if I would like to take on this café. I've thought about it hard and long. My first impulse was to say yes. The idea of staying here permanently seemed great. Then I thought about it for a while and I wasn't so sure."

"Oh Mum" said Timmy "you can't possibly want to leave here, it's so lovely and we've made so many good friends. Please...."

"Alright Timmy, I haven't finished. What I was going to say is; the more I thought about it the more I came to like the idea. So, yes Dad, I'd love to take up your offer. I'll need help and advice now and again I know, and you may find it difficult to watch me doing things in a different way from yours. It will mean that I won't have as much time to spend on you Timmy, at weekends and during the holidays, except when you are helping, working as a waiter."

"That's alright, I don't mind doing a bit of waiting if the pay is good. If not I can always go and work for Mick" he said with a happy gleam in his eye.

"Well I can't think of a better way of celebrating your birthday; thank you for accepting. Mum and I would have hated just closing down and having to watch regular customers, who have become friends, walking away disappointed." He got up and walked around the table and put his arms around her.

"It really is welcome home now, isn't it?"

"Can I go and tell Mick?" asked Timmy, pushing back his chair and getting up from the table.

"No, as I said, I'll go and see him tomorrow and when I say 'I', you know full well that I mean 'you and I'. Now off you go and play, Granddad and I have a lot to talk about."

As a birthday treat that evening, Walter took them all to a Chinese restaurant. He knew that Jacqui would like it and Jessica also loved oriental cooking. Besides, he didn't want to cook, he wanted a bit of a treat as well.

The next morning Timmy was up with the lark, itching to go to see Mick and tell him that they were definitely staying. That would mean that Dillon would be staying at Braggator for him to ride whenever he wanted. At last they set off; Jacqui insisted on walking saying that it would do Timmy good not to ride in the car. Walking wouldn't hurt his head and he was a lot stronger now. His unsteadiness on his legs had been the only reason for taking the car before.

Mick had probably seen and heard them coming as Timmy was chattering away excitedly all the way down the lane. He was standing in the yard waiting for them. Jacqui went straight up to him and putting her hands on his shoulders pulled him towards her and gave him a kiss.

"Thank you so much for my lovely flowers, they are wonderful."

"Flowers, what flowers?" he said in mock surprise.

"We know it was you Mick. Come on Mum, tell him your other bit of news."

"Give me time to get here and catch my breath Timmy."

"Other news, what other news?" asked Mick.

339

"You remember when you said about the possibility of keeping Dillon you asked if we were going to stay here. I said that my dad wanted to have a word with me, and I would have to wait a while before I could give you an answer. Well, he has asked me to take on the café, and after a lot of thought I've decided to say 'yes'. That's why Timmy here is so excited, he's been awake most of the night, wanted to come and tell you yesterday."

"Well I'm very happy to hear it."

Timmy meanwhile had run over to the gate and had called to the horses. It wasn't long before they were all at the gate with him stroking their heads and rubbing them behind their ears.

"Come on over here Mum, come and make friends with Dillon, he's lovely."

Jacqui and Mick strolled over and she stroked Dillon's soft velvet like nose.

"I can't wait 'til Easter, I'm longing to get on him again and ride across the field here."

"Why don't you have a ride?" said Mick to Jacqui. "You could ride Ptarmigan, she's lovely and quiet."

"No I couldn't, besides she looks awfully big."

"Well, ride Dillon then, he'd carry you" and then almost as an after thought Mick said

"Have you ever ridden before?"

"Yes, but only once. It was when we were staying on that small campsite at Lanscombe Farm. My friend Charlie and I went for a ride, they were all quiet ponies. We just walked along the lanes in a long line. The ponies knew where they were going, they had probably done it a thousand times. We were supposed to be going again, but we decided that it was more fun to go to the end of the lane and wait in case those two boys I told you about came along."

"Yeah" said Mick "those old ponies belonging to Jimmy Lightfoot were right old plodders."

"That's right, Mr Lightfoot, I remember now.....Hey, how did you know his name?"

Mick was laughing, his whole body shaking. He just stood there laughing and laughing as though he had never laughed before.

"Don't tell me....you were one of those two boys, I can see it now. You were the one who was obviously the better rider. Why didn't you say the other night when I told you about it? I said that one of them was the son of a man who worked on the big estate, that was you wasn't it? Your dad was the gamekeeper."

She punched him playfully on the shoulder and he grinned at her.

"I knew when you were telling me about it, although I have to admit, I don't remember you and your friend Charlie. At that time, when you were telling me, I couldn't say anything. Now...well...you understand. Now, let's get you up on Dillon and see how much you remember of that childhood ride."

"Oh yes Mum" said Timmy who ran to the stable to get a halter.

"I don't seem to have much option do I? Will I be alright in these clothes, it's hardly riding gear is it?"

"Jeans and boots, they're fine" said Mick as they all three walked back to the stable with Timmy leading Dillon. It was only a short ride, just once around the small field with the sheep in it. Timmy walked along beside her, proud to be helping and looking after his mum.

"Very good" said Mick when they got back and she dismounted. "You've got a good seat, I think you'll learn quite quickly, if you want to that is. You could certainly ride Ptarmigan."

"Yes, and then we could all go out riding together" said Timmy excitedly.

"Not so fast young man, I'll be working in the café remember, and so will you."

"Yes, but there's always the evenings, the days are long in the summer."

"It seems like he's got an answer for everything" said Mick as he unsaddled Dillon. The three of them walked Dillon back to join Osprey and Ptarmigan in their field. Mick was joking and laughing with them both. More relaxed than Jacqui or even Timmy had ever seen him. They stood watching the horses for a while and then Jacqui said

"I know that Timmy here is very happy today, and I know the reason why. You also seem to be very happy today, may I ask why?"

"Since I spoke to you the other night it's as though an enormous weight has been lifted off me. I don't feel so sad anymore. I feel….free."

342

"You had built a barrier around you to protect yourself" said Jacqui, taking his hand, "now you've broken that barrier down and you've escaped."

"You're like that gall wasp that you told me about" said Timmy. "You were hiding in your oak apple to keep yourself safe, now at last you are out...flying free."

"Kids" said Mick with a smile and turning to Jacqui he said

"I told you he had an answer for everything, didn't I?"

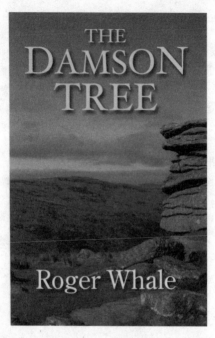

THE
DAMSON
TREE

Roger Whale

Frank Narraway is home on leave for his father's funeral. Friends and neighbours all seem to think that he will now come back to live and help his mother run the family farm on Dartmoor.

Does he have the expertise and self confidence to take on his father's job?

Will his love of the moor be great enough for him to give up the career in the army that he has followed for the past fifteen years? Will he miss the camaraderie of the regiment?

He knows that he will receive a warm welcome in this small community, and in some ways feels that he owes it to his mother, but is all this reason enough?

And what about Linda?

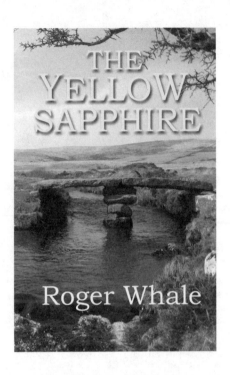

The Yellow Sapphire is the second book of Roger's Dartmoor Trilogy. Several new characters, together with some old friends return to tell of more goings on in this Dartmoor village.

Piers Silverton from San Francisco is visiting Dartmoor to see if he can find where his ancestors lived. He is lucky enough to enlist the help of local girl Beatie who is also researching her family tree.

They are not the only ones in the village to find surprises in their family cupboards.